D0397173

BL· 6'5 —
AR Pts: 13·0

Quiz No. 162833

MVFOL

THE GIRL WHO SOARED OVER FAIRYLAND AND CUT THE MOON IN TWO

by Catherynne M. Valente

with Illustrations by Ana Juan

FEIWEL AND FRIENDS
NEW YORK

A FEIWEL AND FRIENDS BOOK
An Imprint of Macmillan

Feiwel and Friends books may be purchased for business or promotional
use. For information on bulk purchases, please contact Macmillan
Corporate and Premium Sales Department at (800) 221-7945 x5442 or by
e-mail at specialmarkets@macmillan.com.

Library of Congress Cataloging-in-Publication Data Available

ISBN: 978-1-250-02350-6 (hardcover)/978-1-4668-4853-5 (ebook)

Book design by Elizabeth Herzog and Barbara Grzeslo

Feiwel and Friends logo designed by Filomena Tuosto

First Edition: 2013

10 9 8 7 6 5 4 3 2 1

mackids.com

*For all those who take the hand of a brightly colored stranger
and journey back to Fairyland once a year*

*and everyone
whoever thought
they were too young
or too old.*

Dramatis Personae

SEPTEMBER, a Girl

Her Parents

AROOSTOOK, a 1925 Model A Ford

BOOMER, a Lineman

BEATRICE, a Gentleman Greyhound

The Blue Wind

PEASEBLOSSOM, a Puffin

THE CALCATRIX, a Strange Crocodile

Several Untrustworthy Winds

BALLAST DOWNBOUND, a Klaubautermann

The Moon

The Black Cosmic Dog

RUSHE, a Black Jackal

WAITE, a White Jackal

NEFARIOUS FREEDOM COPPERMOLT III, a Lobster

SPOKE, a Taxicrab

ALMANACK, a Very Large Whelk

ABECEDARIA, a Periwig

A-THROUGH-L, a Wyverary

CIDERSKIN, a Yeti

SATURDAY, a Marid

VALENTINE AND PENTAMETER, Two Acrobats

CANDLESTICK, a Buraq

MARIGOLD, a Lamia

TAMARIND, a Lamia

A Certain Leopard
TURING, a Tyger
TEM, a Child
Her Parents
ERRATA, a Wyvern
THE PEARL, a Thaumaturge
A Fairy

THE INVISIBLE CLOAK OF ALL THINGS PAST

In Which a Girl Named September Tells Several Lies, Hoards Money, Turns Fourteen, Wears Trousers, and Goes on a Joy-Ride

Once upon a time, a girl named September told a great number of lies.

The trouble with lies is that they love company. Once you tell a single lie, that lie gets terribly excited and calls all its friends to visit. Soon you find yourself making room for them in every corner, turning down beds and lighting lamps to make them comfortable, feeding them and tidying them and mending them when they start to wear thin. This is most especially true if you tell a very large lie, as September did. A good, solid, beefy lie is too heavy to stand on its own. It needs smaller, quicker, more complicated lies to hold it up.

September would be awfully crushed to hear us call her a liar, but it cannot be escaped that she and honesty had not got on well for some time.

There are many sorts of lies. You could fill a shop with them. To be sure, lies are terribly common. Few would pay particularly good money for fibs when they are so busy making their own at home for nothing. But if you peek inside the shop door of the heart, there you will find a full stockroom. Lies to conceal dastardly deeds stack up smartly along the shelves. Over in the refrigerated section hang lies told so long ago and so often that they turned into the truth and get taught in history books. Lies told to make oneself seem grand pile up high on a special four-color display. And in the front windows, laid out so nicely no one could blame you for having them, snuggle up little harmless lies told to spare feelings or save face or keep a friend from trouble.

Of course, nothing is really harmless. Sometimes telling the truth can bang the world about its ears just as much as any lie. But you must always be careful when you visit that little shop where lies are kept. They are always looking for a way out.

The first lie September told was very simple indeed. It was such a tiny lie, in fact, that if you were not looking carefully, as we are, you would surely miss it. She told it on a rainy, blustery, squalling day, which is just the right sort of day to start down a strange and secret path. Long, cindery, smoky-colored clouds rolled and rumbled over the Nebraska prairie. The storm fell in silver streamers, stirring the thirsty earth into a thick soup. September sat in her mother and father's house, looking out the window at the sloshy drops plunking into mud puddles the size of fishing ponds. Everything glittered with the eerie, swirling light of the heavy sky. Her familiar fields looked quite like another world.

September had a book open on her lap but could not concentrate on it. Her cup of tea had gone altogether cold. The pink and yellow flowers on the handle had worn almost to white. A certain small and amiable dog rolled over next to her, hoping to have his belly scratched. September did not notice, which deeply offended the dog. Her mother read the newspaper by the fire. Her father napped quietly with a checkered blanket thrown over his poor wounded leg, which never could heal quite right, no matter how many long trips into the city they took to visit his doctors. A bubble of thunder burst and spat. September's mother looked up, leaving off an interesting article about a modern new road that might run very near to their house, and asked her daughter:

"Whatever are you thinking about, dear? You seem quite lost in your head."

And September, very simply, answered, "Oh, nothing really."

This was wholly, thoroughly, enormously untrue.

September was thinking about Fairyland.

Now, you might say that September had been lying all along, for certainly she never told her parents about the magical country she had visited twice now. That is what grown-up sorts who are very interested in technical terms call a lie of omission. But we will be generous and forgive September for leaving her adventures out of suppertime conversation. How could she ever explain it all? *Mama and Papa, you might be interested to know that I flew away to a land of Witches and Wyverns and Spriggans, fought the wicked Marquess who was in charge of it all, and won—please pass the roast beets?* It would never do. *Papa and Mama, not only did I do all that, but I went back! My shadow had been making trouble, you see, and I had to go to the underworld to fix it all up again. Shall I do the washing up?*

No, it seemed best to leave the matter where it lay. And where it lay was deep inside September where no one could take it from her and ruin it by staring at it too closely. When she felt afraid or alone, when her father was in such awful pain he could not bear to have anyone near him on account of the terrible racket of their breathing and thinking and swallowing, she could take her memories out and slip them on like a shawl of fabulous gems.

Poor September. Everyone has their invisible cloak of all things past. Some shimmer and some float. Some cut all the way down to the bone and farther still.

If you could only hear the little trumpet of that lie, calling all its brothers and sisters to muster!

And muster they did. What was September to do when her teachers asked her to write a composition on how she had spent her summer vacation? Five paragraphs on *I brought my father's shadow back from Fairyland-Below where my own shadow had pulled it over from the war in France and I carried it all the way home to put it back together with his body again*? Certainly not. Like all the other students, she wrote a nice essay on the unusually hot August she had spent bringing the harvest in, learning lacework and how to repair the brakes on Mr. Albert's Model A.

Yes, Mrs. Franke, that was all. Nothing interesting in the slightest.

And when Mrs. Bisek, who taught physical education, remarked on how fast September could run nowadays, could she possibly pipe up and announce: *I have had good practice while migrating with a herd of wild bicycles, as well as escaping several alarming creatures?* Out of the question. It was all up to helping her father learn to walk properly again, of course. Together they made endless circuits of the acreage so that he could get strong. And worst of all, when Mr. Skriver, the history teacher, asked if anyone knew the story of Persephone, September had to bite the inside of her cheek to keep from crying out: *I went to Fairyland on a Persephone visa and I ate Fairy food and both of those put together mean I shall go back every year when the seasons change.* Instead she let one of the girls whose fathers worked at a bank in Omaha and wore smart little gray hats answer, and get it wrong at that.

All around her, the children September had known since her first days of school were growing up. The girls loped tall through the hallways and talked about their boyfriends in the same thrilled and thrilling tones you and I might use to discuss marvelous flying dragons. They shared the mystic secrets of keeping one's golden hair perfectly golden and one's ivory skin perfectly clear. Some of the boys had bits of beard or mustache coming in, of which they were very proud. September was excluded from the mysteries of golden hair and ivory skin, having neither. Nevertheless, she was getting taller, too. She would soon find herself taller than all but three or four girls her age. Her face was turning into the face it would be when she was grown. But she couldn't see it, for no one can see themselves change until they have already done it, and then suddenly they cannot remember ever having been different at all.

And above all the bustle of thirteen-year-olds becoming fourteen-year-olds floated the great and powerful rumor: The war would be over soon. Everything was going to go back to normal.

Spring melted over the farms outside Omaha like butter in a pan. Sharp, green days full of bold white clouds. September could not help smiling a little smile, all day long and in her sleep, too. Waiting for Fairyland was like waiting for a raspberry bush to fruit. One day you thought the whole thing was dead and hope lost, and the next you were drowning in berries. But the fruit always came. That is what September told herself. Of course, faith and patience are very hard tricks for a heart to learn. It would be easier for our girl to learn how to somersault off a trapeze than to believe that the dastardly, dashing world tends to do things whenever it pleases, on its own persnickety timetable and not that of yearning young people. She watched April rumble through like a bright, wet train and May burst in close behind, warm and noisy and full of wheeling, boisterous birds.

Her fourteenth birthday came.

September's father felt well enough to help with her present. It was a present so wonderful it came all the way round again to terrible and so terrible it sped through to wonderful with a quickness. September felt so nervous and excited her skin flashed cold and then tingly and then hot as a stove.

September was going to learn to drive.

On the morning of September's birthday Mr. Albert's creaking, cranky Model A Ford sat out in front of the house like an old horse ready for the races again. A little orange ribbon fluttered in the wind, tied round the burlap Aroostook Potato Company sack that covered the spare wheel. The Model A could not claim to be young nor fast nor good-looking, but it made fantastic snarling noises. Alongside her mother, September had worked her fingers into almost every part of that engine. Now those fingers twitched with eagerness, remembering valves and pistons. With some coaxing and bargaining, she knew, the aged beast would roll down the road to town, grumbling plenty all the way.

And now it was *hers*.

At least for the afternoon.

The moment it became her own, September saw the Model A as quite a different animal. It was no longer a chore to be finished by supper, but a glorious monster, a puzzle smelling of gasoline with a lot of parts like teeth. She touched the battered, accordioned vent—the paint had not won its battle with fifteen Nebraska winters. Once it had been pure, dark, wintry green. Now it looked like a pelt, with spots and stripes of naked metal and rust showing through. The black fenders curved up and over piebald front wheels, hoisting the near-flat spare and big froggy headlights. The chrome had not dreamed of shine since Mr. Albert had whacked it up against a beech tree a month after he bought the thing. The cracked windshield sparkled in the hot sun. It had a cloth top you could pull over your head, but the day glowed so warm and still that September knew they wouldn't bother with it. Not today. She would drive with the wind in her hair and get a marvelous roadster's sunburn.

"Hullo," September whispered to the Model A, just as she would to a crabby old horse who didn't want her apple, thank you very much. "Don't be afraid, I shall try very hard not to crunch you or whack you in any way. Of course, I cannot promise, but I am usually quite careful when dealing with terrible engines."

Her father eased himself into the passenger seat, his face a little red and flushed with the effort and the sunshine and the bustle of a birthday. He tightened the straps of Mr. Albert's driving goggles over September's head and pulled the extra pair down onto his own big, lovely nose. September could hardly breathe. Her excitement leapt and sputtered in her as though the car were already speeding down the road.

Now, a Model A does not start and stop the way automobiles whose acquaintance you and I have made do. It has a good number of levers and valves and switches, and operating one is something like puppetry, something like lion taming, and something like dancing. September's mother pointed and explained the peculiar workings of the rusty creature with an engine for a heart.

"Now," she said brightly, her warm, firm voice full of confidence in her daughter. "There are important rules in driving an automobile, rules from which no one, not even your own mother, is exempt."

"Tell me the rules," said September with that secret little smile her mother could not interpret.

"Some are easy: Go on Green, stop on Red. Use your mirrors,

they're there for a reason. Look both ways before turning. Brake into a turn and accelerate out of it. But most of the rules have to do with not killing the car while trying to get it started. Getting things started is always such a difficulty! But, like so: the brake must be on before you can begin. This seems backward, but it's important. Turn on the gas valve and push the spark lever—that's the one on your left, dear—all the way up. It's fire that makes a car go, my love, fire and fuel. Now pull the throttle lever—on your right, darling—a little ways down. Imagine a clock, where the throttle is the hour hand. Put the hour hand at four o'clock. See how at four o'clock the accelerator pedal goes down all by itself? That's how you know you've got it right. You must turn the carburetor—that shiny knob there—one full turn closed, then one full turn open. Put the gear in neutral—neutral means neither forward nor backward nor fast nor slow, and it is the place from which you must always begin. Closed before open. Brake before beginning. Now, at last, turn the key to ON. But it is not ON yet, no matter what the key says! Pull the carburetor rod back, and press this button on the floor which is the starter. Wait for the engine to turn over—that sound like it is clearing its throat and will soon begin talking up a storm—and let the rod go."

September thought the rods and buttons would slide smoothly into place with satisfying sounds and clicks. Once you knew what to do, well, doing it would be no trouble! But it was not like that at all. It took all her strength to drag the throttle lever into position. She thought her wrist might snap before the gearshift would agree to grind into neutral. The Model A spat and gargled and shuddered awake, but not all at once. First she gave too much gas; then she was too slow to press the starter after yanking back the carburetor with both hands and her shoulders put into it in earnest. No wonder Mr. Albert thwacked that beech tree.

September's father put his warm brown hand over hers and let the spark lever down a little. There were more strange words—*clutch* and *choke* and *shift,* like the car was a body and quite alive, if a little sick with bellyache or cough.

Had she been less excited by the phlegmy roar of the Model A, September might have noticed how much she had grown in order to touch the pedals with her feet and see out the windshield while sitting up very straight and proper and not boosted on heavy books. But the car jangled and her heart jangled with it. When she released the brake, there certainly was much clutching and choking. September let out a whoop of joy that was swallowed up in the raggedy protestations of the engine, and off they rattled down the dirt road, bouncing and jostling and knocking and bonging. When it came time to shift gears, the Model A bolted forward ungracefully. When it came time to slow down, it whined and sputtered. September did not care. She leaned into the road, mud spattering her goggles, laughing into the May wind.

It was, after all, so very like riding a Wyvern.

Nothing else happened that day.

The sun set without peculiar happenings and no sooner than she could blink, September once more lived in a world without the Model A, as if none of it had ever happened. The wonderful, monstrous, noisy car vanished back to Mr. Albert's garage. No Wind of any color came rushing up behind the exhaust-blast of the car. When she lay in bed that night, she could still feel the vibration of the engine in her bones, like when you have spent the whole day swimming and the sweet rocking of the water lulls you to sleep long after you're good and dry. *I shall not worry just because the Green Wind did not come today,* she thought over the echoes of shifting gears shivering her skin. *Aunt Margaret says worry only turns down the bed for bad news.*

Instead of fretting over a day here or there, she would prepare. The place that fear took up in her heart she would fill with provisions and readiness. She was a seasoned Adventuress now, after all. It would never do to keep turning up in Fairyland like a helpless lamb with nothing but the wool on her back. Grown-ups didn't just wait around for things to happen to them. They made plans. They anticipated. They saved up and looked out and packed in. September slept very well that night. She dreamed of neatly filled suitcases and lists with every item checked off.

The first and most important of these preparations began with a mason jar under her bed. September had been saving pennies for some time. She was her mother's daughter and that meant a frugal girl with a weakness for hoarding what she never knew if she might need. But now her efforts had a clear purpose: September was quite fed up with the problem of having *needs* in Fairyland but no *means*. It was no better than her own world! Worse, in fact, since she hardly had a notion of what money meant over there at all. But she would have no more First Kisses traded on the open market this time, nor rubies wedged out of a Fairy sceptre that might well have been an oversized log back in Nebraska. She would never be a rich girl, neither here nor there, but she could at least make a go at convincing magical folk that a bit of copper was as good as a kiss.

And so September offered herself up to all her neighbors: no chore too big or too messy, guaranteed no complaining! She fed sheep and chickens and weeded kitchen gardens. She pinned up washing like blowing white sails on seas of long grass. She wrote letters for Mr. Killory who couldn't read and wasn't about to start learning now. She looked after the dusty, crabby Powell workhorses, fed and watered and combed them while they snorted in pointed disapproval. Mrs. Powell gave her a half-dollar as pretty as a plate when the big roan turned up pregnant after they'd long given up on the notion. She took over her mother's errands for Mr. Albert, driving round the county to fetch or deliver or purchase. Dimes and nickels and pennies went into her jar, filling it up like glinting jam.

Being prepared meant standing at the ready at any moment, should Fairyland come for her—and this was how she conceived of it in her deepest heart: a whole world drifting ever closer in a beautiful chariot of air and light and ocean, a whole world coming to collect her. Thinking everything over and laying her fairy-habits out one by one like butterflies in a tray, September had to admit that shifts and dresses were not the most practical of traveling clothes. She had only one pair of trousers, but they became dear to her—wearing them meant that she would soon be tumbling over stone walls and chasing down blue kangaroos. They meant going and doing and daring.

September also took her father's temperature every day, though when he offered her a dime for being such a steadfast nurse, she would not, could not take it. She asked after his pain as though it were a visiting relative and recorded the answers in a little book given to them by his doctors. He went to Omaha every three months. Ever so slowly those doctors were straightening his leg. There was nothing to be done about the piece of bullet lost somewhere in his thigh. September watched him go each time from her window, disappearing in the long, sleek Packard sent by the Veterans' Association. Each time she had the peculiar thought that he was under a spell just like hers, compelled to leave home and return to a strange city over and over again.

While she did her small work from farm to farm, September thought often of the Sibyl who guarded the entrance to Fairyland-Below, where her shadow had made its home. The Sibyl had loved her work, how she had known since she was a child that the work was as much a part of her as her own heart. *What is my work?* September thought, and not for the first time. *What can I do that is useful? What have I done since I was small that comes as natural as guarding to a Sibyl?* She did not know. It was probably not planting kitchen vegetables or driving a car. The Killorys' bleating sheep and half-blind rooster seemed to tell her with their black eyes that she was not so good at looking after them that she should make a life of it. The pregnant roan did not deign to share an opinion in any fashion. September considered herself quite good at reading and thinking, which was mostly what her father had done in his classroom before the war. She could, it certainly seemed, depose monarchs fairly well. But these did not seem to add up to what one might call a profession. September knew that some girls worked hard at training to be a quality wife and a mother to children that would one day be born. But her mother did all that and also made airplanes fly with just a wrench and her own good brain. September also wanted to do wonderful things with her own good brain. It was no easier to wait for such a profession to become clear than to stop looking for signs of Fairyland around every stone wall and fence post.

September tried to fill up her good brain with these sorts of things, to fill it so full that she simply could not think about anything else. May relaxed into its flowers and songbirds. June took the summer's baton and sprinted down its dry, golden track. The big hay wheel of the Nebraska moon looked in through September's window at night. And once, but only once, she held her jar of coins in the moonlight and thought finally the terrible thing she had not allowed to come in, no matter how it knocked on the doors of her heart. *Maybe it's because I am getting old. Maybe Fairyland does not want me because I have been trying so hard to be a grown-up person and behave in a grown-up fashion. Maybe Fairyland is for children. I am fourteen now, which is ever so much more than twelve. I have jobs even if they are not very good ones. I can drive a car and remember* to record Father's temperature at the same time every day. Maybe I am getting too big—no, worse, maybe I am getting too usual to be allowed to go back.

She woke that night with a start, sure she had heard a Wyverary's deep *haroom* right next to her.

But there was nothing. In the warm, still dark, September cried.

CHAPTER II

EXEUNT, PURSUING PUFFINS

In Which September Fails to Mend a Fence, Runs a Border, Misuses Prepositions, and Meets a Very Nice Dog Named Beatrice

The first day of July got out of bed hot and contrary. September woke early, so early that the sky still had a little pink and yellow in it when she shut the door softly behind her. She headed out to the neat line of trees at the far edge of their property. She was wearing her beloved green work-trousers, which, truth be told, had gotten both threadbare and too short for her, and a faded buttoned shirt with a pleasant red and orange checker on it. She carried a hammer hooked into her belt loops and, in her deep olive pockets, a little case of nails, two pieces of butterscotch candy as well as a paperback book concerning Norse mythology which she'd had to bend nearly in half in order to fit. Her jam jar of coins rested in the crook of her arm. September aimed to read about mistletoe and eight-legged horses for a while, then mend a space of fence that had blown down in the last rainstorm. The fence in question divided their property from Mr. Albert's much bigger spread. Her father had mentioned it the night before, absently, sadly, as though there were no point in trying to fix it, what with the world going on the way it was and rains coming anytime they pleased. When September finished with the fence, she was to take the Model A into town and purchase a good number of things on a list her mother had made out. Mr. Albert had a list, too, and Mrs. Albert and Mrs. Powell and Mrs. Whitestone down the way as well. For herself, September had decided to spend some of her precious coins in order to buy a compass and perhaps some other provisions that might prove useful in Fairyland.

With all the lists neatly tucked into her back pocket, September looked out toward the ribbon of leafy birches in the far distance, their white trunks showing starkly like capital letters. Their shade beckoned gorgeously, black and deep and cool. It was a long walk and September could not whistle or anything of the sort. Instead, she took out her book to read as she walked, spying her path out of the corners of her eyes. September could do nearly anything while reading: walk, brush a horse, pull ragweed out of the herb-bed, scrub the teacups and gravy boats which by now had almost no paint on them at all. The writing was very dry, but it hardly mattered when Valkyries and goats with mead in their udders were afoot. A lady named Skadi was going about choosing a husband just by looking at the legs of all the gods when that rich, thick shade fell over the pages. Time to walk along the fence until the ruined bit spilled out its wire and wood all over the place. September took out one of her butterscotches and popped it into her mouth.

All those gods' legs and butterscotch and hot morning sun might have kept September from ever seeing the rather large person and even larger dog walking along the other side of the fence. To be fair to our girl, the other person walked very quietly. In fact, she did not walk so much as sizzle silently into nothing and reappear again a little ways farther down the fence while her dog trotted to keep up. We can only thank the tangle of storm-battered fence for making its entrance just then and not a moment later. For when she saw the wreckage over the top of her book, September put Skadi and her gods-legs away and looked straight into the crackling, electric, blue eyes of an enormous woman and a tall, bored-looking greyhound.

September could not rightly tell whether the woman herself was enormous or if it was only her armor that made her seem so. But how fearfully strong and sturdy she must have been to bear up under it all! Metal closed up her tall, broad body like the grille of a train, twisted up in snarls of wires and bolts and incandescent knobs. In the center, where her heart should be, a great miner's lamp shone with blistering electric light, throwing off the palest blue sparks. Her shoes were made of railroad tracks bent and buckled into shape. Huge black half-pipes prickled with rivets hunched over her shoulders. Her hands, half the size of all of September, sported rough gloves cut out of two single cloudy diamonds. Inside the facets, lights flickered on and off, cold-black and searing white. Even the woman's hair was a tangled mass of electrical wires, bound up in a great knot. A few strands blew in the breeze, sending little sparks hissing down into the dirt. She held a huge, old-fashioned lantern in one hand with a ball of black burning where the flame ought to have been. In the other she brandished a great hook twisted up with intricate, beautiful metals like carvings on an ancient whalebone.

The greyhound, as tall as a lion and twice as lazy, stared with the same fiery blue eyes, but his fur rippled the flies away without armor, soft and gray and white with black speckles. His expression was the mournful, skittish one worn by all his breed.

September stared. The wire-woman stared back, much less alarmed, as September was rather small and not throwing off electricity like confetti.

Then she vanished.

The empty air where the woman stood popped and wriggled for a minute, and then all was still. The greyhound gave September another long, half-interested, houndly look which seemed to say: *A dog's work is never done and is that butterscotch I smell?* He got up, arched his back into a quick stretch, and padded off down the fence line.

September bolted after him. She needn't have; the electric lady crackled back into existence three or four long steps away. She lifted up her hook and seemed to catch an invisible something in the July air, yanking and twisting it against a frightful resistance. Beads of sparkling yellow sweat shot from her brow.

"Good morning!" said September, and felt foolish. Was this woman from Fairyland? She *seemed* Fairyish. She *felt* Fairyish. The air around her boiled with an intolerable heat and she smelled like scorched metal— but also, absurdly, like growing things, mushrooms and dandelion greens and pine sap. What else *could* she be? September had never seen anything like her. For certain she knew how to disappear.

The greyhound grabbed hold of the end of the long hook. He growled and hauled on it, and together with his mistress they worked free whatever had become stuck in the sky. The lady mopped light-sweat from her brow with a very plain checkered handkerchief. The pattern was nearly the same as September's shirt.

"And a good morning to you, kid, though by my clock it's midnight and by my mood it's a nasty one." She dug her massive diamond hand into her breastplate and tossed a bright bit of red light to her dog, who jumped to catch it and crunched happily away. "Too long before my shift's done and too much Line left to spool. Isn't that always the way?" She smiled a weary sort of smile. Her teeth flashed copper.

September simply could not think of anything to say. When that happened the thing she wanted to say but oughtn't usually jumped out of her mouth and that's just what it did.

"You're not a Wind," she said bluntly, and then felt rude and flushed.

"Got that right," the lady said darkly, and guttered out again. September gritted her teeth with frustration. She looked around and scrambled back along the fence to where the electric lady was coming once more into focus. The hound gave a little yip and followed.

"What are you, then?" September said, not less bluntly. She took a deep breath and started again. "I do have manners, I promise. It's only that when manners don't let me say what I want to, I don't have anything *else*. And what I want to say is, well, you *are* from Fairyland, aren't you? You just *have* to be."

The lady stuck her hook into the sky again, but this time, she hardly had to wriggle it twice before she seemed satisfied. She took out another lump of red light, put it into her own mouth like tobacco, and chewed thoughtfully. "Now, *from*'s a funny word for it. It's a preposition and those are a jagged business. Am I *from* Fairyland? No, no, you couldn't say it. You'd be wrong as a pen in a socket. Am I *among* Fairyland? That's closer, but nope, still a bust. Am I *out of* Fairyland? Am I *next to* Fairyland? Am I *regarding* Fairyland? It's no good! The trouble with prepositions is they want to stick pins in you. They want to say how you get on with things, where you are exactly in relation to this or that. Prepositions are the guardians of space and time—and if I use my manners, space and time and I had a row in school and we're not what you'd call bosom buddies any longer. Prepositions want to put you in your place, the little sticklers. In my line of work—oh gracious, there's me punning!—in my line of work you can't let anything hold on to you, not even words. Words are the worst. Everything else runs on words. And there's hordes of them, just running mad all over your business like ants. If you hold still long enough, they'll get you good. So I don't."

She crackled blue and sizzled out again. The greyhound fixed his incandescent eyes on September.

"We are *throughout* Fairyland," he said slowly. His voice was soft as falling ash.

The lady's staticky voice returned before September could see the blue lamp of her heart blaze up in just the same place she'd left.

"You didn't go anywhere!" September exclaimed.

"Well, sure I did," the woman said. "I went a hundred thousand miles. Put a patch on the Line at the Spindle Substation. And now I'm putting a fuse in here at the Pomegranate Junction. Only it's not *here,* see. I'm not *here* at all. S'what I mean about words. I'm on the other side of the rim. But the Line is so backed up here you can see bits of me coming through even though you shouldn't." Her blazing blue eyes narrowed and she bent down to September, shaking one gargantuan diamond finger at her. "Maybe you ought to just go to bed right now, young lady, without any supper. Spying on Heisenbergian mechanics through the keyhole. Kids today!" But then the electric lady laughed. "Don't look so shocked. I'm just having my own little jokes. I don't mind if you see me. Linemen don't mind much."

"What's a Lineman?" breathed September, glad to have something in all of that to hold on to.

"I'm one. My name's Boomer. My old boy there's Beatrice. He's a Cap. A Capacitor if you're inviting him somewhere formal. Keeps me grounded, holds on to the Line while I work it."

"That's a girl's name."

Boomer shrugged. "He likes Beatrice. It's not my business what a Cap wants to be called. Howdy, you are just bound and determined to make me talk, aren't you? Use words like a *person*." Boomer clattered and fizzed as she settled down onto the dirt beside the fence. "Well, I'll try but I don't have to like it. A Lineman works the Line. The line between the worlds. Like when you want to keep cows from wandering out and getting hamburgered by a train or busting ankles on oak roots. If there wasn't a Line, anyone could just jump around between worlds like hopscotch. Toss their marker over the chalk and bounce right through, calling all her little friends after her in a row. Nothing but a mess and I've seen it happen, back when."

"But people do jump," said September shyly.

"Oh, they do! Boy, and *how* they do! That's why I've got a job! The Line's got weak spots. It's old and I've got my suspicions about the morals of those what strung it in the first place. It has to be fixed nonstop. Just while I've been talking to you I've knit up fourteen frays, spackled a blown transformer, spooled up twenty slacks, replaced seven dark nodes, and netted a hole the size of Montana." Boomer squinted one eye. "And I hope you're smart enough to know those are just words, words you understand because you live in a world that has a Montana and transformers and capacitors. It's not what they *are*."

"Of course," said September, who had not realized that at all.

"I'm not from Fairyland. Never been there. But I've seen it through the shop window, you know? I go between, and I mind the Line. There was a bad break here a while back—a while back by *my* clock, not yours. And by *here* I don't mean your farm or Nebraska, really. Just here. *Here* summed up by Pluto and inchworms and balloons that rise because of helium. People have been coming and going like they got shot out of a circus cannon. I do not like it, no ma'am. The Line'll always be weak in these parts. Structural flaw. But it almost wore through completely last year—I think I've got that right. Time zones are my bedevilment and no lie. Last year we almost lost it, and now I've got to tend to the sag."

"Last year! I was in Fairyland then! And my shadow was stealing magic! A minotaur told me the borders would have just melted into nothing if she'd had her way."

"You should always listen to minotaurs. Anybody with four stomachs has to have a firm grip on reality. The Line was all in tatters. It got so bad you could just trip over a wall and end up who knows where? And when the works go that wrong, you get *bandits*. Worse than mice. If you see one it's too late. Beatrice does his best to rustle them good, but what can he do? It's a foundational fact of the universe that everything leaks. What comes out when it springs, that's the only question." Boomer spat. A stream of red lightning glittered out of her mouth.

September looked down at her shoes. "Am I a bandit? I've been crossing the Line. Twice. Four times if you count the return trip."

Boomer looked at her meaningfully. September stuck her hands in her pockets. But she looked up again and held the Lineman's gaze. She wasn't sorry. She wouldn't pretend she was sorry. She supposed that made her a bandit for sure.

Beatrice's eyes flashed like lightbulbs. He began to howl: a long, whistling, hollow note, just exactly like a steam engine.

"Here they come," snarled Boomer, and heaved up, her metal body unfolding like a puzzle.

"Who?"

The prairie stood quiet and green, except for a loose and fitful wind blowing the long grain and the dark green tips of the birches.

"Weren't you after a Wind? I hate Winds. Criminals and fugitives and psychopomps the whole stupid gasbagging lot of them. But for the Winds I could have retired with a nice spread out beyond the edge of time by now. Up, Beatrice! Speak!"

The greyhound rose up on his great haunches and barked once, twice, three times. His voice was no longer a steam engine but a terrible tolling bell. September clapped her hands over her ears—and a good thing, too. The wind whipped itself up so fierce and fast all the grain could do was stand straight up, stretched and taut almost to breaking. The air seemed to tip and totter and finally fall over, spilling out a throng of hollering, ululating, laughing, whooping creatures.

Puffins.

One by one they rolled up into fluffy cannonballs, flapped their tiny wings once or twice, and thudded back down onto their plump bellies, tumbling over one another like a wave breaking. Their round beaks gleamed bright orange and gold. Some were tiny, no bigger than jacks. Some were much bigger, the size of hunting hounds. Their eyes sparkled black and green and red and purple as they tumbled nearer—and at least some of those were not at all the right colors for birds' eyes as far as September knew. One by one they heaved up into the air again, paddling their wide webbed feet against the sky like they were scrambling up a mountainside.

And dancing on top of them, leaping from puffin to puffin, twirled a grinning young lady all in blue. She wore indigo trousers with as much silk to them as a skirt, and when they rustled, ghostly pale blue stars peeked out from the folds. She had on turquoise opera gloves and sapphire-colored boots with crisscrossed icicle laces all the way to the knee. A long, beautiful sky-colored coat spun out like a dress from a heavy silver belt at her waist, swirling with aquamarine stitching, trimmed in wild, woolly fur from some impossible, blueberry-colored sheep. Her long, azure hair flew every which way under a cobalt cap rimmed in the same blue shag. The cap had an ice-spike on top of it, like old pictures of the Kaiser. She smoked a blue churchwarden pipe, blowing great squares and triangles and rhombuses of blue smoke for her puffins to dip and dive through.

A long honk broke up the caterwauling puffin songs. In the center of the flock, half bouncing on the ground and half hoisted, shoved, carried, and jostled by the birds, came Mr. Albert's Model A Ford.

"But that's *my* car!" September corrected herself, but she was quite indignant that someone else—even if they *were* puffins—was driving it. "I mean it's Mr. Albert's car! What are they doing with it? They're going to break it to pieces, that's what!"

"Horse thieves!" Boomer said with disgust. She brandished her hook like an ax. Beatrice growled. It sounded like the turning of gears deep in the earth.

The woman in blue sighted September. Her grin grew wider; her black eyes glittered. They barreled toward the fence. The air wriggled around the Lineman and her Cap, so hot it turned the back of September's legs painfully red. She stood her ground.

"Girl, Ho!" the blue bandit yelled, in the manner of sailors sighting land. She saluted smartly.

September saluted back. A smile broke open on her face like a firecracker. Who could this be but the Blue Wind, a little late, but come for her at last? September forgave her immediately for her tardiness. Her heart hammered around inside her like it meant to get free.

"Wind, Ho!" she cried. Suddenly, all that talk of bandits and holding the Line seemed wholly, entirely unimportant. September laughed and waved giddily. She couldn't help adding: "Have you come to take me to Fairyland?"

The Blue Wind cocked her head to one side and hooted. The puffins hooted back. Now they were nearly on top of her, September could see each little bird dressed in smart, shining armor of the sort you find in books about Spanish explorers. The armor was made of ice and caked in snow. Their own black feathers stuck out of their helms as plumes.

"Hadn't planned on it," shrugged the Blue Wind. "Fairyland's a dreadful place. Why would you want to go there?" She laughed; her laughter rocketed into the forest, echoing and breaking apart against the trees.

Several things happened all on top of each other.

The bandits shot up into the sky: puffins, the Blue Wind, the Model A, and not a few birch trees yanked out of the ground by the fearful, shearing air.

Beatrice vaulted up to meet them, his long silver body arcing like a current, his sharp teeth glowing hot white.

Boomer dropped her hook and undid her hair. It was such a simple gesture September did not know what she was about until the whole mass of it came down and open: a net of wires sizzling with electricity, as wide and strong as the sail of a grand ship.

September cried out and she did not know who she meant to warn: the dog, the birds, Boomer, the Blue Wind? But it did not matter.

Beatrice snapped at the underbellies of the birds. They laughed chitteringly at him. He missed once, twice, three times; they could go higher than he. He fell back to the ground, his snout twitching, yelping frustration like a puppy. As soon as her hound had got clear, Boomer threw her net in the bandits' path. September was certain they'd be cooked to death—but the Blue Wind only giggled. With a wink for September, she spun around like an ice-skater on the back of a particularly large puffin. The stream of birds narrowed and squirmed and shrunk and passed straight through the gaps in the electric net—and so did the Model A, honking tinily as it jumped.

The storm stopped abruptly. All was silent. Boomer stood stock-still, her flashing diamond fist clenched in anger around the wires of her electric hair. Beatrice howled his mournful train-whistle howl once more.

September tried to catch her breath. She looked at the Lineman. She looked at the Cap. She looked after the Blue Wind, vanished completely. A very certain thought came on in her mind. Boomer wouldn't let her cross over. She knew it. It was her job to say no. To bar the way. Just like it was the Sibyl's job to say yes and open the way. Just like it was her own job to record her father's temperature and mind the pregnant Powell horse even when she bit. You do your job and you mind your work. That's how the grown-up world gets along—and grown-up magic, too.

Before the Lineman could stop her, before Beatrice could get up on his haunches again, September clutched her jam jar to her side, darted forward, and leapt with all her might. She dove through the same gap in the net of crackling white-blue wires that had swallowed up the puffins, just wide enough for a girl. She shut her eyes at the last moment, blinded by the showers of glowing sparks and by a sudden sureness— she hadn't jumped hard enough! The wires would catch her in a flash and turn her into smoke. Too late, too late!

September winked out of the world like a firefly.

Boomer sighed. She kicked the fence post, which shattered in terror before her great foot had a chance to touch it. The Lineman dropped the net of her hair like a curtain and promptly blinked out again. This time, Beatrice sizzled away, too, and the only thing left of any of them was a last, lingering wisp of the hound's howl.

CHAPTER III

VISITORS OF LOW REPUTATION

*In Which September Lands in a Familiar City, Argues With the Wind,
Makes a Valiant Stab at Stoicism, and Faces Certain Facts About the
Dissolution of Political and Economic Regimes*

O f all the somersaults ever turned, only a few could be called sloppier than the head-over-heels half-flying cartwheel in which September tumbled out of the sky.

She did not have far to go. The Lineman's net, without ceremony or dignity, dropped her onto a dry, dusty road from just enough height to let her know it was not at all happy with her. September landed on her knees; they jangled and buzzed all the way up to the top of her head. She winced, but did not make a sound. For a moment her eyes would not open, quite convinced she'd been crisped. But even when she could feel her rough trousers and the entirely unbarbecued skin of her hands, she still could not do it. What if she peeked and the world around her was not Fairyland—if it was the woods around Mr. Albert's house or some awful abandoned, star-strewn depot on the Line?

One eye, then the other. September had to say it twice before she could get her eyelids to obey. *One eye, then the other. Then see what you see and face up to it.*

The sky shone neither blue nor black, day nor night, but a fiery, swirling twilight. Light blazed in scarlet, peacock, deep plum, and molten quicksilver, light so thick it seemed to drip from the air onto every surface. September knelt on a faded green-gray line etched, perhaps even *sketched,* into a long avenue. On either side, soft smoke-colored pillars soared up into the bright, twisted clouds. Pillars—but not pillars! Some were very tall and very rickety; some looked like cathedral towers but had no fine bricks, only clapboards and rusty nails. Some were made of lovely stone slabs, but great holes gaped in them, all the way up. And many, many had long silky ribbons tied round them and wax seals in black or white or red or gold. Tears and stains marred each of these. She could see drawings through the holes: lines, houses, funny little dragons with huge nostrils floating in carefully inked seas. They were great scrolls of ashen parchment, each crease and fold and rip tinged in ultramarine. The road, which rustled gently under her knees as she stood up, was paper as well, the lovely old thick and glossy sort of paper that only very beautiful or very important things got written on. Up at the top of the scrolls, September could see little church towers and villas and ranches and gardens. A wooly, horned sheep peered over the edge of one and bleated down; his bleat echoed fuzzily in the paper canyon. Rusted-out cupolas crowned towers here and there.

Just the sorts of buildings where wind howls hardest, whistles loudest, screams highest.

Up ahead, a great pearly-violet mountain range opened up like an infinite library. A stormcloud of squawking birds tumbled and danced toward those hills. Automobile exhaust puffed and sputtered out behind them.

September wanted to jump up and down on the road and shout at the molten-colored heavens. She wanted to turn a somersault, a real, proper somersault. She wanted to exult and sing nonsense at the clouds and kiss anyone who happened to be by, which was no one, but never you mind. But she did none of those things. September raised her hands to her mouth and wiggled in place like a dog wagging her tail. Her face turned red from the keeping in of all the noise and movement her body longed to make. At this moment, her head spoke louder, and what her head wanted was to be as cool and collected as a Wind. To be knowing and canny as they were. When you wear all your insides on your outside, people look at you very strangely. No one had ever told her that exulting and dancing and singing nonsense were childish things, but she felt sure that they were, somehow.

Shall I tell her? Shall I be a kind and merciful narrator and take our girl aside? Shall I touch her new, red heart and make her understand that she is no longer one of the tribe of heartless children, nor even the owner of the wild and infant heart of thirteen-year-old girls and boys? Oh, September! Hearts, once you have them locked up in your chest, are a fantastic heap of tender and terrible wonders—but they must be trained. Beatrice could have told her all about it. A heart can learn ever so many tricks, and what sort of beast it becomes depends greatly upon whether it has been taught to sit up or to lie down, to speak or to beg, to roll over or to sound alarms, to guard or to attack, to find or to stay. But the trick most folk are so awfully fond of learning, the absolute second they've got hold of a heart, is to pretend they don't have one at all. It is the very first danger of the hearted. Shall I give fair warning, as neither you nor I was given?

By now, my dear friends, you know me better.

And so September tried to put an expression of a very proud, noble, solemn adultish sort of wonder on her face, because it was a trick she felt she ought to learn. But that is a lot to contain in two eyes, a nose, and a mouth, and she really only managed her own unhidable leaping, fizzing joy—yet this time the joy was a silent one. It jangled inside her but did not boil over. To be back in Fairyland. To be near magic and thrillingness again. To be in a place where she did not have to lie about the things she wanted most of all—because they were *here,* and she could touch them and talk with them and wrestle with them and ride upon them.

But there was no one to praise September for her restraint.

And where was *here?* It looked so terribly familiar, but September could be quite sure she had never run down a road of vellum or called up to the tip-tops of scroll-towers before. And run she did, to catch the puffins and the Blue Wind and Mr. Albert's poor car who hadn't asked to be bothered with any of this trouble! Her jar of coins rattled and jingled loudly in the canyon of pillars. But hadn't she heard the wind whistling like that before? Hadn't she smelled that dry, sweet smell on the breeze?

Fortunately, now that they'd jumped the Line, the flock of puffins didn't seem to be in any great hurry. The glossy throng of them burst apart, save those hoisting up the stolen automobile on their ice-armored backs. A few shot ahead up toward the sun, cannonballs with orange beaks. Little birdy bullets of pearl and ink fired and spun out to land upon whatever they could find in that wild place. As September bolted up over a rise in the papery road, she found what they found: a little shantytown laid out among the pillars, every rooftop and chimney colonized by the squat, chattering birds.

The road ran smoothly, straight into the village, whose back bunched up against the mountains. The peaks beyond flowed up to impossible heights, traceries of text and compasses and old, old ink disappearing into the distance. A boardwalk ran from the main avenue into the town proper, each slat on the path the fold of a long, thick, heavy map, hanging the way they did in libraries, draped over strong bars so as not to crease or wrinkle. The slats showed the blue of strange oceans, every one. September scrambled to a stop before a ramp up onto the boardwalk: an atlas the size of a boat, open to its frontispiece, which read:

MERCATOR, TOWN OF.
FIRST EDITION PUBLISHED 1203.
EDITOR: KING CRUNCHCRAB I.
LAYOUT AND DESIGN: CADASTRAL CROSSHATCH, ESQ.
ALL PERSONS, EVENTS, CRIMES AND CRIMINALS,
MAGIC, MAYHEM, AND THREATS OF BODILY HARM
USED BY PERMISSION.
VISITORS OF LOW REPUTATION REPORT TO
THE WAY STATION IMMEDIATELY.
ALL OTHERS KEEP OUT.

"Well, I don't *think* I have a low reputation!" opined September, catching her breath.

A wild, bouncing laugh prevented her from further defending her character. September startled: Up above her, crouching on the rim of a spindly, spirally chimney, the Blue Wind pointed at her and kept on laughing.

"Oh, my little sour blueberry, you are just adorable when you don't know what you're talking about!"

The Blue Wind sprang out from the chimney like a bat. She spread her arms for the briefest moment, then pirouetted down to the ground before September. She clapped her blue hands.

"Even if you hadn't entirely deposed (and possibly killed) not one but *two* governments and destabilized all sorts of political regions you couldn't even pronounce, let alone draft up constitutional monarchies for, even if you'd been far more careful about leaving your toys strewn about everywhere when you tire yourself out with anarchy and run on home, I'd say you really are the lowest sort." The Blue Wind grinned wickedly. Her purple lips shone. "A *hitchhiker*."

"I didn't hitch!"

"Oh, come off yourself! You could never have got through without me! When have you ever gotten into Fairyland by your lonesome? Never, because you can't, because you are a *person* and people are *boring* and boring means *you*." The Blue Wind crossed her brocaded arms over her chest, quite satisfied with her logic.

This struck September like a slap. She remembered, suddenly, that the Blue Wind was not loved by her brothers and sisters. The Green Wind had said so, she was quite sure. "You're teasing me. A Wind wouldn't call such names. Winds are . . . well, not kind, but at least they aren't cruel!"

The Blue Wind arched one aquamarine eyebrow. "Have you never known a cruel wind? What an easy, balmy, tropical life you must have! I never tease, madam! I coax, I beguile, I stomp, I throw tantrums, and for certain I *freeze*—I am the Coldest and Harshest of all the Harsh Airs! I am the shiver of the world! But I do not *tease*. You can cause ever so much more trouble by taking folk seriously, asking just what they're doing and doing just what they ask." Her blue eyes glittered. A puffin circled down and landed on her shoulder. He marched back and forth (a very cramped sort of marching) with an icy poleax in his wing.

September burst forth. "You were supposed to come and get me! You were supposed to bring me to Fairyland in the spring! Or if not you one of the others! The Green Wind promised—he promised I'd go back every year and you didn't come and now you're just snapping like an old dog. You don't seem like a Wind at all, in fact! Where is your cat? Shouldn't you *like* stealing folks away? You certainly seem to like stealing everything else!"

The Blue Wind put her hands on her lilac hips. Her voice tightened into a squall.

"Listen, you spoiled, wretched *gust* of a girl," she snarled, "I am not public transportation! Haven't *you* become the jaded little tart! Accustomed to getting what you want and wanting what you've gotten accustomed to." The Wind puffed out her cheeks like a cherub and calmed herself down. She looked out over the boardwalk as if she had much better things to do and to drink. "Expectations are so very dangerous to young humans. I wouldn't give my worst hat for the way my siblings manage their affairs. I don't even attend the reunions. I go my own way—and don't they punish me for it! They took my Snow Leopard away over that nonsense in Tunisia, if you *must* roll out my embarrassment first thing. Hypocrites, the lot of them. As if they've never turned the world the wrong way round just to see it fly! But I never let it get to me. I keep my head high! My puffins are quite the equal of their snobby old tabbies. The Puffins of Sudden Blizzards, my little army. Winter needs her knights, after all." The Blue Wind saluted the stalwart fellow on her shoulder. He saluted back with the tip of his poleax. "No, I do not think I would like to steal you away to Fairyland. I thought about it for a good long while, all through the summer. I watched you scuttle around *boringly* and put my brain on it and I think I just don't like you very much. Fairyland has spoiled you rotten. I suppose you think you're *owed* the trip! The cheek! It's time for you to be a sensible, gracious girl, get good marks, and stop mucking about with Fairylands of any stripe. Learn a trade, hit the road, close the case."

September opened her mouth to protest, panic rising up through her legs and stomach like a stormcloud. What a cruel Wind this was! She did not like her manner at all. September had never thought she was *owed* anything—but hadn't she? Hadn't she felt angry when May passed and the whole summer, too, and nothing, not even a whisper? Hadn't she felt, well, betrayed? But who had ever promised September anything? You can only feel betrayed when you have a right to something. Chagrin seeped up through September's toes and all the way to her cheeks.

The Blue Wind barked laughter. She reached down swiftly and gave September's cheek the tiniest of slaps. It struck her like a cold word. September stared, dumbfounded, her mouth hanging open.

"She who blushes first loses!" the Wind crowed. "I win and that's the match!"

September lifted her hand to her face. She had been struck only once before. One of the older girls in school, whose name was Martha May and who had the thickest, brightest, prettiest red hair anywhere, had walked up to her at lunchtime one day and slapped her. It wasn't a hard slap; at the last moment Martha May shut her eyes and didn't land it quite right. Her fingers brushed September's cheek and her ear. But it stung all the same. Martha's friends had dared her; through her tears and hammering heart September could see them laughing under their hands, which is how folk laugh when they know they oughtn't be laughing. Martha May had stood there for a moment, looking really rather sorry and not at all sure why she'd done it, in the end. But then she laughed and ran off back to her pack, her red curls awfully bright in the sun.

September would not cry this time. She would *not.*

The Blue Wind hooted triumph once more, throwing her Kaiser-hat up into the air and catching it. As she worked herself up, all around them, whirlwinds and flurries worked themselves up as well, spitting and wheeling and scattering apart. September's dark brown hair and the Wind's purply blue hair streamed out around them as though they were underwater. The wind screeched through the holes in the high, rickety towers. September knew that sound! Suddenly she forgot all about her burning cheek.

"Wait!" she cried. "Are we in *Westerly*?"

The Blue Wind stopped short like an unplugged radio. All her gusts died in a moment. She crouched down, balancing on her blue leather toes, tented her fingers, and looked up curiously at September.

"Where else would a Wind call home? Well, not Westerly proper, you know. Not Westerly the Big Fat Club of Rottens That Won't Let You in for No Reason at All. This is the suburbs, girl. The *hinterlands*. Where the criminals and the carnivals and the concatenating counterfeiters of no morals to speak of make a home. Mercator's off the tourist track. It's where you come if you can't go through official channels. If you need to trade or buy or sell or rent or smuggle or feed something you oughtn't. It's the underground. That's what *suburb* means, you know. Under the city. It's Latin, which is an excellent language for mischief-making, which is why governments are so fond of it. This is the Blue Market, where you turn up when the world tells you no."

September turned to look down the book-boardwalk into the murky, twilight town. Folk moved down the streets, but she could not see their faces in the gloom.

"Perhaps you ought to give me directions to Westerly, then. I . . . I met Latitude and Longitude once. They might remember me. I still know all the puzzle pieces to go from one world to another. I think I could get them to open up again and take me through the official way.

I shouldn't like to go sneaking through the back door when I could present myself nicely at the front."

The Blue Wind opened her mouth and closed it again. Her great dark eyes danced with amusement. She patted September's hair. "Oh, my wintry waif, don't you know what happens when the government totters? Or, in this case, gets dropped soundly on its head by a certain spoiled traipsing tourist. Out goes organization and in comes skewered-if-you-do, roasted-if-you-don't, in comes smuggling, bribery, graft, skimming, back alley deals, and might-as-well-do-it-all-while-no-one's-looking. A whole fabulous bouquet of ways and means! It's so sweet that you think Latitude and Longitude look anything like they did when you went ingenue-ing about years back! I think they've re-tired to Paraguay. Now it's Line-jumping and squeezing through by the teeth of your skin and don't forget to bribe the door on the way out."

September felt a chill. "But there is a government! Charlie Crunch-crab is King—it even says so on the sign."

"Oh, the Old Crab is doing his best to pinch it all back into shape. Nice and Imperial, he says, Just Like the Old Days. But"—the Blue Wind spread her hands and shrugged—"what does a bandit care for a King's little hobbies? Now, if you're entirely finished, I've got goods on the barrel and you've quite ceased to be interesting."

"Goods! You mean Mr. Albert's car! You can't just go selling it. It isn't yours!"

"I suppose you think it's yours? Or this Mr. Albert, who sounds even more insufferable than you?"

"Well, yes, of course, it's Mr. Albert's!"

"Don't you 'of course' me, my blueberry-brat! You're wrong three times over!" The Blue Wind ticked her fingers off one by one. "It's not *yours* and it's not *Mr. Albert's* and it's not *mine,* either!" She held up her hand. "It's a *Tool* and Tools Have Rights. I'll split the proceeds with the—it's a car, is it? Measly word—fair and square, and we'll have a good sit-down between us and decide which buyer the beast likes best."

September sputtered. "You can't have a sit-down with a car! It's not a Fairyland car with a story and sorrows and sugar on top—it's just a *car.* From my world. It doesn't even work very well. It can't talk and it can't spend money and it certainly doesn't have rights!"

The Blue Wind whistled. She stood up, spreading her satin-gloved hands, washing them of all things September. "Well, I'm sure you're right and I'm wrong and there's absolutely nothing you don't know about anything."

The puffin on her shoulder shook his head disdainfully at September. The Blue Wind turned sharply and marched off down the boardwalk of book spines and into the crowd of Mercator. The scarlet light of the sky caught the silver thread in her jacket and sparkled.

"No, you don't!" snapped September, stomping after her. "I am coming with you and if someone is going to buy that automobile it's going to be me. And then you're going to tell me how to get into Fairyland like a Wind should—" September caught herself. That was not an argument this Wind would like one bit. She wouldn't care at all for what a Wind should do—if she were in the habit of acting as she should she wouldn't have lost her Leopard. And without a Wind, how would she get to Fairyland? There were no others about; it was the Blue Wind or nobody. September took a breath. If the most trouble came from taking folk seriously, she would do just that. "You're going to tell me how to get into Fairyland," she revised, "because even though I am spoiled and you don't like me, it's a good bet I'll stir some manner of consternation up there and kick things over and make a mess, because I'm a *person* and that means *trouble* and trouble means *me*." September drew herself up and grinned, even though she did not feel in the least like grinning. The Winds were mischievous, that was certain—so she had to be as well.

The Blue Wind said nothing. She did not stop. Her blue leather boots made soft noises on the boardwalk. But after a moment, she held out a long turquoise hand.

September took it.

CHAPTER IV
A Professional Revolutionary

In Which September Is Wayed and Treasured, Meets a Well-Connected Crocodile, Learns a Spot of Fiscal Magic, and Becomes an Official Criminal of the Realm

The sun set in Mercator.

But that didn't seem to mean much. The sky turned a sort of lemony lavender, and strange, unfamiliar magenta stars came on between the braided clouds. The stars seemed awfully close. September could see wispy bits of their flames curling out all around them. She supposed it should have been hot, with all those stars just as close as the sun, but instead the shantytown seemed to hunch up under a chill, turning up its coat collar against the constant wind. Sweet little houses lined the streets, compasses stamped on their paper doors—but all the lights in the windows were dark. The boardwalk led straight to the center of town, a great square as full of people and sound and doing as the houses were empty.

The square was a great map, inked in vermillion and viridian and cerulean and citron and bold, glossy black, fairly glowing in the twilight. A thousand countries crowded in upon it—and most of these were being stepped on and jumped on and jigged on and fallen on and stamped on by some fellow or other. September would have liked to have spent hours crawling over every line and legend—was Fairyland there, the dear island she had sailed all the way around? Was her own home? But she would not get the chance. Folk hustled everywhere, dressed in long, thick coats with brilliant buttons and deep pockets. Some wore hats and some wore helmets, some wore scarves and some wore smart little caps, but no one went bareheaded. September touched her own dark hair, feeling suddenly unprotected. She could not help but notice how many of the shadowed and shadowy faces were as blue as the Blue Wind's. Music ballooned up here and there, though September could see no instruments. It made a disorganized sort of tune, as though it grew wild as a mushroom in the forest, where songs and ballads and symphonies got themselves planted nicely in sweet little rows and watered from a clean spout every morning. Drums *whump*-thumped, horns squwonked, piccolos trilled, concertinas went squeezing in and out, but there was no order to any of it, only the occasional and wholly accidental harmony.

"That's a pleasant sort of noise, even if you couldn't sing along," September ventured.

The Wind nodded her blue head, her own furry hat gleaming wet with melt. "Music has more rules than math or magic and it's twice as dangerous as both or either. There's plenty here to buy and barter, to have and to haggle, but don't you go bothering instruments—I haven't got time to clean you off the Till."

For in the middle of everyone and everything, where the map's colors pooled densest and darkest, squatted a hulking old-fashioned cash register as big as a Roman fountain. It was the old-fashioned sort, with a hand crank, which September had only seen in books. It gleamed all over, its wooden cylinders and brass keys polished till it all shone like a candelabra. The glass of its display bore not a streak or a smudge. Within, on black squares blazing with curly white letters, the words NO SALE could be clearly read for miles.

On top of the Till sprawled a long, coppery crocodile.

As they drew closer, September saw that his scales were not scales at all but pennies, some green with age, some clean and new. His tail wrapped around himself and cascaded over the Till—not a crocodile's tail but a fan of deep emerald-colored feathers like a beautiful rooster. Deep, emerald-colored bills, folded so expertly they flowed and ruffled like feathers, showing their denominations when a breeze blew by. The crocodile watched the commotion below with glinting silver eyes: clusters of dimes, pale fires behind them, golden glass spectacles before them.

"Well, on you go," said the Blue Wind testily, pushing September a little closer to the register. "You saw the sign. I've brought you to the Way Station safe and sound. You should thank me and buy me supper and tell me how fetching I look in these shoes. Just look at that croc! Scary as a stormfront, isn't he? You should say: *What wonder! What majesty! That nasty old Green Wind just dumped me in the ocean, but you, you have outdone him flat-out!*"

"What wonder. What majesty," September said with a little sneer. She had never tried on a sneer before. It felt rather nice.

"Oh, aren't you just the rottenest wet blanket who ever spoiled a sport," snapped the Blue Wind. "You ought to try to make it nice for me. This is my first experience with smuggling humans across the border. If you rain on my fun I shan't bother again. Why, I didn't even make you solve a puzzle or stand in line!" The Blue Wind crossed her arms and spat, a coil of icy snow splattering onto the map of the square.

But September was not listening. She had sighted the Model A, surrounded by long-coats who were pressing their ears to the hood and trying the horn and sucking bits of air from the tires. "They'll spring a flat if they keep that up! I'll see about the crocodile in a moment—"

"No, you will not!" hollered the crocodile in a barreling, jingling voice. His feathers flicked over the NO SALE tiles. "Present yourself or I'll have you audited faster than you can blink those big, wide, *my-goodness-gracious* human eyes!"

The Blue Wind gave her a much firmer shove and September tripped forward toward the brass plates below the Till.

"Now then," began the copper crocodile. When he spoke, bits of green feather popped out of his mouth like punctuation. "I am the Calcatrix, Agent of the Crown, Excellent Exchequer, and Chief Beast of Imp-erial Ways and Treasures, which is a *very* new department and thus *very* fashionable. I get into all the best dancing halls just by flashing my scales. I will be conducting your Inspection this evening. And you are?"

"September." She clutched her jar of coins a little tighter.

"That's not very many titles," frowned the Calcatrix. "I'll bet you don't get invited to parties at all."

September bit the inside of her lip. "That's true," she admitted, rather more bashfully than she meant to. "I was a Knight for a while. And then a Bishop."

The Calcatrix leaned forward eagerly, his pennies clinking against the Till. "Now, now! We must not dwell on what we were in our salad days when soup days steam now upon the table! I see deep vaults of tragedy in you, young lady! No parties, and no banquets or saturnalias, either, I'd wager! Whereas I have feted the fetid and fabulous alike at every ballroom with two flutes to rub together. Even before I rose to my current position, my family were in low supply and high demand. We are all of us Numismatists of great potency—Finding Magicians, Collectors of Coins and Currency, Sorcerers of the Imaginary. I keep my collection on my person, where it is safe and sound and specially displayed. A Bank is but a college of Fiscal Magic and one never likes to be the rabbit in a beginner's first disappearing lesson. We ourselves, each of us, wore the Vestments of Investment and Brandished the Bursary! We practically invented the whole field of Fiduciary Glamours. I see you are an enthusiast, if obviously an amateur." The Calcatrix nodded at September's jar of coins. "Therefore I feel kindly toward you, though we hardly know each other. I am generous by nature and miserly by nurture. You are lucky that today I am feeling naturally."

"My savings certainly aren't imaginary," said September, curling her arm protectively around her net worth.

"All money is imaginary," answered the Calcatrix simply. "Money is magic everyone agrees to pretend is not magic. Observe! You treat it like magic, wield it like magic, fear it like magic! Why should a body with more small circles of copper or silver or gold than anyone else have an easy life full of treats every day and sleeping in and other people bowing down? The little circles can't get up and fight a battle or make a supper so splendid you get full just by looking at it or build a house of a thousand gables. They can do those things because everyone agrees to give them power. If everyone agreed to stop giving power to pretty metals and started giving it to thumbnails or mushroom caps or roof shingles or first kisses or tears or hours or puffin feathers, those little circles would just lay there tarnishing in the rain and not making anyone bow their noses down to the ground or stick them up in the air. Right now, for example, as much as I admire your collection, your coins aren't coins. They're junk."

September opened her mouth to object—the hours she had spent earning them! They were most certainly not junk! She had exactly seventeen dollars and thirty-seven cents in her jar and every one of them was as real as a roan with a bellyache! But the Calcatrix held up one coppery claw and continued patiently.

"Ah, my pecuniary petunia, but they are *not* real, because no one here would take them. To the denizens of the Blue Market, they have no power. What would they do with them?" He shook his head from side to side to make it clink and sing. "Why, without magic, they're nothing more than crocodile scales. None of them came here looking to trade their wares for copper with a human head on it. But I can wave my claws over them and *make* them coins, just by saying a few words, because I am the Exchequer, which is another way of saying Wizard. I can take your junk and make it wealth simply by saying: *One of these is worth this or that much.* The coins will still be coins, they will not have changed. But suddenly they will have power. And my dear, when you can change something just by saying a word, that is magic. Or I can take them and give you a certain number of Crabs in return, which is the *very* new and *very* fashionable currency of Fairyland—but then we are fully in sorcery's grip, for who are you to say I reckoned it right? When a thing becomes so simply because a person in shiny clothes said it with conviction, that is also magic. If you argue, then it is a wizards' duel! If a very silly one, because I am the Calcatrix and you are not."

September thought very carefully. "Maybe that's so for Fairy money," she admitted. "But human money is just money. It's quite serious stuff. And even if it weren't, it doesn't *matter* whether or not money is imaginary, if everyone agrees that it's got power. If we can't pay the bank every month we'll lose our farm, and I daresay they wouldn't like it if my mother told them to square up for a duel."

The Calcatrix grinned, showing all his silver teeth. "Just because it's imaginary doesn't mean it isn't real." He flared his green tailfeathers and settled one great penny-clad paw onto the Till's hand crank. "Does your human money not make objects appear at your whim? Does it not change a person from one thing to another, perhaps from a frightened child in rags to a haughty industrialist in a suit? Does it not heal you when you are sick? The doctor must be paid, after all. Can it not strike down your enemies at your command? Keep some folk on one side of town and others high on the hill as sure as briars round a castle? Create a coal-fire in the hearth where there was none, whisk you away to a tropical clime when you are so cold you cannot bear to watch another snowflake fall? Oh, do tell me what wonders human money would have to muster to earn the awe with which you treat the littlest Fairyland bauble!" The Calcatrix laughed, the coins of his throat tinkling. "And hie ye not to the Stock Exchange, child! There sneaks so much sorcery, crackling along the ticker tape, that if enough men all together believe a Company has heaps of money, why, suddenly, it will swim in a sea of Conjured Cash! But should those same men turn their faith away, that Dinero Diabolick will vanish as fast as the first abracadabra ever uttered. All that gold, just—presto!—turned to sticks and seeds and pinecones. Now, call the Calcatrix a liar."

September blinked. It looked like the truth, if you scrunched up your eyes. Hadn't it happened just that way just before September was born? Hadn't Aunt Margaret's husband, that unhappy Uncle of whom they all so rarely spoke, gone from a great man with fur on his coat and squeak in his shoes to a pauper with only a dust farm and a lot of suddenly powerless paper in the space of a night?

The copper crocodile nodded curtly, seeing his case made. "But enough of all these free lessons in my rarefied speciality! How clever of you to get something for nothing—and here's me hardly noticing. Well! Let us begin." His feathered tail swept over the till as he bent down to get his stubby hands into the works. "We used to be dreadfully backwards about this, you know, weighing your soul against a feather and all that. But now we have a *Methodology*. Now we have *Tools*. It's such a good lot of fun. Commence! Yes! First Inquiry!" The Calcatrix puffed with the effort of pushing the crank into position. "What is your profession?"

September's shoulders fell. "I . . . I haven't got one yet."

The copper crocodile blinked his silver eyes. "Excuse me," he said, "but that's just ridiculous. How can you have a Way if you haven't got a profession? And how can we put you down in our books if you haven't got a Way? Surely you're employed *somehow*."

"I go to school," September offered. "And I do odd jobs for those that need it."

The Calcatrix scowled. "All jobs are odd, or they would be games or naps or picnics. Well, let's ring this up item by item. What sort of thing do you like to do best?"

September did not have to think about that. "Traveling. To Fairyland—and back, but that's not nearly as good."

The Blue Wind scoffed. She and her puffin had dozed off, their heads leaning against each other, but the crank's creaking woke them. "That's not a thing you do, it's a place you *go* to do things *in*."

The Calcatrix ignored her. He continued indulgently. "And what sorts of things do you do when you get to Fairyland?"

September spoke very quickly in hopes that she could tell the truth without it counting against her. "Well, the first time I made friends with a Wyverary and a Marid and a Hundred-and-Twelve-Year-Old Lamp and got a magical wrench from a casket in the Worsted Wood and sailed all the way around Fairyland and defeated the Marquess."

The Calcatrix quirked a copper eyebrow. "So you're a revolutionary."

"No!"

"But you've already admitted to consorting with known mutinous rebels, and you're keeping *very* dubious company at present. Whereas I number among my peers Magicians, Ballerinas, Cockatrices, and the King himself. What does that say about the pair of us, hm? You said the first time—what about the second? Perhaps there's something there."

"I went into Fairyland-Below on account of my shadow being Queen there and almost shot her with a Rivet Gun—but I didn't do it! And she's still Queen, I think. . . ."

"So you're only an attempted murderer," the Calcatrix said. He seemed uncertain what to do with the crank, given this information.

The Blue Wind laughed so hard the puffin on her shoulder flew off in consternation.

"Don't forget that you *stole* that wrench and *did* shoot a Minotaur and pummeled that Marid you love so much half to death just to get your way. You even lied just to get into Fairyland in the first place!" She was bent over with giggles now, trying to catch her breath. Snow-flakes flew from her eyes like tears. "And look here!" she cried be-tween gales, "Contraband! She's a smuggler to cherry it!" The Blue Wind grabbed the wooden hilt of the hammer hanging from Septem-ber's belt loops and snatched the nails, remaining butterscotch, and book out of her pocket, as deft as a cutpurse thief. She rattled the nails in their little tin box.

"These here are *iron,* or else I'm an elephant. Weapons grade! Would an innocent girl just wander around with iron in her pocket? She's a hoodlum, your Excellency, up to no good and down for nothing nice. I'll vouch for it—I knew her for a brat the second I saw her. If you don't believe me, call for a phrenologist! There's one for sale next to the water pump. She's got a delinquent skull, just look! There, in her left temple! That's insurrection, plain as a stamp. Sedition written all over her face. She can't help it, poor kidlet. However good she tries to be, which isn't very if you ask me, if you let her open her mouth, chaos comes tumbling out and makes itself right at home on your doorstep."

The Calcatrix shook his green tailfeathers huffily. The pennies along his spine ruffled like an attack dog's scruff. But when he spoke his voice was merry. "I think the matter is clear. You'll have to go down as a Criminal. At least it's a growth industry. And you can work anywhere."

September wriggled out from under the Blue Wind's fingers, which prodded her forehead for further evidence of devilry. "But I'm *not* a criminal! I know all that sounds bad, but there were such good reasons for it all! What else could I have done? The Marquess was terribly cruel and my shadow would have driven all the magic out of Fairyland. And as for lying, the Green Wind told me to do it!"

The Blue Wind patted her shoulder convivially. "Oh, we all have such good reasons. It's the reasons that make it sweet."

"I am not a criminal," September repeated, pulling away from the Wind. "Just calling me one doesn't make it so."

"Well, of course you're not a Criminal!" chuckled the Calcatrix. "Not *yet*. You're not licensed to commit crimes! A fine place we'd be in if we let just anyone go about infringing and infracting."

"Excuse me," September interrupted, quite exasperated with being discussed as though she were on trial. "But all this seems awfully official! I thought things were different now, without the Marquess making the rules. I thought this was an underground market with back alleys and things! I'm quite sure someone told me that, in fact." She glanced pointedly toward the Blue Wind, who looked smugly delighted.

The Calcatrix scrunched up his long copper snout. "There's got to be some official claptrap, or else how would you know the unofficial when it came along? How would you recognize dastardly clandestines when you meet them in that dark alley you mention? It's no fun at all to break the rules if there aren't any. And for *really* convoluted rules and breaking, I tell you, child, there's nothing like a Fairy running things again. It's been ages since one of those buzzers had the chair! We'd all quite forgotten the games they do so love to play. King Crunchcrab wants to get things straightened up, get the works going right and proper again, the way it was in the Old Days when he was a boy. And that means doing the old Imp-erial foxtrot, if you catch me. Can't have much of an Empire without Standards, and that's why I'm stationed out here between Fairyland and Everywhere Else, to bear the standard. Certainly not for the latest cuisine or the local theater. King Charlie came to me personally, right up to the greenback door of the Numisma-tarium. I rolled out the frogskin carpet for him, nothing but the best: mug of mint, doubloon sandwiches with just a scrape of butter, and the key to my Executive Swamp. The King and I took a marshbottom con-stitutional together, and lucky for me I had fresh peat on hand! Once we were nestled down in the boggy mud, he laid it all out for me. Thruppence, he said, which is my personal name and I'll thank you not to use it until we know each other better, Thruppence, he said, if I'm to go about Empiring, I won't make a half-job of it. I was taught if a fellow takes up a sport he has to begin with fundamentals, with classi-cal technique. A proper Empire wants a border and a currency and some who are high and some who are low, says the Crab. And a *really* proper Empire, the best and most enviable kind of Empire, has Crimi-nals. You're not doing Empire right if there aren't loads of people who don't like it one bit! It's all well and good to establish a market economy and purely decorative Parliament, but you're just lying down on the job if no one's trying to bring the whole thing down and pass things under the table and cheat the whole business! The trick is, you don't want freelancers doing the job. A person, on their own, raking up trouble be-cause they enjoy it, well, that's nothing but dangerous. What's wanted are Official Criminals, Professional Revolutionaries, Accredited Scoundrels! That way, we always know where we've left our toys, if you catch my meaning, and I caught the King's meaning right in the teeth. So he started handing out licenses, lovely big writs and papers with curlicues and seals on them that said people had to go be wicked in the name of the Crown. I've got a stack, I could fill in your name. Oh! And you could bribe me! That'd be a marvelous way to break in, don't you think?"

"But I don't *want* to be a criminal," September insisted. She could hardly believe that the Charlie Crunchcrab she knew, the cantankerous ferryman who had taken her across the Barleybroom River into the capital city so long ago, could have thought of all of this nonsense. And even if she had done all those things the Blue Wind had said, that didn't mean it wasn't nonsense. Finally, she said, more softly: "I certainly don't want to do it professionally."

The Calcatrix was beginning to tap his hind claw in irritation. "Well, then what are your intentions toward Fairyland? I'm supposed to ask that anyway, but it's out of order—see, you're already breaking the rules!"

September thought for a moment. She didn't have any intentions. Her intentions had only been to get there, to be there. It had filled up all her heart and her head and her waking hours.

"I suppose I mean to find my old friends there, that's all. I miss them, and it's been ever so long."

The Blue Wind snapped her head back around. "Now you told me you aimed to make trouble! You can't take it back! I testified on your behalf! I told him you were 100 percent delinquent!"

"She fully admits to seeking out her ne'er-do-well comrades, so I hardly think she can avoid doing what comes naturally." The copper crocodile smirked—and jumped down onto the Till faster than a penny dropping. He landed on a key that read AGITATOR. The crank turned and the *chunk-chime* of the register sounded. He leapt, emerald tail flying, onto another that said CONSORTING WITH ROGUES. *Chunk-chime.* Finally he heaved onto LIAR.

"Step onto the scale, please!" the Calcatrix ordered.

September bit her tongue against the monstrous unfairness of all those words and stepped up onto the brass plates. The black tiles in the register's display began to whir. The keys moved up and down like carousel horses. She started to say that she was a good girl and if they had to call her something, couldn't it be Knight or Bishop or any of the things she'd been called before? But the Calcatrix had already rung up the sale.

"You have been accepted into the Treasury as a Contracted Villain with all the rights, privileges, and dashing uniforms due. Please take your receipt."

The tray of the register opened with a loud chime. September had to stand on her tiptoes to see over the edge. Inside was a long scroll with her name written in little calligraphy and *Charles Crunchcrab* written in large calligraphy. Underneath, several words glowed with scarlet finality:

Royal scofflaw,
professional revolutionary,
and criminal of the realm

A goodly number of illuminated ravens and rats and wolves and raccoons danced in gold and silver ink in the margins. Beneath her writ lay a suit of black silks, trousers and shirt and scarf and shoes that had never dreamed of squeaking, the very best any Criminal could ask for.

CHAPTER V
A Pitchfork Said No

*In Which September Is Formally Introduced to Her Car,
Learns of Strange Doings in the Kingdom of the Giants,
Hears Two Nos and One Yes, and Receives a Lecture
on the Care and Feeding of Tools*

"Sell you a Way, miss?" a voice hissed.

September smoothed her hands over her Criminal's finery—
quite the richest and softest fabric she'd ever known. Even the Watchful Dress had not clung to her this way, almost as though she was wearing nothing at all. But her new clothes were not in the least tight. The silk hung loose and sly and knowing, as if the very stitches were promising to keep her safe, no matter what she might get up to. Though the air crackled with chill, she felt warm and light. She did not want to wear it. She did not want to be marked out. She did not want to let them

decide what she should be called. But they did get to decide. This was their place. *My dear, when you can change something just by saying a word, that is magic.* And it felt so lovely against her skin. She did not want to admit that, but there it was. September pulled the last piece down over her head: a black cap with earflaps and long ribbons meant to tie under her chin. She let them hang free.

"I got all kinds right here, come see," the voice wheedled. His breath brushed her ear, even beneath the Criminal's cap. September whirled around.

One of the blue-faced folk in long coats stood behind them. He had the same purply blue hair as the Blue Wind, sticking out under a policeman's cap. His eyebrows stuck out spikily, stiff with frost. When he spoke, his cheeks ballooned like a cherub's. The man opened his coat surreptitiously, his eyes shimmering in a wild and wily way. Beneath, his clothes flashed—long periwinkle trousers with teal patches and curling cornflower shoes like a jester's. But what his coat hid within flashed brighter. September gasped. Planets hung on the lining of that thick jacket—small globes full of swirling clouds or shifting seas, continents like tiny chunks of ruby or topaz, cool silver moons and boiling purple suns. Light poured out from the depths of the coat, bathing her in colors. She could hardly look away. But she had to look away, she *had* to—the creaks and the groans of the Model A being prodded by prospective buyers would not let her stay. September dragged her feet away from the glitter of planets, mumbling apologies she did not mean.

"Come back, miss! You won't find better Ways than mine if you've lost yours. Or if you just want to jump the track and grab hold of someone else's . . ." he called after them, even more softly, but the softer his voice, the clearer September could hear it. She pulled the black silk cap around her ears.

The long-coats crowded around Mr. Albert's car had blue faces, as well, wild hair and frost curling over their fingers. Men and women not in the least blue milled around, picking up shadowy bits and chunks from rickety stalls. None of them could squeeze through to get a peek at the automobile. September saw some brown faces, a few pink cheeks, and one blazing golden fellow with hair like sunbeams. But the blue folk knew their business and jostled for position. The golden fellow drew aside, lured by a young girl with robin's egg pigtails and a cigarette seller's tray full of desirables. The crowd closed behind him. When the long-coats breathed on the car, the paint peeled just a little more. When they brushed up against the driver's door, the metal creaked forlornly.

"They look awfully like you," September said, and not without disapproval. One of the Blue Wind was quite enough.

The Blue Wind rolled her dark eyes. "I told you, this is the Blue Market. We're all Winds here. Surely you saw them rushing about when old Greeny threw you over the world like a baseball. Or was he too busy dazzling you with poetry and nicknames? The world is too big for one Wind or six—there's scads of us. One big, terrible, unreliable, tantrumy family. The Blues, well, he'll have told you. We're the cousins they don't set a place for at holidays. Sneaks and dastards. Freaks and desperadoes. Bitter, freezing, furious gales. Think on the coldest day you can remember, when the icicles hung off your roof like snaggle-teeth, when you took one step outside—and the wind stole your breath. That's me, that's us, that's our nature and our nurture. Can't help how you're made. Here's where we ply and sell, where all the things we've stolen away end up. It's the only place we can swindle fair and square. It's too easy elsewise. Your lot thinks you've got hold of the right end of a deal if you get what you want at a fair price. That's how we spell losing out. How much better to get what someone else wants and cozen them so sweet they pay you to take it! It's a game, a sport, a contest—and the prize ribbons are all blue. And you just can't play at our level."

"I can haggle just fine. I had the better of a Goblin in her own Market." September crossed her arms with pride.

The Blue Wind looked pityingly at her. "First off, the littlest lick of a Wind can get the better of a Goblin while sleeping in on a Wednesday. Secondarily, I'd bet you haven't. The best cheats and chicaneries won't drop you on your head until they're good and ready and rested and ravenous. But go on ahead. Buy your little car. It'll be precious. The going price is two hurricanes, a nor'easter, and a thundersquall."

"I haven't got any of those!"

"Wouldn't be much fun if you did."

September looked helplessly as the Blue Winds started hollering at one another over the Model A. She heard cyclones tossed into the pot, then an ice storm. *I can't buy it,* she thought, her mind racing to logic it out. *I can't steal it with all of them standing about like that. They certainly won't give it to me. . . .*

September smiled sweetly. It is easy to be sweet when you have figured out something to your advantage. "But you can't sell it to just anyone. It's a Tool and Tools Have Rights. Whatever that means."

The Blue Wind scowled. "It means you ought to stop saying *it. It* has a name."

"Oh, it does not! I've known it for ages, and if it has a name it's *Model A Ford* and that's the beginning and end of it." September was quite tired of being told how a human car from the human world worked. She might not know much about Fairyland or Lines or magic or even money, but she knew about this.

One of the other Blue Winds stared at her as though she had just said the sun was called Robert.

"She's called Aroostook," the other Wind said. She pointed a long, indigo finger at the spare wheel's burlap cover and the Aroostook Potato Company's potato-flower logo. "Can't you read?"

"Of course I can read!"

The Blue Wind picked at something on the furry hem of her rich sleeve. "You humans treat your Tools very shabbily. It's not stealing at all so much as liberating. The Old Crab says: *Use a Tool as you would use your own heart. Ask its leave, hold it gentle, keep it scrubbed, and put it away nice when you're done.*"

"It's not a tool, anyway; it's a machine," grumbled September. "It came off an assembly line at the Ford factory with hundreds of others just like it."

"Oh, and I suppose you weren't born in a building with hundreds of others who look just like you?" a short, squat Blue Wind snapped, his beard as thick as ice cream.

"That's different!"

"Only because you're squishy and ugly and useless and it's fiery and shiny and useful!"

A little Blue Wind, hardly more than a child, his big blue eyes full of silver flecks, took pity on September.

"It's on account of the Pitchfork," he piped up. "Happened in Parthalia, where the oyster-trees grow and the rum rivers flow black and deep and the Giants pummel their mountains into cities. A Giant's pitchfork—more like a trident, the size of a cedar—woke up."

"Was it a hundred years old?" asked September, who recalled her friend Gleam, a Tsukumogami—a lovely festival lamp who came alive on her hundredth birthday.

"Well, yes, but it didn't hop up and talk and walk and complain about the state of modern literature. What I mean is a different sort of waking altogether. It didn't stand up and run off to seek its fortune. It didn't join the Giants' country dances. It didn't even move to a sunnier part of the barn. One day the Pitchfork just wouldn't work. If Cundrie Cattail went to stick it in her hay, the prongs just bent aside and went dull. Once she let it be they sprang back into shape again. Cundrie wrestled with it all morning and into the evening but there was nothing for it. The Pitchfork would not pitchfork. Well, things in Parthalia go funny-side up sometimes. But by spring it had spread to her hairbrush—and a Giant's hairbrush is as good as a Knight's mace to anyone else. One evening it just sucked all its bristles up into its back and wouldn't have a thing to do with Cundrie's long mossy hair."

"I don't know if that's what I'd call waking up exactly—"

But the little Blue Wind did not let her finish. "It's saying *no*. That's your first hint that something's alive. It says no. That's how you know a baby is starting to turn into a person. They run around saying no all day, throwing their aliveness at everything to see what it'll stick to. You can't say no if you don't have desires and opinions and wants of your own. You wouldn't even want to. No is the heart of thinking. The news went faster than a trade wind: In Parthalia, a Pitchfork said no. In the country of the Giants, a Hairbrush declined. When the Old Crab heard it heralded, he locked himself up in his Thinking Foundry for days and days. When he came out, he had built a new law. It still glowed red-hot in his royal tongs. *Tools Have Rights,* it said, and he hung it up on the wall of the Hue-and-Cry, which is what he calls the new Parliament most days." A canny smile crossed his cerulean lips. "You can say what you like; machines are how humans do magic. They're Tools as sure as I'm Blue. And the law says if you can't deal fair with them, we have a moral duty to set them galloping. And just look at that poor thing. Hasn't seen fair since the factory. Our cousin did a noble deed by liberating her. Don't worry, one of us will continue her education—can a Tool say anything else or is no the limit of their notionals? All of Fairyland wishes to know."

September heard suddenly in her heart every sputter of the engine and backfire of the exhaust, every stubborn lever and screech of protest from the brakes, every broken part or sprung leak. Were those no's she hadn't even known how to hear? No, *no,* whatever the Pitchfork said, this was not a Fairy car, it was not magic, it was not alive, it was Mr. Albert's second-best automobile and that was all. But those growls and snarls and wheezes and clutches and chokes would not stop echoing in her heart.

"If all that's true," she said, "then it . . . then *Aroostook* knows I have taken good care of her over his years. My mother and I patched her tires and kept her fluids fresh and when she looked near to . . . to death, we made her well again. If you ask her, I am quite sure she would rather be with me than with any number of blue-in-the-face fellows who don't know a gearshift from a grape."

"Too late!" wailed a tall Wind with a splendid plum-colored miter on his head. September's own Blue Wind had slipped off and was now clapping him merrily on the back. "Two hurricanes, a nor'easter, a thundersquall, an ice storm in Perth, and a cyclone in Brooklyn. On the barrelhead, spit in hand, stamped and damped and done and deeded!"

The tall Wind hopped up, turned a nimble flip in the air, and landed neatly in the driver's seat. He looked flummoxed at the levers and pedals, pulling and pushing in a madcap whirl of blue hands and groaning metal. The Wind seemed to think just this was wonderfully exciting and well worth the price. September hid a smile with her hand—but she also winced, for she could hear the poor engine chewing on itself as the Wind mishandled all its parts. Finally, finally, he pushed the button and turned the key.

Aroostook the Model A said no.

Or at least she gave a loud splatting cough and refused to start.

The little Wind who had explained about the Pitchfork darted away and leapt into the air, floating like a hummingbird, battering the tall Wind about the blue ears with his blue fists until he spilled out of the automobile.

"If you can't manage it, let a better bluster have a go!"

The little Wind was not so rough; he moved gracefully and September only shuddered a little when she heard an awful whine as he forced the throttle lever all the way down instead of just the easiest bit. He gave the throng of Winds a triumphant azure smile and an even more triumphant, even more azure whoop. He turned the key.

Aroostook the Model A said no.

Or at least she gave an unhappy squeal that ended in a flabby sputter of smoke.

September could bear it no longer. She stomped over, opened the driver's door, and would have hauled the little Wind out by the lapel of his long-coat if he had not simply wafted up out of the seat, crossing his legs in the air to watch her attempt what by now was clearly impossible. The Winds had begun to drift off, looking for something more interesting and less stubborn. September dug the driving goggles out of the glove box and pulled them on. She closed her eyes behind them for a moment. She pushed in the brake. *One eye, then the other. Then see what you see and face up to it.* She opened her eyes and turned on the gas valve. She pushed the spark lever all the way up. *It's fire that makes a car go, my love, fire and fuel.* She put the throttle smartly at four o'clock. Hardly breathing—would it work for her? *Was* it alive? Was this all a lot of silliness and you really couldn't expect a Wind to know a thing about cars anyway? She turned the valve one full turn closed, then one full turn open and put the gear in neutral. Key to ON. Carburetor rod all the way back—and then let go. September waited for the engine to turn over, not daring to make a sound of her own.

Aroostook the Model A said yes.

Or at least she erupted into sound and life and the blast of exhaust blew several lingering Winds fluttering into the sky like autumn leaves. The engine quieted into a grudging idle.

The Blue Wind, her Kaiser-hat glinting in the magenta starlight, looked down at her with a fuming frown pulling at her face.

"Tools Have Rights," said September brightly, though her body vibrated with relief. She could hide it. She was learning to hide it. To show a different girl on the outside than the girl she was on the inside. "You can't have him back now, she's made her preference quite plain."

But had she? September had known how to drive a Model A, that was all. It was nothing special. It wasn't magic, and it wasn't alive. She pressed on. "Now, *I'm* a licensed Criminal, but do *you* have a charter that says you can thump me one and break dear old Charlie's new law across your knee? I don't think you do. You seemed very attached to it a moment ago."

The Blue Wind colored with fury. A white flush like frost forked over her face. September looked the Wind in the eye and pointed at her blazing cheeks.

"She who blushes first loses," she said evenly. "I win and that's the match." September made her gaze hard and put her hands on the steering wheel. "Now get in."

CHAPTER VI

Everything You Have

*In Which September Loses Her Savings but Acquires Unusual Cargo,
and, at Long Last, Hits the Gas and Lights Out for Fairyland,
Whereupon She Is Alarmed by a Flower, Abandoned by a Wind,
and Awed by the View from the Top of the World*

The Blue Wind's mouth twisted into a sneer—but then it untwisted, and unwound, and unfolded into a secret little smile. She walked around Aroostook's rumbling front end and climbed into the passenger seat just as a person might who expected a nice Sunday drive. September's heart banged and guttered all around her insides. Being stern was like being underwater—she could do it, but never for long, and how her whole body burned to come up for breath!

The Blue Wind put her hand out the window and crooked a finger. In half a sigh, the Wind who'd tried to sell them the planets in his coat appeared at September's side.

"Now, miss. Now you'll be wanting your Way," he said firmly, soft and clear.

He opened his coat again and the mingled light of the planets poured out its rainbows. On the other side of the coat hung little books with silvery purple papers in them—magic ration books! But surely there was no need for them any longer.

"Collectibles, miss. *Vintage*. But that's not your speed at all. You came to the Way Station. You need a Way."

"But I haven't lost my Way—I'm only beginning! I lost it once, but that was on purpose."

"You haven't met your Way yet. It hasn't so much as kissed your hand. You haven't even knocked at the door of the hall where your Way dances. But look here, look see, I've got them, I've caught them up just for you, a big bouquet of anywhere you want to go. Just pick a bloom, my girl, hold it to your pretty nose."

"I want to go to Fairyland."

The Blue Wind tapped the dashboard impatiently. "She's very stubborn on that point, brother. Dense as a foot, this one. Personally, I detest Fairyland. Something is always brewing there, some frantic task that simply *must* be done, some despot who cannot be borne another moment, some bauble that demands fetching. It's exhausting! Wouldn't you rather have a nice race across Antarctica instead? Or a Grand Tour of the Gulf Stream? We could skip stones across the North Pole. Besides, no one ever asks *me* to go running off on a grand adventure. No one ever says: Blue, darling, wouldn't *you* like to go away to Fairyland and skate on the clouds there? One *does* like to be asked."

But the squat Wind had already plucked a silvery, iridescent moon from his coat, a crescent hanging from a fine chain. Ruby starlight caught in its horns.

"Fairyland's on special tonight, as it happens," he purred. "So cheap my little baby typhoons in Tokyo will have to go hungry. A bargain fit for a beggar."

"How much?" ventured September.

The Wind smiled. His woolly, frozen eyebrows waggled. "Tonight only, my Midnight, Blue-Light, You-Heard-It-Right, Close-Out deal: All it costs is Everything You Have."

September looked down at her jar of coins, nestled in her lap. "That's not a proper price at all. How do you know how much I have? What if all I had was a shoelace and a spare button?"

The Wind's smile got deeper and wider and bluer. "The point's not what it costs; it's what it costs *you*. Everything You Have. That's my price, that's my prize, that's my ransom, and that's my rune. The only price in the world that matters is the one that hurts to pay." He let the Moon spin on its chain. "You want it; I have it. There's no duel here. If you had a shoelace and a spare button, that'd be on the tag."

September sighed. She had saved it all for this, she supposed, to be able to pay her way respectably. She held her jar, heavy as all the days she'd spent earning it. She was paying with Hours again, she realized, just as she had with the Goblin Glasswort Groof. The coins didn't mean five or ten or twenty-five cents, they meant time. They meant half a day on the Powell farm or four letters for Mr. Killory or every morning getting rooster scratches on her arm just for trying to feed the Whitestone chickens.

All money is imaginary.

September lifted the jar up and handed it over.

The whispering Wind scoffed. "The rest, too, little holdout. I'm not your fool."

September grimaced as she handed over the book of Valkyries and mistletoe and hairy god-legs and her last butterscotch. Being more or less an honest girl, she would have given him the hammer and nails as well, but when she offered them, the Wind hissed and recoiled, smelling their iron. He rose up into the air in a hurry and, turning slowly upside down, hung the Moon around her rearview mirror. It whirled and glimmered, cool and pale. But the Wind was not finished. He pulled something out of his coat—a huge, long, ornate box, perfectly white, with strange scrimshaw tangled up all over it: horns and crab claws and hearts and ears and stars and flowers and open, grasping hands. It was emphatically locked.

"What's this?"

"I said it would cost you Everything You Have." The Blue Wind in the passenger seat chuckled gleefully. "Take this to the Whelk of the Moon in Almanack—that's a city. Ask anyone, they'll point you. And no peeking." The Wind waved his fingers at her. "You didn't really think a jar of small change was all you had, did you? How sad."

He closed up his coat and stepped lightly up and away, as if climbing invisible stairs. September looked at her own Blue Wind uncertainly.

"Well?" she snapped. "On your Way, then. Hoof it, or wheel it, or however your personal phraseology would handle the fantastical notion of *getting a move on*."

September gave Aroostook a little gas. The engine boomed; the rods shivered. The little moon hanging from the rearview began to swell up like a balloon filling with water. It got bigger and bigger, and brighter and brighter, and more and more silver, and the engine boomed again and again, each boom shaking September's bones until she thought they would come apart.

Then the Model A careened forward and Mercator, suburb of Westerly, slammed shut around them like a door.

. . .

A howl of fine cold powder sprayed up and over the windshield like an ocean wave. It whipped across September's lips, sharp, vicious—and sweet.

It was snowing sugar in Fairyland.

September and the Blue Wind found themselves driving along a high mountain road. Jagged violet peaks shot up into the night, dark silver cliffs dropped dizzyingly away on either side of the path, and if we are honest, the Model A was not designed with such conditions in mind. They shuddered and jiggered and teetered, and the journey would certainly have been cut dramatically short if the car were not somehow, valiantly, driving itself. We may be very grateful for this, as young girls who learn to drive upon the great plains are no more designed for wintry mountain roads than convertible automobiles for snow, and it is in our interest and September's that novels last longer than their beginnings.

Stars clotted the sky above, peeking out from behind gusts of confectioner's snow. It streamed down in blazing ribbons of white and blue and green that made the Milky Way—or whatever Fairies might call the wild cord of starlight tying up the heavens—look rather like a scrap of old newspaper. And far below, where any fall from the high passes would abruptly end, roared a sea of cold turquoise fire, biting at the mountain's feet and throwing little meteors of sugar-ice against the battered cliffs.

The Blue Wind sang out in joy. She put back her head and howled and it was just the same sound as the awful winter wind screeching all around them. They were still rushing up, up, up, the speed incredible, the sugar-snow lashing September's face with electric prickling pain. Sugar is not nearly so soft as snow and not nearly so nice as dessert. Every crystal bit into her skin and having found warmth in the wound, melted there with a tiny sting. September, once more, wanted to cry out in joy, to shout, nothing in particular, but the wordless hooray of relief and delight when one finally gets what one has looked forward to for so long. But when she opened her mouth to crow, the sugar-snow flew in and choked her.

"Isn't there anywhere we might get out of the storm?" September yelled over a shearing updraft that nearly upended the lot of them. A few spare puffins scrabbled against the blizzard, paddling their feet for purchase on the dark backseat.

"Out?" hooted the Blue Wind, laughing. Her laugh sounded like icicles breaking all in a row. "Why would we want to get out? This is my favorite vacation destination! The most splendid spot in all of Fairy-land! The balmy beaches! The luxurious yurts! The mashed-rice cock-tails! How I have longed to lay out on the slopes of Mount Chiaroscuro and Moon-tan!"

The Blue Wind hopped up on the seat, hardly able to contain her-self. In one grand sweep of her arms, all of her lovely warm clothes vanished: her ice skates, her brocade coat, her spiked cap. She now wore a spangled cerulean bathing costume and a pair of large silver sunglasses—which September supposed were called moonglasses, if the Blue Wind meant to Moon-tan while wearing them. The Blue Wind flashed a dazzling robin's-egg smile.

"That's better! Your bauble whisked you to a dreamy, exclusive spot, September! Ever so much better than a nasty old beach lousy with witches." The Blue Wind flicked the silver Moon still hanging from Aroostook's mirror. It rocked back and forth listlessly. Whatever it had done, it had done it and would now like very much to be left alone.

A lump of sugar-ice rocketed out of the sea below and landed in September's lap with a hard crackle and thump. September thought the witches were rather brilliant, and how she would have liked to have seen the wairwulf again, and tell him how she'd got on in the capital.

She opened her mouth to say so—and could only cough in a cloud of stormsugar.

"Oh, VERY WELL! No one appreciates a good squall anymore." The Blue Wind turned up her face to the sky. "Shut it!" she hollered.

And the sky did.

The snow laid down on the ground like an obedient dog. The wind went suddenly, utterly silent. The cold fire sea still crashed and pounded below, but it only made a distant, hushing sound like radio-static. The Model A rounded a rill and rolled out onto the wide, flat table of the summit, a glassy dark shard of land mounded up with sweet, crystalline slush on all sides. September pushed her driving goggles up onto the black Criminal's cap like an aviator. They had fogged and frozen so quickly she'd hardly been able to see until now—and now that she could, two extraordinary things showed themselves immediately.

The first extraordinary thing was this: Without any warning at all, without any *reason* at all, the steering wheel of the Model A—of Aroostook—had turned into a bright green sunflower. The petals felt hard and sturdy under September's hands. The green of them shone with oily swoops of purple. Aroostook's body was no different than it had always been. The same peeling dark paint, the same cracked head-lamps, the same piebald tires. Even the same half-deflated squeeze bulb of the horn still sported its pink rubber patch. It all still smelled of gaso-line and rust. But inside, the green flower of the steering wheel glinted undeniably as it caught the light of the second extraordinary thing.

A great road ran up out of the mountain. It began on the summit, its passage flanked by two silver streetlamps as tall as elm trees. On ei-ther side curled bony rails like briars, canted and corkscrewed at strange angles. Here and there on the bone briars, clusters of cool green berries bobbed and swung, glowing as brightly as lightbulbs. It ran so far and so high September got dizzy just trying to follow it—for the road did not run straight, either, but looped and spiraled and doubled back on itself, a long snarl of silk yarn thrown up into the sky. Ice glittered on the rails and the long lanes—and so did moonlight. For the road led far and high indeed, all the way up to the Moon, which hung above them in the sky, distant and beautiful, a giant crescent the size of a world. The last of the puffins bounced up out of the backseat and rose to meet the Moon, honking softly all the way.

"What happened to Aroostook?" September stared at the improbable sunflower which should not, should *not* be there. Of course all manner of improbable things happened in Fairyland, but September herself had never changed. Her clothes stayed the same, her face, her hair, her shoes, whether she came wearing one or two.

This was different.

If September knew anything, she knew what happened to you when you jumped or ran or swam or fell or flew into Fairyland. She and the girl who had crawled out of the kitchen window two years ago were one and the same, that was certain. Yet she could not explain the sunflower. She felt her own skin with her hands; she seemed quite herself. Her essential September-ness had not turned into a strange flower.

The Blue Wind ignored her quiet distress. She had somehow pulled a spyglass out of her bathing costume. It glittered, hollowed out of an icicle. Through it, she peered up at the road to the Moon. September followed that icy gaze with her own naked eye. She remembered what her friend Taiga, the reindeer-girl, had said in the glass forest: that the Moon was a rich and fertile place where all manner of folk lived. The road to the Moon dazzled her eyes and all the rest of her, too.

The last time she'd come to Fairyland, she had seen trouble right away and no mistaking. From the moment her foot landed everything was wrong and required mending. And in that glass forest, the wrongness came from her own fault and by her own hand. Until this moment

September had not realized how wound up her heart had got, how prepared she had been to see some other wretched consequence of her adventure come to bite her in the dark. But she was simply here, and could go somewhere, see something marvelous. She could spin around three times and dash off in whatever direction she faced, if she wanted to! And deliver the long, tooth-colored box, yes. But that was quickly done and quickly forgotten. Hand it off and find A-Through-L and Saturday and then—Anything Magic. Possible Magic. And how many other sorts she could not think of right now, in the delicious moment when it was all still in front of her and not in the midst nor behind. Boomer was wrong. What gladness dwelt in prepositions!

September drank in the starry sky with a longing and a tugging and a sigh. All the way up, to that enormous crescent in the black.

"You can see the prongs of Almanack from here. And the Sea of Restlessness all couched in dragonfly beaches! I shall have to remember to make off with a few of those marvelous cabanas come my next Moon twister." She retracted her icy spyglass with a snap. "Well," the Blue Wind said cheerfully, "that's me then!"

"You're not coming?"

When the Green Wind had taken September away, he had not been allowed to come with her. The Marquess had banned Harsh Airs from Fairyland. But no longer—the ban had vanished with the old regime. September had planned to ask the Blue Wind along. *One does so like to be asked,* she'd said. September wanted to be the kind of girl that would invite her, even if the Wind had been nasty to her and she still felt sore on it. The best way to be the kind of girl you want to be is to do what that girl would do. Truthfully, September had been looking forward to showing off how gallant and gracious she could be.

"I'm very busy," sneered the Wind, who wore a sneer beautifully, dashingly, better than September ever could. She tossed her long blue hair as if it mattered not at all. "I've baskets of hail to deliver to Broce-liande and a truly spectacular bout of thunder-snow overdue in Maine. And you! You've got work to do, my little postal service! You be sure to go straight to Almanack, now. No dawdling or stopping for straw-berries on the side of the road. You're on the clock."

"But I don't know how to get there!"

"Look, you sour gimlet of a girl. I think I've done more than my part. I don't know why the other Winds make such a to-do over this hauling-off business. It seems very unsatisfying to me. And if it's unsat-isfying at the start, it's sure to be unsatisfying at the stop. I don't think we'd be the best of traveling companions, anyhow. I am certainly in-trepid and splendid and sordid and strong; I can see why you'd want me! But I'm afraid I've left the kettle on or whatever it is people say when they're bored." The Blue Wind pushed her moonglasses up onto her head and winked one dazzling dark eye. "And while they do make a smashing cocktail, the Moon really is awfully provincial if you ask me, but you didn't, so I do hope you all fall off of it. Ta!"

The Blue Wind put her fingers in her mouth and whistled as high and sharp as metal tearing. A great puffin, bigger than any of the others but encased in the icy, thorny Spanish armor, soared into view. The black comet of his body hurtled down to the Wind's side. She gave a little pirouette on the ice of the summit, leapt into the air, turned a double flip, and landed on the puffin's back. In half a moment they had become no more than another blue star against the black.

CHAPTER VII

THE ROAD TO THE MOON

In Which September Suffers the Following: An Ascent into the Heavens, the Attentions of a Somewhat Surly Otter, a Lack of Fuel, and a Sudden Earthquake Which Is Not an Earthquake

Ice ground like glass under Aroostook's wheels. September felt sure they would spring a flat at any moment, but somehow the Model A soldiered on. The long, blue-white highway soared up ahead of them, arching and falling, a diamond roller coaster tick-tick-ticking up into the night. Soft shadows flickered on the corkscrewing rails.

The road to the Moon ran on quietly except for September and Aroostook. The Model A made her old, familiar, frightful noises. She wasn't about to stop now, just because she had sprung a sunflower. After a little while, September began to see creatures traveling in the other direction, back down to Fairyland proper. Which, she supposed, was

Fairyland-Below from where she stood now. A motley troupe clattered by in a covered wagon—but the cover was all of stained glass and the wagon floated in the air on a thatch of ragwort stalks puffing green pollen behind it. September thought she saw a witch with her face pressed to the glass. At least the face behind the ruby-colored pane wore a great pointy leather hat with a buckle on it. An enormous, upside-down paper umbrella drifted by, pasted together from the funny pages of some very expensive newspaper, for ever so many more than four colors gleamed on the umbrella tines. A family of bright red raccoons peered out from the bowl of the umbrella, their striped tails quite on fire and quivering like rattlesnakes. The papers did not seem to be any worse for it. They must have brought along drums on their journey, for September could hear a wobbling beat grow nearer and then pass them by as the umbrella slipped down the slope of the road, eight pairs of bandit eyes regarding her suspiciously.

But for long, luxurious stretches, September had the road to herself. The giant crescent Moon sailed closer steadily but slowly, for it is a very long way from earth to the Moon. She looked nervously backward at the long, white box in the backseat. What could be in it? How she would have loved to crack that carved lid and look inside! But it was locked good and tight. She had brought parcels from one farm to another so many times. Aroostook's seats were quite accustomed to boxes and baskets and barrels. And though she knew she oughtn't, she always peeked inside. Just pulled up a bit of the paper so she could see what Mrs. Tucker had ordered from Scars and Roebuck. Perhaps, if everyone meant to call her a Criminal, she ought to learn to pick a lock. September was reaching back to see if she could work her fingers under the ivory corner of the box when a clatter of bells and moaning startled her out of it—a Spriggan in a sturdy suit of blue clovers was driving his cow herd down the road from the Moon. The cows' hides shone clear as glass—and inside, September saw moonshine stills bubbling away where their guts ought to be. The cattle lowed, begging for milking. The Spriggan touched the side of his long, skinny nose in greeting as Aroostook stopped to let them pass.

"I should have thought there would be a fearsome traffic jam all the way there and back!" exclaimed September. The hard green sunflower of Aroostook's steering wheel turned gently under her hands, keeping them in their glowing lane. She patted the dash, talking to the car as she often had. But now she felt as though she ought to wait for an answer, which was out of the question, of course. She hurried on. "Who would not want to visit the Moon? I believe if anyone back home had a choice between California and the Moon for visiting, they would choose the Moon every time!"

A great black road sign reared up, blazing with silver letters: FALL-ING FORTUNES: EXPECT DELAYS.

September laughed a little. It *had* seemed harder and longer to get into Fairyland this time. Like a door that has always swung smoothly suddenly sticking. Perhaps Boomer and Beatrice had got the Line sturdy again. Another sign drifted by: CAUTION: YETI CROSSING. This alarmed September, and she held tighter to the green sunflower of the wheel. She could not tell if she was doing the driving or Aroostook or the road itself, but she held on anyhow.

"I hope we won't find the Moon empty when we get there. I met a whole family of reindeer-girls and reindeer-boys who said they'd once lived on the Moon. The way they talked about it, it seemed like the most wonderful place—but I suppose it was frightening, too. They had to leave, after all."

The pair of them, car and girl, came up over a rise in the road. A long straightaway opened up before them, miles and miles before curving off and up sharply, the last turnoff to the Moon. Aroostook opened up her throttle and roared out onto the thoroughfare—and sputtered, choked, coughed, and promptly went silent. September caught the wheel before it spun wild. They rolled on a little farther as there was no wind to slow them down, but the engine stayed stubbornly mute.

"What's happened, Aroostook?" And this was the first time she had used the Model A's name out loud, if that was her name. "Whether or not you're alive, you do seem to be acting very strangely, and until I know why, I shall tread very lightly on your feelings—should you have any."

September clambered out of the car onto the silver paving stones. There was no sound at all on the road to the Moon. The dark air wrapped her head like cold wool. Even when she spoke, the sound seemed to fall apart as soon as it left her lips. The starlight shone down as strong as party lanterns.

"Poor Aroostook, what's troubling you?"

September opened the hood of the Model A. Bits of paint and rust flaked off and fell, winking, into the blackness below the road. She had been over every cog and pat of grease in that engine with her mother. It was as familiar to her as her own bed. She tugged on her black cap to keep out the cold and tapped her finger on the gas tank. It bonged out a desolate clang.

September sighed heavily. There was a pack of tools in the trunk for fixing just about anything but this. "I expect we used up the whole tank coming across," she exclaimed. "I know I'm starving! Eating's always the first trouble in Fairyland." She patted the Model A's headlamp in sympathy. "It feels like you've never eaten before and will never get the chance again when you set foot—or wheel!—here. And if I'm hungry, you must have been running on fumes all this while! Well, there's nothing for it but waiting. Someone else will come along presently—where there's folk, there's always more!"

And so they did. September settled down beside the forlorn Model

A, drawing pictures with her fingers in the frost that coated the road. She pulled a few of the pale green fruits from the briar-rails to satisfy her own stomach. She bit slowly, in case they tasted foul. Their pulp glowed oozily—not foul but not sweet, rather like a very juicy onion that had once met a heap of black pepper and had a grand time. Her Criminal's silks slid against her like hands rubbing her skin to warm it up. September squeezed Aroostook's horn. Perhaps someone would hear it and put some speed on. The horn wheezed like a throat clearing. It *oompah*ed bravely, but the sound died just a breath beyond the bell of the horn, just as her voice had. It was no longer entirely an *oompah,* either. The horn sounded hard and urgent, almost like a real voice, but the space ate up all the sound the horn could feed it.

Finally, at last, thankfully, a shape approached, creeping toward the stranded car with incredible slowness down the long crystal straight-away. As it drew nearer, September saw that it was a ship. A real sailing ship, with lines trailing everywhere and a tall, squarish black sail crossed by white poles like bones. Nearer still and it was not so much a galleon or a schooner but a merchant's barge, flat and broad, its prow a great pair of scissors sticking out point-first. It cut through the still dark air, not sailing but flying, scissor blades lazily opening and closing, eating up the miles. Barnacles of every color crusted the bottom of the boat: honey and lilac and cherry and bottle-green, tiny as pen-points, huge as beer barrels. Holes honeycombed the rudder; striped ultramarine fish with long, fine fins like a girl's hair swam slowly in and out of them. Even nearer and a mariner, the captain, perhaps, held up a hand in greeting, throwing lines over and wrangling the wheel to come around. The fish in the rudder all darted into their hiding places at once and the sailing barge stopped abruptly, neatly parked alongside them. The mariner peered over the rail. Light from a tall sign crackling with violet sparks scrubbed them all in shine: B.D.'S MOONDOCK SALVAGATION.

The mariner had an otter's round, furry face, sporting a beard of crusted icicles and whiskers that clinked when they twitched. But her lower half was a long, gnarled fish's tail, wound around itself as tight as a bolt. Her scales flowed in wild patterns, dull and gray as old metal, dripping with bony, knife-shaped fins. On her shoulders glowed two ancient glass lanterns. Their brass netting had turned green and misshapen with the junk of years. The candles within blazed a pale, uncanny green. A thousand nights of grizzly wax had busted out the lantern panes and spilt onto the creature's fur, so thick and so much that her chest vanished completely inside a cuirass of the stuff, a hundred shades of white. She wore a battered, threadbare Admiral's hat all tangled with white seaweed.

Half-buried in the wax of her chest was a stitched nametag. It read: *Ballast.*

The otter-fish blinked one dark eye slowly, then the other. Her fuzzy cheeks puffed out and she barked up at the crescent Moon. Then she turned her back, a ridge of salt-crusted fins glittering on her spine, and began banging on a thick copper pipe with her fist in time to a rough, grumbly tune.

> *Bully for Ahab and Blackbeard and I*
> *We've got a doomed ship and a death to defy*
> *We've got us a maelstrom and a hook in our eye*
> *We've got our salt souls all baked up in a pie*
> *Oh, bully for Blackbeard and Ahab and I!*

"Pardon me," began September. "I don't mean to be any trouble—"

The otter-fish cut off both her song and September. "Ship's broke," she sniffed.

"I think it's lovely!" September protested. The colored barnacles seemed to breathe gently, swelling and shrinking, swelling and shrinking.

"Not mine, thine. Mine'll swing anchor at the end of the world." Ballast threw down a heavy, wet rope. "Yours won't make tomorrow. Tie her on and we'll see what we see."

September hefted the rope and, with much pushing and hauling, got it knotted around Aroostook's bumper. She caught the salt-caked ladder Ballast humped over the rail and came aboard. Everything on the barge stood very neat and tidy: boxes and barrels and vases and pots and chests, but each one closed, well polished and maintained, and stacked in orderly pyramids. Ballast seemed to have used up her store of neatnickery on her cargo. When she moved, making smart, efficient little hops on her wound-up pewter-colored tail, bits of wax broke off and crumbled away. The barge began to sail again, upbound toward the Moon. The ultramarine fish blossomed out of the lacy rudder once more, their trailing fins floating in space.

And a moment later, Aroostook, too, was floating in space, trailing behind the salvagation barge as a winch slowly hauled it the rest of the way on board.

The great rope lashed barnacled barge and rusty Ford together into one awkward vessel. Ballast rubbed her furry cheeks. Her pelt was the color of good, old rum.

"Do you know anything about cars?" said September shyly, once they were away.

The otter-fish blinked her eyes again. "If that's what you want to call your ship, then I know everything there is to know. And *ship* is just another word for what bears you up and keeps you safe. So if you stop your yapping I'll do yours. It's my job, anywhat. Ballast Downbound, that's me, B.D.'s Moondock Salvagation, sundries and subtleties, answer to every SOS and IOU."

September clapped her chilled hands in relief. "How lucky that you happened along!"

B.D. snorted. Wax and ice sprayed. "What's luck? Luck is for lubby-landers, leprechauns, and lazybones. I told you it's my job. More'n my job, it's my body and soul. I'm the best Klabautermann you'll ever meet. Can patch a hull in a hurricane, sew a sail in a zombie fight. Or let them all drown, if a ship's got tired of living and wants a nice patch of seafloor to retire in. Raise anenomes. Take up with a fancy fish. Not so many of us working the routes anymore, mind you. On account of how you can get attached to the sailors. They're sweet, I suppose. Nice tattoos. But they keep their loyalty in their false legs. Better pay, nicer berths? They're off like shots fired portside. A Klabautermann's love is for the ship alone. I'd guess some'd call me old-fashioned but that's as I see it. You can always get more sailors." B.D. hopped over to a stack of round boxes, rather like hatboxes made of copper and stone. She opened one and rummaged around inside. "I make the run up and down this road day and night. It's a good current, steady work. Heard you distressing loud and clear. Sounds like a buoy knocking in a storm, the alarm that sounds in a Klabautermann's heart when a ship's about to go down."

"Go *down*?" September said. "She's only out of gas!"

"You'd never even see me if your ship weren't on its last leg. S'what a Klabautermann is. An early warning system, I guess you'd want to call it if you're mechanickly inclined, which I am." B.D. pulled a case from inside the copper hatbox. It was quite flat and thin and shiny, like the chrome on cars much newer than Aroostook. "See, I bet you don't know anything at all about shipcraft. Take me for a lesson and a cheap one at that. I'm named for the secret, vital core of a ship. *Ballast* is the weight down in the deep of you that keeps a vessel upright in dark water." The mariner bent over Aroostook, speaking to the car more than September. "Oh, the cargo you carry will do it for a while, or even the heft of a crew, mates and mettles, if you love them enough. But a ship's not a ship till she's got ballast of her own. Down in the belly, a big massy mess of rope and wood and hardtack and love letters and harpoons and old lemons. Anything that ever fascinated the ship, made it sail true, patched it or broke it, anything the ship loved or longed for, anything it could use. Bo'sun gets in a fistfight with a deck-hand over a missing cannonball and they bloody each other up some, but that ball's just circled down into the baby ballast. Some'll tell you a ship's not born till she gets a name or has a bottle of wanderwhiskey broke over her bow, but it's not so. Without ballast, she's just wood." B.D. ran a tender paw over Aroostook's burlaped wheel. "It all just sort of sinks down and jumbles up together into something hot and heavy inside you, and the weight of everything you ever wanted in the world will keep you steady even when the worst winds blow. Me and mine, we get born when the ballast gets born. Come out of an egg if you want to hear private details, if it's still an egg when it's a good hemp Turk's head knot. We don't peck our way out, we *untie*. When the ship despairs, we feel all those old ropes tearing us apart until we get to fixing what's fouled."

September touched her chest softly. *What have I got, where a ship has ballast?* she thought. But what she said was: "I don't think Aroostook has anything like that. I've taken her apart and put her back together pretty often and I've never found anything that wasn't meant to be there, apart from a squirrel that up and died in the manifold one time."

B.D. blinked her great otter eyes. She shrugged. Wax snapped off from her lanterns and drifted down like snow. "I'm not the arguing kind. I won't go poking about in her just to show up a girl and make her feel wrongly. Little tugger deserves her privacy. I think there's more under there than an empty belly, but that's her business. Mind your own charts and no copying, my mother always said. And if it's only gas you want, I've got it, any kind you please." The Klabautermann nuzzled the hood of the Model A with her furry cheeks as if she was a cat. "I'll cook it up special for you, my scruffy wee seadog. No charge for strays."

Ballast Downbound popped open the shiny case and pulled out a tap, the kind you'd use to open a keg of cider. She bounced up onto her tail and crossed the barge, leaving September to scramble behind her toward a stained oilcloth, draped over something with a great number of points and corners and humps. With a tremendous spring of her tail, the Klabautermann caught the top of the cloth and hauled it down, revealing a soda fountain with a clean chrome counter. It was just like the one in town run by Mr. Johansson the pharmacist. When September needed medicine for her father, she would always stay and watch Mr. Johansson mix up sodas for his customers. Once, she parted with one of her precious dimes and he'd whipped her up an orange fizz. It looked like fire in the glass.

Of course, it was not exactly like Mr. Johansson's soda counter. A silver soda-water fountain took up most of the space, carved into the shape of a huge, ancient fish with spines all down its back. It bent over, its wide mouth pointing downward, its hundred fins aroused and bristling with sticky splashes of old syrup. Row after row of bottles racked up like bowling pins behind the counter: little round globes sloshing with dark, rummy stuff, tall flutes so caked with barnacles September couldn't begin to guess what bubbled away inside, big-bellied casks fairly glowing with luminous goop. Where Mr. Johansson would have stacked his tall, clean tumblers sat two gas cans all of crystal. Glass spigots arced gracefully out of them, ready to slip into a thirsty tank. September suddenly felt deathly thirsty herself.

"I don't suppose you have orange fizz?" she asked without much hope. "Or anything to eat?"

Ballast Downbound snorted. Bits of wax blew clear of the lanterns on her shoulders. "S'not for you! This here's my Memory Fountain and I'll be mixing up an Egg Bygone for your boat."

"But what my *car* needs is gas, not memories! How can you make a car go on memories?"

B.D. scratched under her Admiral's hat. "What'd you think gas was, girl? 'Course there's all sorts of fuel, wind and wishes and chocolate cake and collard greens and water and brawn, but you're wanting the kind that burns in an engine. That kind of gas is nothing more than the past stored up and fermented and kept down in the cellar of the earth till it's wanted. Gas is saved-up sunlight. Giant ferns and apples of immortality and dimetrodons and cyclopses and werewhales drank up the sun as it shone on their backs a million years ago and used it to be a bigger fern or make more werewhales or drop seeds of improbability." Her otter's paws moved quick and sure, selecting a squat, square bottle here and a round rosy one there. "It so happens sunshine has a fearful memory. It sticks around even after its favorite dimetrodon dies. Gets hard and wily. Turns into something you can touch, something you can drill, something you can pour. But it still remembers having one eye and slapping the ocean's face with a great heavy tail. It *liked* making more dinosaurs and growing a frond as tall as a bank. It likes to make things alive, to make things go. And that's what's in my bottles here—sirops of sunshine, sunshine that remembers so fierce it burns itself right up. Strong stuff, not for the faint! Drink up yesterday to make today go faster."

Ballast cracked the cork of a copper-strapped globe and let it trickle thickly into one of the gas cans. The liquid glowered dark gold. She tipped in two glugs from a brown beer bottle in a brown bag; it bloomed bloody when it hit the first sirop. "Pleistocene Concentrate and a swallow of Pure Pre-Seelie Dawn." She broke the cream on a milk bottle—what slid out was black and full of stars. A mere tangerine drop from a test tube; a whole wallop of bronze, greasy bourbon from an oil can. "The trick is in the mixing. Anything you use changes you. I could turn a pixie into an umbrella stand with the wrong sirop at the right time. Go sparing on the Atlantean Applejack, double down on your Cretaceous Demiglace. That's all it takes—but don't you go snip-ing my recipe, girl. Who knows where you'll end up when you've got fancy combustibles in you, and if it'll be raining when you get there?"

Ballast wedged the gas can under the mouth of her fountain-fish. A stream of bubbles shot out of its silver lips, splashing into the sirops and turning them into a swirl of changing colors blazing with light.

"Just what's wanted." She nodded at her cocktail with pride. "Downbound's Own Nosh of Nostalgia and Antediluvian Antifreeze."

When B.D. hoisted up Aroostook's hood, September peered into the maze of the engine, looking for a tiny, growing ballast, a knot of something, anything. She saw nothing, and did not know how she felt about that. The memory-gas flowed silkily into the battered tank, making little delighted gurgles as it drained from the can. When it was done, September turned the automobile on once more and hoped for the best. She did not recall anything about the intersection of sunshine and werewhales in her geology textbook. Nevertheless, Aroostook blossomed into life. The engine fired without argument and fired more strongly and smoothly than September had ever heard it, as though it had never been whacked about the nose with a beech tree in all its days.

She turned to thank the Klabautermann and found that otter's face suddenly very close to her own. She could smell the smell of Ballast Downbound: salt and the sea and kerosene and rummy sirops. She placed something in September's hand.

"Call it an orange fizz, mixed just for you." She chuckled.

September held a small bottle shaped like an egg. Patches of barnacles and pearls grew all over it, sealing in a black cork. Deep campfire-colored spirits bubbled inside.

And then, with a roar, everything shattered.

September felt it in her stomach before it started, like the shadow of a quiver. Earthquakes are not common in Nebraska, or else she might have had something to compare it to. This was not, however, an earthquake.

It was a moonquake.

Ballast's neat boxes tumbled down; the bottles in the Memory Fountain burst and smashed. The barge groaned horribly as it veered into the briar-rails of the road. The ultramarine fish in its rudder flopped up onto the decks, hoping for safety. The Moon drew very close now. The last off-ramp announced itself cheerfully on a broad sign: WELCOME TO THE MOON! PLEASE WIPE YOUR SHOES. But as the heavens seemed determined to shake itself apart, the sign split in half, falling down into space along with bits of broken railing and silver paving stones and ivory wagon wheels. September screamed, clutching for Ballast Downbound—but her hands met empty air. The Klabautermann was bouncing over the barge trying to keep her boxes and her bottles and her fish and her ship from skittering out into the endless black sky beyond the road. September caught her terrified eyes as she scooped up an armful of rudder fish and dumped them into an old bathtub that was sliding downdeck as the barge heeled at a sickening angle.

"It's Ciderskin," Ballast hissed. "It's the Yeti coming for us!"

The Model A's door swung open and September's legs tumbled out sideways, her feet kicking in space. She wrapped both arms around Aroostook's sunflower steering wheel, her teeth jarring, her legs scrabbling for purchase on the stepboard. Up above, the crescent of the Moon stopped being a crescent and became a wide countryside, full of silver mountains. It was all there was to see. Aroostook lost her grip on the barge and tumbled up, or down, or sideways—who could tell? But the land caught them with a crash and a cloud of fine silver dust.

September had made it. She was on the Moon.

But the shaking went on and on and on.

THE BLACK COSMIC DOG

In Which We Examine Perspective, the Geography of the Moon, and a Very Busy Canine

Sometimes it is hard to see the shape of things. The world is frightfully big, and you can only ever see the part you're standing on. Even if you could find a ledge or a tower so high up that you could see everything from New York to Budapest to Australia and back again, the cosmos is so much bigger and wider than that. You cannot see from your doorstep that the world is rolling along in space with its brothers and sisters, which we call Venus and Jupiter and Saturn and the Sun, but it is so. No matter where you stand, everything is always and forever so much bigger than you can tell.

If September had found such a ledge or tower, she might have seen herself, inside Aroostook the Model A, moving up that long silver road that led from the mountain to the Moon. And she might have seen the mountain itself, a great, gorgeous spire of rock rising out of the fiery cold sea in the shape of a woman with long flying hair and wings like a fish's many fins on her back. She might have seen the woman's craggy hand pointing up toward the sky and from the tip of her longest finger the road winding out and up like her own long breath. She might have seen the frozen face of the mountain pursing her lips and puffing her cheeks, blowing Moonbound travelers off her hand like dandelion puffs after some secret stony wish.

But if our girl could have climbed the tallest ladder you or I can imagine and stood upon the topmost rung with her lunch in one hand and binoculars in the other, she might have seen something even stranger and more interesting.

The Moon over Fairyland is always waxing. Because of all I have just told you concerning the difficulty of seeing things as they are, it sometimes *looks* full to sailors on the Perverse and Perilous Sea or lovesick Physickists in the woolly towers of Pandemonium or young girls walking along intent on some goal or other. They see the vast curve of the crescent turned fully toward them, so vast it looks nothing at all like a crescent. It is on this outer edge that the folk of the Moon live and scheme and play the harpsichord. It is here the Whelk of the Moon looks out over the Sea of Restlessness. It is here the Hreinn once lived, where Moon-walruses practice one-tusk calligraphy and two-tusk billiards.

No one lives on the inner edge of the Moon.

Well, not anymore.

But there is someone there now. Rooting around in the ruins, sniffing at smashed-in statues and pawing at dark, broken houses where nobody is having supper. Somebody is walking around a shattered herald's square, picking things up, turning them over, weighing them, staring at them with a terrible sharp eye. It's a long job—no one bothered to clean up after themselves. Objects lie here and there and everywhere, very fine but very forgotten: sledgehammers, rakes, chisels, straight-edge razors, sickles and scythes, spades and hammers, jewelers' glasses, telescopes, wheels, abaci, longshoremen's hooks and seamstresses' tape, wrenches, knives, swords, fishing rods and wrenches, shears and knitting needles and frying pans and brooms and axes and typewriters and film projectors and dead lightbulbs and clocks.

Somebody is investigating all of them, one by one. He is tall and handsome, with thick, curly black hair and a long, noble snout. He is alert and careful. His ears stick up straight so as to miss nothing. His nose is very wet.

His name is the Black Cosmic Dog.

In the middle of the square he pushes a pile of old spectacles aside and begins to dig, furiously, in the soft soil of the Moon.

CHAPTER VIII

Where There's a Whelk There's a Way

*In Which September Walks on the Moon, Is Accused of Sundry
Wickednesses by a Lobster and Two Jackals, Hails a Crab,
and Meets a Very Unusual Mollusk*

W e have said before that the world is a house.

You and I have gone together into the basement where the
underworlds are kept. We have lounged comfortably in the front room
and shared our familiar tea with all things familiar: Omaha and Europe
and cruel schoolmates and spy movies and airplane factories and amiable dogs. We have played such wonderful games in the upstairs bedroom,
where Wyveraries and Marids and witches and giant talking cats peek
out from behind the bedpost and the Lamp is always on. You might
think that I will take you to the attic next, where the heavens of a

house get bundled up with twine and draped with muslin and wait quietly for our footsteps. But it is not so. In the house of the world, the heavens are not in the attic.

They are on the roof.

Shall we crawl up there and see?

Why, here is everything that soared up high and got lost, everything that wanted to keep safe from marauders below. The tenderhearted old world catches everything thrown too far and too hard, keeps everything fragile whole: baseballs and stuffed bears and birds' nests and last autumn's leaves, zeppelins and Icarus and Leonardo's flying machine, Fairies and pterodactyls and cherubim and hot air balloons and a Russian dog or two. It's hard to get up there, harder than the stairs down into the basement. It takes longer; you must climb out a window and shimmy up the chimney and pull yourself over by your fingernails without breaking the gutters. Gravity is involved, and unbreakable spells concerning escape velocity. After all, anyone can go down into the cellar if they are not afraid of the dark. Any tale you care to tell calls for a quick trip to the underworld to bring up another bag of flour and a working knowledge of your darker nature. The surface of the world is like a great black net; any moment you could fall through and fall deep. But for every underworld there is an overworld, an upper world just as strange as the lower, just as bright as its cousin is brooding. The snow that falls in one splashes down as rain in the other—and brightness is not less perilous than shadow. An Italian poet got himself a ticket good for both shows once and came back to tell us all about it, which shows excellent manners.

Everything that goes down must come up again.

When you leave the world, the going gets tough, whether you are a chemical rocket or a little girl. Take my hand, I know the way.

Narrators have a professional obligation not to let their charges fall onto the pavement.

Aroostook and September idled, each in their ways. The Model A's rumble mellowed into a thick purr as Ballast's soda-gas flowed through her insides. The light of the sun on the Moon blazed pure white; the pearly sand beneath those four piebald tires sparkled sharply, purposefully.

September stared. Specifically, she stared up. She could not quite put a name to what she saw towering above her. Even after climbing out of the car and putting the handbrake carefully on, she still could not get her head all the way around it. Her hands shook even though the Moon had stilled some time ago. In the end they had only fallen a few, embarrassing feet. The off-ramp hung miserably behind her, broken off in midair, jumbled and cracked and twisted by the quake. Bits of ivory briar crumbled away into the starry black; an awful metallic whine wheezed out of the silver paving stones. B.D.'s Moondock Salvagation drifted back downroad, righted and ruddered, looking for wrecks. But September barely heard the sounds of the barge and the creaking road. What clanged behind her could not possibly be important.

In front of her yawned the mouth of a seashell the size of a mountain.

It lay on its side, a sea-snail shell tapering for miles into a slender point on one end and a massive knobbly spiral crown on the other. Along its spine rose great prongs tipped with glowing white flame. It seemed to be every color at once, jade-green and amethyst and quicksilver at the crown, swirling into deep blue and indigo and bright fuchsia, and then into white-orange and copper and gold as its tail swept away up the shore. For the off-ramp emptied out not only directly into the giant shell but onto the shore of a scarlet, frothing sea, its waves washing the curve of the sea-snail and leaving pink rinds of salt behind. The height of the thing made September dizzy. Polished mother-of-pearl lined the shell's wide mouth. It opened gracefully inward like a smile. A steep coral staircase led up to the lip of the entrance and what could be inside September would have ventured no guesses.

"It's all right to gape, girl. I love it when people gape! Means they recognize the spectacular when they see it."

September startled. The great snail shell had so swallowed up her attention that she'd noticed nothing else, not even the trio of creatures guarding that steep staircase. On the left side of it crouched a black jackal with great dark ears and bright silver eyes. On the right side perched a white jackal with a long, pale snout and piercing dark eyes. Between them, a large, muscular, and very green lobster stood watch. In her thick, powerful claw she clamped a long, two-pronged fork whose tips glittered as if to assure September of their sharpness. Her antennae and the jackals' tails wafted to and fro in the same rhythm. Two of the shell's fiery prongs framed the three of them. It was the white jackal who had spoken.

"If you need more time to be amazed, just give us an estimate, love," said the black jackal. Their voices were quite high and human-like.

"What is this place?" whispered September. The shushing sounds of the sea seemed to rub against her, making her skin feel prickly and hot.

The lobster cleared her throat—do lobsters have a throat? September wondered.

"Welcome to Almanack, the All-In-One! Sanctuary, Safehouse, Home of the Stationary Circus and the College of Lunar Arts, Number One Tourist Destination on the Heavenly Circuit and Capital of the Moon! These are my associates Rushe and Waite, Knights of the Crepuscular Girdle, and I am Nefarious Freedom Coppermolt the Third, Lobster of the Watch."

"*This* is Almanack? There's . . . a *city* in there?"

The white jackal laughed, a shrill yip and cry.

"What else would it be? The highway leads here, after all."

"But highways might lead anywhere!"

Nefarious Freedom Coppermolt the Third stamped her fork. "They might, but they don't. King Crunchcrab decreed that in a proper Empire, all roads lead to capitals, and they couldn't have rogue roads just lying about leading anywhere they pleased. A road has to go to a city at the least, or else it will be arrested and sent to the countryside for rehabilitation."

September could not quite believe this, but she could not quite disbelieve it, either. She thought she ought to visit Charlie, and sooner rather than later.

"Of course, the Moon isn't strictly speaking part of Fairyland," Rushe, the white jackal, growled.

"No it is *not*," harrumphed the lobster. "My great-great-grandmother, for whom I am named, would pinch her own gravestone rather than see it happen. She fought in the Battle of the Whelk when the Moon washed its hands of Fairies and threw away the bucket. Wrestled a basilisk to a standstill, my gran! Lost her claw in a Fairy's mouth, but it was mostly turned to stone anyway. Lived to lay her eggs and shed her shell and show no mercy to collaborating crayfish. Now I serve in her name and in her place! Nobody throws a fork farther. I also juggle better than you might expect," she added confidentially. "Just to pass the time."

"But the Road starts in Fairyland, so it's theirs, too, and they get to order it about and tell it its shortcomings and send it to sit in a corner and think about what it's done," finished the black jackal Waite.

"For now," said Nefarious Freedom darkly. She clapped her pincers together.

"Well," said September, taking a deep breath, "if this is Almanack, this is where I'm meant to be!" She pulled the long, carved box from the backseat and held it before her like a shield. "I'm to take this directly to the Whelk of the Moon."

The Lobster of the Watch tapped on the lid with her claw and listened for an echo. If one sounded, September did not hear it.

"Well, I don't think that's likely," barked Waite.

"You must be joking," growled Rushe.

"You do know the lee side is riddled with holes and tunnels?" Nefarious Freedom added in a low voice. "I don't know why you'd even try to come in by the front gate in broad daylight. Bold of you! But goodness, why? Has someone told you we were easy marks? That we could be bought? It's not so, or my name isn't—"

September leapt in. "What on earth are you talking about? I only want to put this thing down where it belongs and be on my way!"

Rushe narrowed his dark eyes. "You mean smuggle in some sort of device or weapon or counterfeit or . . ."

". . . stolen property or wicked beastie or bomb," finished Waite.

"Certainly not!"

"But you're a Criminal!" snapped the Lobster of the Watch.

"Oh, I'm no such thing," September sighed.

"But you're dressed like one," whined Rushe, his pink tongue lolling out of his muzzle.

"Well, if you're going to go passing judgment on those what wear black," retorted Waite, thumping his black tail, "then so am I."

"What's in there?" Rushe sniffed at it, his ruff bristling.

"I . . . I don't rightly know, but a Wind gave it to me specially and though Winds can be rather rude sometimes, they're very rarely nasty. I'm sure it's nothing like what you said!" But *was* she sure? It was terribly heavy.

Nefarious Freedom clapped her pincers again in exasperation. "If you're wearing silks, you're a Criminal of the Realm. Tell me you haven't got a writ in your pocket!"

September could not. She pulled it out of the deep, soft slits of her black trousers and unfolded it for the guards to see. Nefarious Freedom covered her eyes and would not look at it.

"We don't go in for Fairyish decadence up here. Commit your crimes under cover of darkness like an honest crustacean, I say. Folk down below might treat you fancy just because you've got a dash of official danger on you—and danger approved and accounted for is hardly danger at all if you ask me and my grandmother—but here on the Moon, we call them like we see them and I see *you* plain as the tide! No Writ of Rascalry recognized! Petition denied! Take your trash elsewhere, missy!"

But the lobster could not help being at least a little curious. She peeked through the rough teeth of her green claw at September's scroll. Then she opened it wider. And wider still.

"Professional Revolutionary?" she cried, reading the writ. "Do you mean to say you've led revolts? Real rebellions? In Fairyland?"

September demurred. "No, no, it's all a misunderstanding, everything's got twisted round. . . ." But she saw the jackals' ruffs rise and the lobster stiffen. She cleared her throat and changed her tack. "What I *mean* to say is that I brought down the Marquess who ruled over all of Fairyland, but it wasn't a revolt, it was just me."

"Don't be modest!" roared Nefarious Freedom with delight. "Any enemy of the Fairy establishment is a bosom companion of mine. My gran would drop her shell if she caught me treating rough with comrades-at-arms!"

Rushe bowed, stretching his legs in front of him like a cat. "Right up the stairs, ma'am," he purred, "and watch your step."

Waite licked his chops. "And if there's a thing we can do to aid and abet you just howl and we'll hear it. Excellent acoustics in Almanack."

September did not like using the Marquess as a strange sort of password. It had been so much more complicated than that. And it felt like bragging, which was not at all nice when you considered the consequences of it all. Nor could she understand how these beasts could hate Fairyland so—and Fairies, who were nearly as extinct as dimetrodons, save a few stray orphans like King Charlie and Belinda Cabbage and Calpurnia Farthing. But she had little to barter with but her reputation. The sooner she finished with this nonsense, the sooner she could set about finding A-Through-L and Saturday.

"You could winch up my . . . my friend. I fear she won't make it up the steps." September did not know what to call Aroostook, but what use might a lobster and two jackals have for the word *car*?

The lobster-knight looked dubious. "Your friend would crack the pearl! Smash it right to bits. We've got strict preservation codes. No Alien Conveyances Allowed. But never you worry. You'll find Almanack has taken care of all your needs, I promise. Travel by Public Tram, Taxicrab, or Regularly Scheduled Trapeze! See the Grand Moonflower Lawn from the sack of a luxury lunar pelican! You'll have no cause to complain, friend."

"I can't just leave Aroostook. What if someone made off with her or vandalized her parts? Oh, I'm sure they wouldn't mean to, but she's a complicated machine. A Tool, really, and Tools Have Rights." September fell back lamely on the only law she knew by name.

The jackals exchanged glances. "Who told you that?" they said together.

"Never mind, never mind!" cried Nefarious, waving her emerald pincers in the air. "We'll watch over her nice and snug. Safe as seahorses. It's what we do, after all! Come back for her when you're finished."

September felt very reluctant indeed to leave the Model A. Fairyish folk seemed so terribly fascinated by the automobile. But faster in, faster out! September turned off the engine and pocketed the key. She patted the burlaped wheel. "I won't be long," she whispered. "Don't go running off this time! You can't trust just any old person who comes along with a hundred puffins and a pretty face!"

Aroostook settled into silence as September walked up the coral staircase and into Almanack.

When she was quite out of sight, a peculiar thing happened. The big, rusty horn nestled into the driver's-side door melted away into hot steam. In its place billowed up a huge cobalt and white striped phonograph bell. A squeeze bulb ballooned out from the bottom of it, looking a bit like a tulip bulb, delicate and coppery and sheathed in gauzy layers like a live thing.

The jackals sniffed at it. It smelled of sunshine.

September stepped inside the snail-shell and onto a long shimmering street full of sound and tumult. It spiraled down and in along the floor of the great shell—but up and down had clearly become such good friends here that it hardly mattered who was who. Almanack was all mother-of-pearl, silver-green, and blue-violet chasing each other in gleaming ribbons. Houses and streetlamps and storefronts and skinny bright towers and fountains and bridges and pavilions sprung out everywhere: not only out of the floor of the shell but sticking out sideways from the walls and upside down from the misty reaches of the ceiling. It looked as though they had grown there, budded out of the shell itself like mushrooms. Every bank and gambling hall and bakery and public house flashed with the same mother-of-pearl. Everything was Almanack and Almanack was everything. Fishwives cast nets in a pearly river that ran across a curve of spiral wall and should have spilled out all over the avenue and September herself, but somehow did not. People and creatures and carts walked and rolled along, chatting merrily, the men wearing fabulous anemones like corsages, the women tipping coral top hats to anyone they passed. A great pelican whose tail sported no feathers but flapped a long, diaphanous goldfish's tail behind it wafted overhead, its hefty pouch filled with a tumult of mermaids splashing in a specially provided pool.

With a skittering thump, something barreled toward September, nearly crashing into a lovely, tall mother-of-pearl candelabra that lit the way into Almanack, only righting itself with a wild thrashing of four of its eight legs as it careened up on its side. It brought itself in hand with a thud and a scrabble and looked up at September with piercing, intelligent eyes: a broad, polished, black-and-white-checkered crab.

"Afternoon," he said crisply. "Name's Spoke and I'll be your Taxicrab on this fine day. First visit to Almanack? I can always spot a first-timer. Can't stop gawking at the ceiling. Sometimes they throw up! Please don't throw up. I've just had a wash."

September looked from the checkered crab to the green pearl ceiling and back again. "But I didn't call for a . . . a Taxicrab," she said softly.

"Who calls for one? Screamingly inefficient, if you ask me! Almanack takes care of all your needs. I suppose if you felt like insisting on it I could fetch you a walking map, but they're a devil to catch and take at least four hands and an opposable tail to operate so it's my professional opinion as a crabbie of venerable years that you ought to climb on and let me scuttle you wherever you need to scut!"

Indeed, a very comfortable-looking cushioned chair was strapped to the crab's chessboard back with a number of enormous black belts. Throw pillows in all the shades of mother-of-pearl plumped invitingly along the seat.

"I'm afraid I haven't got a fare. . . ." September bit the inside of her cheek so as not to show the fullness of her embarrassment. How hard she had tried to avoid this! How carefully she'd saved!

The Taxicrab's slender claws went *snick-snick-crunch*. "Fare? I don't know the meaning of the word! You're a fair young girl; I'm a fair old crab and I pinch my children equally when they've been wretched. But if you mean paying your way, like I summed it, Almanack looks after your littlest need before you know you've got one in your pocket. Hup, hup, hup! In you go, don't be shy, I won't drop you—well, I won't drop you far. I'm low to the ground, which is how *I* spell safety!"

September could not help smiling. After the Blue Wind, she felt the crab's cheerfulness wash over her like a hot and happy bath. She put her foot in one of the belt loops like a horse's stirrup and hoisted herself onto the plush seat.

"Where to, my four-legged maid?"

"I haven't got four legs! I think you must have miscounted."

"Sure you have! Just like I've got ten. Oh, the ignorant will say eight, but my claws are for walking as well as snatching and pinching and digging. I daresay you could walk around on your hands and knees if you had a hankering to do it. And why slow yourself down by only using your body parts for only one thing each? Very limiting!"

September laughed and held a little tighter to the arms of her chair, suddenly not entirely certain of the sort of locomotion Spoke intended to use on her. "I've got to see the Whelk of the Moon, if you please," she said nervously.

The Taxicrab made a burbling sound somewhere deep in his shell, an uncertain sort of giggle.

"Pardon and all but you'll have to be more specific. Where there's a Whelk there's a way, I always say! Well, we all say. I can't take credit. It's the Taxicrab motto."

"I . . . I don't follow, sir. But I've got a lovely long casket"—she felt it best to talk up the box a little so no one would think it suspicious—"and I'm meant to bring it to the Whelk of the Moon and I hoped someone else would know who that was. I'm not from these parts—I'm not even from the parts this part is part of!"

The Taxicrab bubbled again. "Nup, nup, I've got you now. Don't spin your head about it. I'll spin it plenty on my ownsome!"

Spoke reared up like a pony, stabbed his fore-claws down into the stuff of the street, and launched forward with a tremendous vault, clearing streetlamps, a skating rink, and a throng of little Naiads with ribbons in their seafoam hair, who squealed in delight and waved their hands. They came down with a chin-jarring crunch near a shop full of round rice candy in the windows and skittered away so fast September's hair blew back and her eyes watered. The Taxicrab obeyed no logic at all. He dashed up one wall and swerved toward the ceiling until September cried out in terror, having no seat belt and hanging nearly upside down. Then he leapt out, checkered legs splayed wide, and landed in some poor soul's back garden, shredding their delicate snow-colored grapevines—which tore off and trailed out behind them like streamers when he leapt again.

"On your left you can see the Stationary Circus in all its splendor! Not far nor wide will you find dancing bears more nimble than ours, ringmasters more masterful, Lunaphants more buoyant!"

September looked down and leftward as best she could. She could see the dancing bears, the ringmaster blowing peonies out of her mouth like fire, an elephant floating in the air, her trunk raised, her feet in mid-foxtrot—and all of them paper. The skin of the bears was all folded envelopes; they stared out of sealing-wax eyes. The ringmaster wore a suit of birthday invitations dazzling with balloons and cakes and purple-foil presents; her face was a telegram. Even the elephant seemed to be made up of cast-off letterheads from some far-off office, thick and creamy and stamped with sure, bold letters. A long, sweeping trapeze swung out before them. Two acrobats held on, one made of gro-cery lists, the other of legal opinions. September could see Latin on the one and *lemons, ice, bread (not rye!),* and *lamb chops* on the other in a cur-sive hand. When they let go of the trapeze-bar, they turned identical flips in the air and folded out into paper airplanes, gliding in circles all the way back down to the peony-littered ring. September gasped and clapped her hands—but the acrobats were already long behind them, bowing and catching paper roses in their paper teeth.

"Up top you'll find the College of Lunar Arts—home of the Lop-sided Library and the Insomniac Coliseum. Oh! Too late, we've passed it—look faster! If you practice, your eyeballs can move so quick you can see yourself go by before you've even thought to leave!"

Everything flew by in a sleek swirl of color. September's eyes swam. "Maybe a crab can!" She gasped.

"A Taxicrab must be as limber as time and twice as punctual!" Spoke rocketed over a vast expanse of pale, milky flowers waving sweetly. "Straight lines are a loser's game! I once picked up an old lady hobgoblin, no bigger than a stump, eyes like a lantern fish! Got her to an appointment she missed when she was a maiden, just in time to give a man a donkey's head, kick him twice, and still turn up early for supper."

"You don't mean to say—"

But they reared up again, dizzyingly, the house-cluttered ceiling of Almanack yawning into view and out again—and then the crab stopped short, claws clicking triumph.

"Here we are, Central Almanack, Executive District! Off you hop, no need for thanks, I'm wanted down the circus, careful now, my belts do like to tangle, there you are, safe and sound, and here I go—check your watch, I'll get to the off-duty bear before she sees her bicycle's sprung a flat! All in a day and a night, my girl, just look sharp and you'll find your mark."

And the Taxicrab was gone. His checkered body zoomed off faster than September's eyes could follow.

Spoke had left her in a little grotto so thick with mother-of-pearl it humped up in stalagmites and antler-points and great dark bulbs. A thin filigree net stitched with tiny specks of light like fireflies hung high up above her head. Bowls of liquid lay on every flat surface, as though a great party had just ended and no one had finished their drinks. Down in the heart of the grotto stood a very pale, very small, very beautiful person. After a moment, September caught her breath— how jangled and bashed about she felt after the quake and the crab!— and started down the rills and hillocks of hard, slick colors. The person stood in a kind of alcove, very still.

"Welcome." The voice seemed to come from all over, an echo of an echo. "I am Almanack."

September could not tell if Almanack was a man or a woman. The creature had long, silken hair the color of rosewater candy, and a delicate, pointed face. Long, peach-pale tendrils uncoiled everywhere, looping like vines around draped satin and gauze that covered its body, dipping into the bowls wherever they found them. Almanack had at least six hands, four folded gracefully and two open, held out toward September.

"I beg your pardon," she said shyly, a little out of breath and a little overcome. "I thought the city was Almanack."

Almanack smiled; its lips colored deeper to a dusky ginger. It spoke very kindly. "The city is Almanack, little one, but Almanack is me. It is my shell; it grows out of me, more and more and longer and wider each year. When one of my folk needs a thing, I provide. I squeeze shut my eyes and push out a house for them, or a mountain, or a museum for umbrellas. Almanack," it said softly, "takes care of all your needs before you know you have them. I am the Whelk of the Moon. What is it you need, little rushing bashful two-legged beast?"

"All of this, all of it, the circus and the college and the lawns and the river—it's all you? Your . . . your body? People are living inside you?" After a moment, September added: "And I am not a beast."

A rosy ripple moved through Almanack's cotton candy hair. "A Whelk will grow as big as it's allowed before it is eaten or crushed or starved. Give it a little crystal bottle and you will have a little crystal Whelk. Give it an ocean and who knows where it will end? Give it a moon and you get . . . me. I have never been eaten or crushed or starved." One of its tendrils found a fresh bowl and sank into the burgundy liquid there. Almanack shut its eyes in joy. "Forgive me, I am hungry. I am forever hungry. It takes so much to feed me now. I am vast. Vastness longs for vastness, don't you find?" After a moment, the Whelk added: "And we are all beasts."

September nodded shyly, perfectly willing to defer to the Whelk's opinion on such things, not being very vast herself.

Almanack opened its four folded hands, holding them out, pearly palms showing. "I was once unvast, like you. I dimly remember it. But even then, barnacles and mussels lived on the outside of me and little marine mites lived in me, so tiny you couldn't see them—but I could *hear* them, their invisible briny holidays and squabbles over philosophy. *We are safe in the shell; outside the shell we are not safe.* There is not much to a mite's mind, but what there is, is gentle and uncomplicated. As I grew, I could hear them less and less, and I became lonely. One day a bishop-fish walked into me—I'd grown so large she thought I must be empty and available for a nice hermitage. She wore a miter on her trouty head bigger than she was, and her legs were a jumble of fish-hooks with but a little skin left. We got on very well. Her philosophy had more starch in it, dialectics and philippics and things, but it came to the same in the end: *We are safe in the shell; outside the shell we are not safe.* More and more came, and they needed so much. The first time I made a hut grow I thought I would die from happiness. I watched my bishop-fish fall asleep in it and I sang to her. Haven't you ever wanted to give someone everything they needed, to make them safe within your own arms, to feed them and keep all harm outside?"

September thought of her father and the soreness in his leg and his heart and his memory. She thought of her mother, so worried and tired all the time. And she thought suddenly of Saturday, who had once been locked into a cage so small he could not stand up.

"As I got bigger, that feeling got bigger in me until it was big enough for all," Almanack went on. "My heart is a house with room to spare. I wanted to make the marine mites' philosophy true. Perhaps my philosophy is not so sophisticated. It goes: *Come inside. I love you.* A Whelk's love will grow as big as it's allowed." Almanack sipped a distant bowl of inky black syrup with one of its tendrils. "There. I have turned the lights on in the college dormitories. A whole bank of lamps in the shapes of their least favorite professors, just to make the students laugh."

"Aren't you afraid they'll use you all up? There's so many people, and only one of you!"

Almanack closed its pink eyes. "They are all hungry, too, you know. At the bottom of philosophy something very true and very desperate whispers: *Everyone is hungry all the time.* Everyone is *starving.* Everyone wants so much, more than they can stomach, but the appetite doesn't converse much with the stomach. Everyone is hungry and not only for food—for comfort and love and excitement and the opposite of being alone. Almost everything awful anyone does is to get those things and keep them. Even the mites and the mussels. But no one can use you up unless you let them." Almanack gave a great and happy sigh. "The whole point of growing is to get big enough to hold the world you want inside you. But it takes a long time, and you really must eat your vegetables, and most often you have to make the world you want out of yourself."

September's eyes tingled with tears. Of all the Fairy strangeness she had known, this seemed suddenly both the strangest and least strange of all. How she would have liked to be looked after like that, cared for and watched over. And yet at the same time, she understood the Whelk, and wished she could grow big enough to hold on to everyone she loved at once. To keep them safe and with her always and know their secret needs well enough to answer them. When she spoke, her throat had got thick and tight.

"And what do you eat?"

"I eat their hunger. When a soul inside me longs for something, a bowl fills. As I make a hut or a streetlamp or a hippodrome or a cabaret, I drink up their need and am satisfied when they are satisfied. I am sustained by Being Necessary."

"That's very strange."

Almanack's deep green eyes shone. "Is it? Have you done a long, hard thing for the sake of someone you loved, so long and so hard that your body shook with the difficulty of it, that you were thirsty and aching and ravenous by the time it was done, but it did not matter, you did not even feel the thirst or the pain or the hunger, because you were doing what was Necessary?"

"Yes," September whispered. She could feel the salt of the Perverse and Perilous Sea on her skin as if it still caked there. As if she were still sailing around Fairyland to save her friends.

"Then it is not so strange. Being Necessary is food no less than cabbages and strawberry pies. And surely if you have come all this way, you need something from me. Say it and I will do my best. I cannot do everything, but folk who can do everything are terrible bores."

September's heart sang out inside her: *I need to find Saturday and A-Through-L, I need to touch them and see them and smell them and hear them and to not walk in Fairyland alone. I want a lovely adventure where no one carries a hurt around with them like a satchel or tries to force a country like a door.* But she did not say it. She remembered her errand. *You do your job and you mind your work.* Besides, she did not live in Almanack. She was not one of its folk—it would not be right to go about bellowing demands, and selfish demands at that. September held her heart down while it trumpeted its desires and bit her cheek until she felt she could speak safely without blurting it out.

Oh, September! It is such hard work to keep your heart hidden! And worse, by the time you find it easy, it will be harder still to show it. It is a terrible magic in this world to ask for exactly the thing you want. Not least because to know exactly the thing you want and look it in the eye is a long, long labor. How I long to draw the curtain through this grotto, take September by the serious and stalwart shoulders and tell her the secret of growing up! But I cannot. It is against the rules. Even I am bound by *some* rules.

"A Wind asked me to bring this to you," September said instead. "I don't know what it is, but I came an awfully long way to give it to you."

Almanack's elfin face opened up in an expression of enormous delight and gratitude. "Thank you, child! How wonderfully thoughtful of you." Using all six of its rosy hands, the Whelk of the Moon pried at the lid of the carved ivory box.

But it would not open.

Almanack explored the lock with several of its tendrils. It put its tongue between its teeth as it worked at the mechanism.

But it would not open.

Suddenly, the Whelk of the Moon thumped the box hard with its uppermost right fist. September laughed at the peaceful Whelk's pummeling.

But it would not open.

"I am so deeply sorry, my small friend," it said, holding out the four arms which did not still cradle the casket. September stepped into them, hardly knowing why. The Whelk of the Moon wrapped its arms around her. Its skin was warm. Shaking its head, it murmured finally into September's hair:

"I fear you will have to take it to the Librarian."

CHAPTER IX
THE CURSE

*In Which September Meets an Old Friend Unexpectedly,
Discharges Her Postal Duties, and Is Nearly Burnt to a Crisp*

September rang a bell.

She brought her hand down on top of it again—a big glass buzzer-bell like the one in the principal's office at school. This one did not buzz; it rang clear and high, shattering the silence of the Lopsided Library.

No one answered. A loud *shush* sounded from the depths of the stacks, but September could not see the shusher, even if she stood on tiptoes.

Whoever named this place got it in one, September thought to herself. It was a very lovely library, a great circular room with a high glass chair on a dais in the middle of it all, from which, when such a one was on duty, a Librarian might glare down most effectively at noisy nellies and book-swipers. Pale blue and green pillars studded with round moonstones separated the sections. Neat rows of green-black stone desks and black-green study lamps stood at the ready. Bright stained-glass stacks sparkled as they bore up books of every possible size and type, rising all the way up through several floors to a domed ceiling strung with round lanterns. But all the books seemed to have lurched to one side of the building, as though they had all gotten a good fright from whatever sort of beast haunts the night terrors of books. They piled up on top of each other, wedged in tight to bursting, and if there was an order or a logic to their arrangement it, too, had had a good scare and run off. The stacks on the other side stood nearly empty, stained glass dustless and forlorn, a few lonely tomes leaning over, falling down, huddled in twos and threes for warmth.

"Hello?" September called. Her voice bounced around the rotunda.

This time, an answer came.

It was a roar that was also a shout that was also a laugh that was also a screech that was also a deep, resounding *haroom*.

A huge ball of red scales, claws, and wings shot up out of the rear stacks and landed on the Librarian's chair. The ball had bright turquoise eyes that danced and shone and long orange whiskers.

A-Through-L, the Wyverary, crouched on the great glass chair and grinned as wide as any Wyvern ever has.

"September!" he trumpeted—and before September could answer him by vaulting over the circulation counter into his welcoming wings, a strange and awful thing happened.

A plume of indigo fire erupted from the Wyverary's throat. He threw back his head toward the domed ceiling. The flame flowed thick and oily through the air, coiling and sizzling as it rose. Several lanterns burst into purple sparks and charred chunks, raining back down onto the books. The roof blackened—but it could not get much blacker than the black blast-stars which already scarred it. Finally, the flame sputtered out, leaving A-Through-L looking mortified. He hid his head in one scarlet claw.

And then, without warning, he shrank.

September was sure she saw it: One moment he was as gargantuan as always, towering, a great red beast who could eat two barns for lunch and still have room for tea. The next, he had dropped a foot or two, and cinched in a foot or two, and even lost a foot or two of tail.

But September could not make the time to worry about that. She cried out in joy, finally, a mighty whoop swelling up in her and bursting out at last, a popped bubble, a cut rope. Fairyland at last, even if it was the Moon, and her friend, impossibly, brassy and bright as ever, nothing lost, and not one fig given whether or not she had grown up a little. She laughed and reached up her arms to the Librarian's chair. Ell looped his tail around her and hauled her up, nuzzling her face and blushing furiously. *She who blushes first loses,* September thought. But her own face flushed anyhow and she was not sorry.

"*I'm* very well, thank you," snapped a little piping voice. A final glop of indigo flame hissed from Ell's mouth, landing on the glass chair and sizzling away into lavender steam. A puffball festooned with ribbons yelped and stamped at a smoking book some falling nugget of lantern had stove in. "Oh, why *shouldn't* you take on a Wyvern, Abby? Everyone deserves a claw in the door. He'll be aces at shelving, with those wings!"

"September," said A-Through-L with deep embarrassment, "may I present Abecedaria, the Catalogue Imp. Who is really very nice when there are patrons underfoot . . ."

The puffball hopped over the cairns of books and perched on a stack of periodicals. Abecedaria was a large powdered wig. Her curls and tiers were as splendid as any of the Founding Fathers or French

Kings September had read about in her history books, fastened with black velvet ribbons and little black rosettes. She had no head beneath the wig; several of those sausage curls and corkscrews and puffs formed themselves into waggling eyebrows and a noble nose and a mouth. Two fat poodle-puffs made for legs, which ended in tiny black slippers.

"But what do you see?" the wig wailed in despair. "Do you see patrons?"

"She's a Periwig," Ell whispered. "Aldermanic Order, from the Fox-tail Haberdashery. Very crispable, but a wonder with figures and sorting and classification and fiddly things that take patience that people's heads just don't have. Periwig begins with P, but *she* begins with A and we know each other quite well anyhow by now. Oh, I am so happy to see you!"

"An empty Library!" cried Abecedaria. "A silent Library! Can you imagine anything more miserable?"

September blinked. "I thought Librarians liked silence! I'm sure someone shushed me on the way in!"

"I can't help that I make shushing noises when I walk! It's a far sight better than squeaking loafers! You poor girl, what sort of aged, unfriendly Libraries have you met in your short life? A silent Library is a *sad* Library. A Library without patrons on whom to pile books and tales and knowing and magazines full of up-to-the-minute politickal fashions and atlases and plays in pentameter! A Library should be full of exclamations! Shouts of delight and horror as the wonders of the world are discovered or the lies of the heavens uncovered or the wild adventures of devil-knows-who sent romping out of the pages. A Library should be full of *now-just-a-minute*s and *that-can't-be-right*s and scientifick folk running skelter to prove somebody wrong. It should positively vibrate with laughing at comedies and sobbing at tragedies, it should echo with gasps as decent ladies glimpse indecent things and indecent ladies stumble upon secret and scandalous decencies! A Library should not *shush*; it should *roar*! And that is why I *did* think a Wyvern would be a perfectly boisterous and bombastic Librarian. I have only myself to blame."

A-Through-L groaned in sorrow. "Oh, A is for apology and F is for forgiveness and I hope that you'll take the one and give the other, for I am as sorry a beast as ever flew! You know me, September, as well as anyone who ever walked on toes instead of claws. I *never* use my fire unless I mean to! At least I never *did*! Why, before a year ago I could count on one foot the things I'd scorched. See, I'll fess up to all of them: a certain real estate office, a flock of gillybirds when I was *very* hungry, a bonfire at Midautumn, and *On the Criminology of Fairies* by Quentin Q. Quince, Volumes II–IX. I only meant to burn up three of those and they did ask me to do the bonfire and I'm very sorry about Mr. Quince. I am not a vicious beast! It is only that I cannot help it! Lately, when I am excited or frightened or feeling things very strongly it just comes bellowing *out*. I try to keep it in, I swallow snow by the drift and gargle salt water and eat plenty of greens, but it's always there, just waiting to come out, and I am so awfully, terribly sorry that I hurt our poor lanterns and damaged property and gave September a nasty shock, I'm sure! If you both hate me for it, I shall understand, but you mustn't hate beasts for things they can't help. I do wish books weren't so burn-up-able! But we must all live with our weaknesses." A single orange tear dropped from Ell's eye.

"The Quince was practically his first act as Assistant Librarian," sighed Abecedaria. "All my patrons run away and gone, in a spectacular display of Wyvern!"

"I shall wear a muzzle if I have to," Ell said miserably. "And turn my face to one side."

"Oh, you big stove, don't take it so hard. What would I do without you? I'm getting on in years, I can't even reach the romances anymore." The Periwig patted Ell's ruddy flank. "There, there," she crooned. "That's what curses are for. You'll get the better of it, I just know it. And then you'll be ready for a circulation of your own."

September gasped herself. "You've *cursed* Ell?" She was ready to stand for her friend right there and call the imp a dozen kinds of rotten, nasty, no-good tyrant.

"Yes, I did, young lady, and I'll thank you not to judge until he turns your house into a purple fireworks display and explodes every book you could call your own!"

September turned to look at Ell, who clearly wished he could pull up the whole Lopsided Library over his head and disappear.

"It's a Pedagogickal Curse," Abecedaria said defensively. "Simple Severe Magic. All Librarians are Secret Masters of Severe Magic. Goes with the territory. A Library at its ripping, roaring best is a raucous beast to ride. When he learns his lesson it'll snap like fingers. Every time he fires off like that, he shrinks. It doesn't hurt him and I daresay he's got a ways to go before it makes a difference in his lunch portions. No use whining; it can't be undone till you undo it."

"Oh, poor Ell!" September threw up her arms and the Wyverary lowered his long red snout so that she could hold him as best she might. He was so much bigger than her that it always felt like hugging a building; she did it all the same. His warm skin smelled just as it always had, was just as leathery and dry as she remembered. But it was not the same—not quite. Her arms had never been able to reach quite so far around his neck before. But she would not shame the Wyverary by blurting out how much smaller he had gotten.

"Fire begins with F," he wept, "and so does Flame. Perhaps it's hopeless, in the end."

"Nothing's hopeless! After all, I've found you on the Moon—I can't think of anything more unlikely in the world and yet here we are!" September gave him her warmest smile.

"Oh, but it's not so unlikely!" cried Ell excitedly, his curse forgotten in his eagerness. "September, you only left a few months ago! You left us dancing with the shadows, and *that* went on for a good while. I had quite a lot to say to my shadow, it turned out! And so did everyone else! It took so long King Crunchcrab called a national holiday so the whole business could get a proper hash out. I had breakfast with the other Ell every morning. Radish tart and goblin quiche! But then Belinda Cabbage sent for me—or rather her Automated Elecktro-Whiskered Apprentice did. That's a sort of mechanickal meerkat fueled by worry. The more you fret about a thing, the harder they work to fix up the trouble! Miss Cabbage built a whole mob of them and they all came running when she popped up in Fairyland-Above again. So many anxious folk milling about! Well, that little bronze meerkat flashed and squeaked and trilled and rolled back and forth on her tiny wheels and then spat out a little curl of paper that said Miss Cabbage and some creature called Avogadra had done some Questing Mathematickals and that when you came home—I'm sorry, I don't mean to say *home*; I mean to say when you came *back*—you'd land on the Moon or thereabouts. And here you are! Mathematicks are wonderful things, even if they begin with M."

"I don't think I shall ever understand how time manages its affairs in Fairyland," said September, shaking her head. "For me a whole year has gone by, and a little more besides. But . . . you keep saying I," September said softly. "Where is Saturday? Did he come with you to meet me? I left you together."

Ell put his scarlet head on one side. "Haven't you seen him yet?"

"No!"

The Periwig interrupted them. "I'm sure it's all deeply mysterious but I've got soot to scrub and you've got a box under your arm so let's have at one or the other of them, shall we?"

September wanted to talk about Saturday. She wanted to ignore everything but Ell. She wanted to snap at Abecedaria and tell her to leave them alone already. September took a deep breath, pushing her temper down like purple fire. Give over the box and no more demands on her but to sit with her friend and talk about everything, everything that had passed since they'd seen each other.

"A Blue Wind asked me to bring this to the Whelk of the Moon, but the Whelk couldn't get it open, so I'm to bring it to you for lock-picking or smashing or however you can manage it." With a sigh of relief, September put the long ivory casket into two long, sturdy locks of the Periwig's hair that had shaped themselves into puffy, tightly curled hands.

"Ell, my love, fetch us *The Manual of Safe-Cracking and Assorted Mechanickal Naughtiness*. Spring Edition."

A-Through-L rose up, flapping his long, bright wings. He glided toward the nearly empty side of the Library.

"If you don't mind my asking," said September, "you've got so much room on the one side, why have you packed everything in so close on the other?"

The Periwig turned the black rosettes of her eyes to heaven and the Wyverary. "That's why it's the Lopsided Library. The books, you know, they have opinions. Factions. Pitched battles. Right now, the Fictionals have the advantage—they're the flashy ones, after all, and whatever they say in their pages goes, even if it doesn't make a lick of sense and rhymes besides. Non-Fiction has to abide by the rules of what really is, and that is just exhausting. In retaliation, the Nons are gussying up with fanciful notions and fabricated histories written by the conquerors and grandstanding about with metaphors and parables and other unsavories. So they've got to be stacked with the Fiction, nothing to be done. They dash over to attend parties and be seen with the right popular novels. Give it a week and Non-Fiction will be on the up again. The Fictionals will fall all over one another to expunge their pretty prose and their tall tales and their impossible Physicks and elegant motifs. It'll be a race to the realistic, mark my words. A dance to the dreary if you ask me, but you haven't. Then it'll lurch to the other side and at least we'll have a chance to dust the shelves before they go hurtling back because a social history of changelings tried on a sonnet for size. You'd have to be a champion racer to outrun literary fashion."

Ell returned, holding the volume gingerly in his claws. The Periwig began turning the pages furiously, chasing notations with her black velvet ribbons, marking her place with a fuzzy, powdery curl.

"Oh!" she exclaimed. It echoed in the Library. "Now just a minute! It's no trouble at all. I should have guessed when you said a Blue Wind. Come on, Ell, get your eyeball up to the lock. You have to show it something blue and speak very sternly to it. Poor Almanack couldn't stern a minnow."

A-Through-L put his huge orange eye to the lock. He stared it down for several minutes, never blinking once. Finally, a great turquoise tear welled up in his eye and fell with a splash to the floor of the Library. He stood up and looked expectantly at Abecedaria—but September took a deep breath and stepped up to the lock herself. She squared her shoulders and frowned as deeply as she could. She had put on her sternness once today already, it ought to be warmed up and ready. September glared at the lock and hollered, "You open up RIGHT THIS INSTANT or I shall call your mother!"

The box popped open in a hurry.

Inside lay a stethoscope.

It gleamed blue, naturally. The stethoscope had a certain burliness to it: thick, strong rods and a tube like an elephant's trunk—and all of sapphire. The cup would have engulfed September's head. It seemed made for someone Ell's size, or whatever creature could dwarf a Wyvern. Almanack itself, perhaps.

Abecedaria hissed and drew away.

"The Sapphire Stethoscope! No, no, I won't take it! It's yours, you brought it here, it's none of my business!"

Sterness melted and flew away from September's face like snowflakes after you've rushed inside out of the cold. "What are you talking about? The Whelk told me to bring it to you! I'm finished with it, my duty is discharged, and I mean to have a jolly time with my friend, thank you very much!"

"No! Take it! Take it back and hide it, please! I'm too little. He'll crush me and braid me till I break. You've seen the Library, September. We can't stand up to Ciderskin; we just *can't*. The ceiling barely stays on as it is!"

"That's the second time I've heard that name!" exclaimed September. "Who is Ciderskin?"

CHAPTER X

THE YETI'S PAW

In Which September Learns of the Foibles of Fairies,
Shirks Her Work (but Only Briefly), and a Very Speedy Yeti
Makes Trouble for Everyone

Abecedaria the Periwig drew herself up to her full height—which was not much higher than September's hip. Her curls glossed up and shaped themselves into a very proud new face with shapely powdered horsehair cheeks. The Periwig was about to give a recitation.

"Ciderskin is the fastest Yeti on the Moon. Now, if you knew anything about Yetis, you would be very impressed. Yetis are so fast you almost never see one, only his footprints in the snow, and even the mightiest photograph can only catch a vague blur as they whizz by. They are even born fast! A Yeti grows from a little furry snowball to a shaggy monster with black ram's horns and burning red eyes and hands that could crush wine out of boulders quicker than you can say, *does that avalanche have teeth?* They love the winter and they love the snow; they love the mountains and they love to eat—and all the things that go with eating: squashing and walloping and tearing and ripping and crunching and gnawing. They were here before the Fairies came—but so were many folk less inclined toward stomping on the ground just to see it flinch. In those long ago days when the Fairies built the road and danced on the Moon in their cackling thousands, they sought to learn the secret of fastness from the Yetis. Perhaps you know that about Fairies and perhaps you don't—they were always on the lookout for the best of everyone else to take and use for themselves."

September remembered what Charlie Crunchcrab himself had once said to her: *Fairies started out as frogs. Amphibianderous, right? Well, being frogs was no kind of fun, so we went about and stole better bits—wings from dragonflies and faces from people and hearts from birds and horns from various goats and antelope-ish things and souls from ifrits and tails from cows and we evolved, over a million million minutes, just like you.*

"I thought everyone wanted the Fairies to come back!" she said. September certainly did. But the lobster and the jackals seemed to have no use for them at all.

The Periwig snorted. Two delicate clouds of powder blossomed from her curly nose. "Oh, life then was a whirlwind of magic and a kettle of fun—if you were a Fairy. It's clear a Yeti is not a Fairy, I think you'll agree. They hunted the wild beasts through the Silver Mallet Mountains and up the dizzying slopes of the Splendid Dress, whose frozen peak you can see from outside the shell, up the trunk of the Tallest Tree, a palm that stretches so high a comet once spent three days' vacation on its fronds, sucking the blue coconuts dry. But you cannot catch a Yeti. You can only be where she is going to be or where she has been. Finally, a Fairy's jungle trap clapped shut on a Yeti's paw—by chance, mere chance and bad luck. Bellowing in rage and pain, the poor hulk chewed it off at the wrist and dashed away, dripping Yeti blood across the snow. You can still see them: a row of round black ponds leading into the lunar wilds. Well, that was the end of it, for the Fairies found that a Yeti's fastness lay in his paw. They used it so much they couldn't stop using it—who wants to wait for the pot to boil or Spring to come or for parted lovers to be joined or for a spell to brew or a plan you've hatched to come ripe? They built a city called Patience around the Yeti's paw, because a Fairy's humor is as subtle as a bullwhip. In Patience, they sped everything up so that they never had to wait. Tea was always on the second you were thirsty, Fairy tricks were schemed in one breath and played the next, festivals were always happening the moment after someone thought up the idea. You never had to pine or yearn, if you fell in love with a selkie down in Fairyland, why, he'd be at your side in a flutter of your wings. You could defeat boredom for all and for good— just skip to the part where a Fairy and her pack have ganged up upon an unsuspecting shepherdess and turned her sheep into suitors! Why should a young Fairy wait around to grow up while everyone lectures her and gets supper first and makes her go to bed at dawn when she is sleepy at eight o'clock and wants her bed? She can bite the paw and be a wicked Fairy adventuress with strength in her toes before she gets done wiping the taste of Yeti out of her mouth. A Fairy could touch milk and curdle it, touch beer and spoil it, touch wine and make it vinegar. And they did it, for delight and for flummoxing dairy maids and for the peculiar relish of spoiling and breaking and knocking things apart."

September looked at Ell, his wonderful red presence beside her, listening loudly—for a Wyvern breathes noisily, having so much breath to huff. She thought the Fairies had it right. She would have given anything for a Yeti's paw back home. To somehow fold up the year and skip the part that lay between her and Fairyland, rub it out with her pencil's eraser so that she didn't have to sit through it, full of longing, while it took its dawdling time going by. Show September a paw in the middle of Omaha to bite and she would be there, bright and early, with her teeth brushed.

How we would like to argue with September, and tell her that in the waiting lies the pleasure! That we here in the world of sensible folk know how to wait without twisted-up bellies and tapping feet and wishing for the sun to hurry up and rise and set. That a clever person is never bored, and a bored person is never clever. But though I am sly, I am a trickster, I am even cruel—I cannot lie.

Abecedaria furrowed her crimped eyebrow-curls. "Oh, fine and fat for a Fairy! Fairies live forever! There's no such thing as a withered old Fairy coughing up regret in her sickbed! They could speed up time all they liked and lose nothing! But the Moon was in her springtime then and teeming with folk neither Fairy nor Yeti! Harpies and Banshees and Kappa and Kitsunes and Chimeras and Hreinn and Qilin and Satyrs! Yet once Patience became a city in full swing, the Fairies down in Fairyland raced up the road to join their brothers and sisters in the sky. They say it was like a rainbow emptying out onto the Moon, so many came and so fast—and another pouring away from it, as folk fled, outrunning the terror of time run mad. Even I cannot deny the lure of having everything you want the minute you want it. And so it went. The Fairies knuckled away even the boring old minutes between falling asleep and waking up. The rest? You could only call it burglary. They didn't toss the time off like a dress—they lost it. It bled right out of them. They grew older, faster. Oh, a night here and there wouldn't have hurt—unless it's *your* day or night and you only have so many saved up against death's accounts! But you have no idea how easily a Fairy gets bored. They Yetied away weeks and months if that's how long it took for the shepherdess's suitors to grow a thick pelt ready to be sheared for the wedding day. They were so hungry never to waste time ever again that they wasted the rest of us away. Half the Moon died of old age before anyone could fix it."

"And how was it fixed?" September asked. "Who fixed it?"

The Periwig shrugged her delicate puffball shoulders. "It was long ago and my books don't know. There were battles, of course—savage and ferocious battles—but the Fairies only bit their paws and skipped to the end of the battle, to the end of the war. They stood over the field still fresh and laughing while the Moonfolk lay gasping and exhausted and bent over with arthritis. The loyalists had nothing to slow down time—the Queer Physickists say no one can do that. But Periwigs came to the Moon afterward, when the Fairies had disappeared and accounts had to be balanced, a mess cleaned up, judgments made, cases argued. Only the very youngest of the Harpies and Satyrs and Hreinn and their kin remained. No one would speak of it, and they pulled down the Yeti's paw in Patience with ropes and cheering."

"But what has Ciderskin to do with it, if all is well now?"

A-Through-L spoke this time, his dear, round nostrils flaring. "Ciderskin wants to be King of the Moon, September. He wants us all to clear off on the double and leave him to be alone in the cold and the snow. After all, the Yetis shrunk up and grew old, too. I have seen a painting in the Inconstant Museum of a city filled with ancient Yetis all bending down to die before their own paw. And all because one of them, just once, was caught! The paw disappeared and the Moonfolk agreed between themselves not to look for it which I think shows nobleness, don't you? But I suppose someone could find it and use it. But really, Ciderskin just hates us and he shakes the Moon to shake us off. All he wants is to crouch up on top of the Splendid Dress and munch on the stones and lord over nothing. And he can do it, too! He is letting himself be seen! In the city of Mochi over the sea, the Harpies say he drove a pair of bone shears as tall as a tower into a meadow that hadn't done a thing to him, all the way up to the handles. The Moon quaked and cracked for a week! He is so much faster than we are, September. And he has his paws! At any time he, and not us, could spool up time like thread again and leave us all with our whole lives leaking away. People have already started to leave. You don't know, you haven't seen the Moon when it's full! Almanack is half empty; only grasshoppers live in Tithonus, all but a few prospectors and ballerinas have fled Sepharial now. But what if he shakes the Moon all to pieces? The shards will come raining down on Fairyland and a fat lot of good leaving will have done."

"We are safe in the shell," whispered Abecedaria. "But with the Sapphire Stethoscope, he could hear anyone, anywhere on the Moon. Even our dreams. We couldn't hide or plan; he'd know in a moment what might scare us the most. I don't know what sort of vicious, biting wind would have sent it here—here, where he could just snatch it away at any time! But you cannot keep it here; it's out of the question."

A-Through-L rocked from one ruby foot to the other. "You've no idea how many strange objects the Moon keeps tucked away. It's like a bank vault up here, only folk stick their spare magic up here for safe-keeping and interest-earning. Such a mess. I do wish they'd cleaned up after themselves when they went."

"Who?" wondered September.

"September, who else? The Fairies. Who else would even want a glittery blue thing that let you hear every whisper? A Wyvern prefers his privacy! Ciderskin went scaring up whatever he could find a little ways ago. He's got a great shaggy dog that goes about with him, a dog who can find anything. He dug up those bone shears out of a cave under the Sea of One Fish—and when One Fish tried to tell him to mind his own, the dog bit her tail and lassoed her round his head three times. He tossed One Fish like a ball halfway down to Fairyland. It took poor

One a month to swim back upstream, bleeding moonstones all the way."

"He means to do something dreadful, mark me," said the Periwig. "Once he's got all the bits of Fairy junk he wants."

"Then all anyone has to do is keep him from finding any more, surely . . ." said September.

"You be our guest and try, little lady," sighed Abecedaria. "A Yeti's mind is made of water—runs so fast and so deep no one can follow it, let alone splash around and have a look at the bottom. But that's all appendices and introductions—the body of the work is I won't take your filthy spying Stethoscope when the Yeti wants it. I won't let him wear me on his nasty ice-liced head, no *ma'am*!"

"I daresay your Library would last longer than I would against a Yeti."

September's heart lay down and rolled over and growled at itself. It found her bones and worried them. She wanted only to run off with A-Through-L and swim in the scarlet sea and gaze up at the stars. This wasn't *her* Moon. She wanted to get into Aroostook and drive right back down to Fairyland where at least she felt as though she knew something about anything at all. She wanted to eat pumpkin pie in the Autumn Provinces again. She wanted to skip to the easy part, the part that sparkled and sang. She didn't want to be a Fairy Knight or a Fairy Bishop. She just wanted to be a Fairy and live only in the moments she liked best. But the other part of her wanted to go tromping after a Moon-Yeti and give him what for. To save the strange and beautiful Moon from shaking apart and crashing down to Fairyland. To stand up to Ciderskin and stare him in the eyes the way she had the Marquess and her shadow. That is the trouble with standing up to people, of course. Once you start doing it, you can hardly stop.

If a wig can narrow its eyes, the Periwig did. Her black rosettes squinted shut; the white mustaches of her mouth pursed. September looked down at her black silks. Everyone saw her as a Criminal. They did it because of how she looked. But that was the whole purpose of clothes, she supposed. Clothes are a story you choose to tell about yourself, a different one every day. Even folk who wore plain overalls every day and didn't comb their hair and knew more about cattle breeds than fashion were telling a story: *I am a person who doesn't know or care about fashion because those aren't things worth knowing or caring about.* September had not chosen this story. She had not even chosen her clothes— but hadn't she? She could have kicked and screamed and refused to put them on. She could have spit in the face of the Blue Wind—and probably the Blue Wind would have liked it! But even if she hadn't chosen it then, she could choose it now, if the *choosing* was the important thing. September felt very much that it was.

"I think I shall have to go and see the Yeti," she said with as much loudness as she could muster. It was also important to announce your intentions at top volume, she thought, or your intentions will think you are ashamed of them. "I am a Professional Revolutionary, after all."

"I rather think you're a shirker of high degree, September," the Periwig said archly. "If I read your silks right, and I always do, for I have read every volume on heraldry and royal codes in my catalogue, you are a Criminal."

"I like Professional Revolutionary better. After all, if a Revolution comes off, it's not a crime."

The Periwig leaned close in. She smelled like lavender and talcum powder. "I see! Your cap has the anarchical charcoal-on-pitch chevron pattern. As clear as yelling."

Ell fretted, rocking from claw to claw. "It won't be like before, September! The Marquess was at least roughly your size. . . ."

But Abecedaria would not let him finish. "Ciderskin wants to be

King of a Lonely Moon and he oughtn't! You're quite right! It is your *job* to go and . . . well, I expect you know your work better than I do. Array the instruments of your craft and, well, craft it. He lives on the inner edge of the Moon. I can tell you the quickest path over the mountains, though it will make me an accessory. I suppose I'll risk it. A Librarian must be stalwart and bold; she must give information when it is asked for!"

"Well then," said September with what she hoped was devil-may-care cheer, "can't you tell me how a girl roughly my size would go about meddling with a Yeti?"

The Periwig wriggled all over, her bluish-white curls fattening and shrinking, unplaiting and plaiting up again. After a moment, September understood this to be how a Periwig performs the sort of frowning humans do when they are thinking very hard.

"I suppose you'll have to find that old Yeti's paw," she sighed, spooling up her locks tight and firm. "You could never hope to catch him otherwise. It'd be like a duckling racing a champion dodo."

"You said it was lost! And big enough to get pulled down with ropes, which means far too big to carry. And I'm not sure I feel quite right about using a nasty mummified paw against the very sort of beast the Fairies stole it from. If you defeat an opponent, that's one thing, but if you beat him about the head with his grandfather's cut-off hand, that's just cruel!"

"It is lost, it is—if it weren't I expect we'd know it by how old we got before teatime." The Periwig's ribbons twisted and untwisted. "As for the bigness of it, I'm sure you'd only need a thumbnail or some such—too much and you'll go speeding through time right with him. But none of my books have an opinion as to where it wound up, which is unusual, since books have opinions on everything."

September noticed that the Librarian ignored the question of cruelty against Yetis.

A-Through-L smiled a toothy smile, his orange eyes glittering. "Orrery, Abby! She has to go to Orrery! And I shall take her!"

The Periwig shook her puffy poms. "What a brilliant beast I hired! I am terribly impressed with my past self. She was naive about the relationship between Wyverns and fire, but what a lovely present she has made our present!"

The Wyverary practically danced with the joy of explaining a thing to September, for explaining things was what he liked best after alphabetizing, and September knew so little she always needed explaining.

"Orrery is the city on the slopes of the Splendid Dress, which is a frightful big and lovely mountain. The Glasshobs built it to keep an eye on the stars, who have a tendency to run off on adventures and forget about how much we down-below folks need to navigate and cast horoscopes and meet lovers on balconies. A Glasshob is a kind of lantern fish with goat-legs, and they carry their breathing parts in silver censers that swing from their fins. And they weep glass! It just comes pouring hot and orange and molten out of their eyes. How sad they must have been to make Orrery! It's a city all of lenses, September! Telescopes and oikeoscopes and microscopes and kinetoscopes and chromoscopes and cameras and spectacles and detectives' glasses and binoculars and mirrors! You can turn the shingle of a roof and see Pandemonium through it. And it's near the Tipping Edge, where the outside of the Moon turns into the inside. Of course, the Splendid Dress blocks the way, but I can fly us over it. We'll spy out the paw in Orrery. I just know it."

September thought of Almanack and its enormous love for the city inside it. She thought of Ballast Downbound sailing up and down the road patching up wrecks because she heard their ruin in her heart. She thought of the strange Blue Wind with his coat of planets grinning darkly at her. *Everything you have.* You do your job and you mind your work.

September stood up and wiped her hands on her black trousers. "Well, what is the good of being a Criminal and a Revolutionary if you don't set off to do ridiculous things nobody in their right mind would dream of? Come on, self, what did we long for all those rainy days if not to jump over the Moon like the cow in the song and cross paths with a Yeti? I'm sure I couldn't fight him any more than a ladybug could fight me, but you can't say it's not an adventure, not for a moment! We'll find that paw and maybe I won't have to crack skulls together with him like a couple of gentlemen deer in the springtime."

"Bully for us, every one," said the Periwig dryly.

It *was* her Moon. It was her Moon because Ell lived there and because it was Fairyland's Moon. Because if she had a shell to comfort and protect things she loved, they would be inside it, tucked in tight. *I suppose,* she thought, *running back down to Fairyland for pie would be as selfish as the Blue Wind said I am. Well, I shan't let her be right about anything if I can help it.*

September took up the Sapphire Stethoscope, folded its tubes and earpieces together, and tucked it back into the ivory casket. She shut the lid; it locked loudly in the great round Library.

"I do think this falls under Guarding the Library from Night-Marauders, which is in my contract," A-Through-L said, by way of asking Abecedaria's leave. The Periwig shook her fuzzy head. Finally she whispered:

"Child, we are dying because of him. The Moon is dying. What can we do? A paw is only a Tool in the end. Whoever it belonged to is long gone. I shall make you a bargain. I shall feel guilty on your behalf. I shall feel wretched in the extreme. After all, it was I who told you about it. That way you can ply your trade with an easy heart. Leave it to the professionals, that's best. I certainly prefer to be left alone at *my* work."

September nodded, but it did not soothe the prickling of wrongness in her breast. She looked up at Ell, her heart stretching to hold the whole sight of him.

"We'll have to go and collect my car before we leave," she said finally, because it seemed the sensible and grown-up thing to say. But after a moment, she added, "It's us again, Ell, you and I off to do something very unlikely."

"Car begins with C, so I shall be thrilled to meet it!" And then he lowered his head like a puppy playing, smiling a secret smile of *I know something you don't know.* "But September," he purred, "don't you think we ought to go and collect Saturday first?"

CHAPTER XI

AEROPOSTE

In Which September Discovers a Friend in the Circus, Reads a Number of Hands, Feet, and Faces, Tucks Into a Most Literate Lunch, and Hears a Perfectly Practiced Tale

A-Through-L swooped and soared down the gentle slopes of Almanack. September clung tight to his back. She had ridden him before—but then he'd walked, his bumpy, two-legged chicken-gait. His wings had been chained down horribly. And in Fairyland-Below she had flown as a Wyvern herself before turning back into a girl mid-flight. But this was the first time she and Ell had flown together. Laughter and tears and shouting got jumbled up on the way to her mouth and tried to come out all at once. A Wyvern was meant for flying—how clear that was now! She could feel delicate muscles under his skin moving gracefully, tipping into the air and dipping under it as if they were such good friends.

Down below, someone else was flying. Many someones—the lovely folded-paper trapeze artists and acrobats and elephants of the Stationary Circus, zooming and twirling and wheeling madly over their wide, boisterous ring. And in their midst, darting between them and leaping among them, was a someone with long black hair in a topknot and flowing tattoos on his back.

Someone blue.

Saturday had joined the circus.

September could not take her eyes away as they circled down. How could she not have seen him before? Saturday spun from the trapezes of the Stationary Circus, catching the slim arms of a newspaper girl, stretching out his long blue body in the rich peacock light of Almanack, his tattoos gleaming, his topknot fluttering behind him. An illustrated boy caught him by the ankles and tossed him up into a gorgeous arc; Saturday bent in half and touched his toes in the air, hanging perfectly still, longer than anyone should be able to hang. Where the tips of his fingers touched the tips of his feet, a blossom of dark seawater gurgled into life and then fell down to the ring below as rain. The Marid snapped flat, snatched the next bar as it came swinging toward him, and came to rest on a high platform, landing on one foot and balancing a sudden huge black pearl on his nose like a seal. He flipped his head back, caught the gem in his mouth, and blew a ball of glittering sea foam into the air like a smoke ring. The roustabouts down in the empty stands applauded with great, strong dictionary-hands. It was only a practice—but what a practice! The Marid smiled—and September had never seen a smile like that on the face of her shy, uncertain friend. His face blazed turquoise with exertion and excitement and exultation. He knew his own strength and it surged through him like a blue tide. He waved at the ringmaster, whose broad body was made of vivid postage stamps folded every which way. She blew Saturday a peony; he caught the deep orange flower with a quick blue hand. He wore long silken trousers the color of tarnished silver with whorls and loops of spangled writing running round his legs and no shirt at all. His muscles moved under that familiar blue skin, lean and long and lithe.

He was beautiful. He had always been beautiful, but now his beauty seemed to collide with September all at once and altogether. Her face burned suddenly. Had A-Through-L not borne her up, she might have staggered. He was beautiful and he was here.

"Just look at our boy," Ell crowed. "It's a new world—everyone flies!"

Then Saturday saw September; his hand went to his mouth in shock. His papery comrades followed his gaze; their faces opened up along creases and folds that said: *Oh, the stories we've heard about this one round the old pulp-fire!* But then Saturday was waving madly and September was calling his name and an overeager memorandum-lion opened his pink-paper mouth to roar, just to be a part of whatever was going on up there. But the roar did not last. The lion bit his tongue and yelped—a jet of indigo flame erupted joyously from Ell's mouth once more, singeing the rooftops hanging down like green bats above them. The folk of the Stationary Circus suddenly creased and shot downward, away from the dripping flame and Ell's apologies, coming as thick and fast as his fire. The mother-of-pearl boasted a wonderful resilience. A few furry, scaled faces popped out of windows to glare and holler, but they were whole and unburnt, and so was the newspaper girl and the illustrated boy, standing on a second, lower platform and looking up at them darkly.

The Wyverary squeezed in so quickly September fell a little as he shrunk beneath her. He scrunched up into a red body no bigger than a large and galumphing elephant. This was the second time in such a short space—worry racketed around September's heart. *But how can we keep him from getting delighted or scared?* thought September desperately. *Especially now we're together again and stirring things are bound to happen? No one can do that!* She found it quite easy to forget how hard she'd tried to do it herself in those last months, practicing her grown-up behaviors. But she could not hold on to her fear for Ell—finding Saturday blew all the worry from her mind like dust. They crowded together onto the platform—that the three of them could fit at all ought to have sounded alarms, but hardly anyone can measure spatial relationships when their farthest and dearest are close around.

"Oh, September!" Saturday cried, and lifted his arms to hug her—but he stopped, shyly, looking to her to see if it was all right. September finished the hug herself, throwing her arms around her Marid—hers, her very own, and not his shadow, who had done all sorts of things without asking before or after. Saturday was taller than she remembered, terribly lean and strong, but his smell was the same: the endless cold sea and dark stones. "I'm so glad I found you first!" he whispered.

"What do you mean?" September said into his shoulder. She pulled away and looked at him as though she meant to do a lifetime's looking all in one long gaze.

But Saturday flushed dark with embarrassment and shook his head. "It doesn't matter now," he said with a careful laugh that he meant to sound careless. He turned to Ell instead, who hung his still-huge head in shame.

"Everyone's all right, aren't they?" Ell said bashfully. "Say it's so! I couldn't help it, I was so happy, to have you both in one place! The happiness gets so hot and big inside me these days it just comes out and I feel like all of me will blow apart! I don't know how the Dragons do it, having this fire in your mouth all the time."

"Perhaps you ought to get out into the open air where there's no roof to blow off," Saturday said with a sideways smile. "Everyone is fine, though I think the lion has lost a tooth to scorch."

Ell could not meet the lion's eye. He nudged them both with his head just exactly like a cat in need of petting. September and Saturday obliged, each talking over the other as though all the time in the world was not enough to say all they wished to. Of course, it was not and could never be. The three of them had not had more than a moment together since that day when Saturday had wished them all well and whole and into that lovely field of flowers where September had left Fairyland for the first time. She had known their shadows, in Fairyland-Below, but her friends, in the flesh and in the world—but so much time had passed. So much had happened. September's heart puffed up like a kernel of corn, awfully full of excitement and memory and the peculiar jangly, jittery sort of contentment that comes when you suddenly get what you've wanted for so long that you forgot what it was like to think about anything but wanting it. And in the jangle and jitter it all came tumbling out: the Yeti, the inner edge of the moon, the Blue Wind and Aroostook and the Stethoscope and the moonquakes and where they were going, which was *out* and *over,* and would he come?

Of course he would come.

"But first come down," Saturday said, holding September's hands as tight as he could, though he was very careful not to crush her fingers. "Sit still a moment. There's so much I want to show you! You must be so hungry, if you've only just gotten here. I know . . ." he flushed a little, blue against blue, "I know how hungry you get, when you are adventuring."

In long, even circles, A-Though-L bore them down from the high trapeze platforms to the main ring. The ring, paved with thick, glossy postcards, gleamed up at them, showing a thatch of beach umbrellas and snowy peaks and the streets of Pandemonium and the whitewater rum rivers of Parthalia and the magicians' cafes of Buyan and a thousand versions of the great crescent Moon of Fairyland, in every season and every sort of weather. Where the postcards creased together, words shouted and beckoned: VISIT! COME! WISH! HERE!

The ringmaster moved to meet them, but before she could get past the greeting-card horses tossing their confetti-manes in the air, a boy and a girl dashed toward them at full speed, hardly waiting until they'd climbed down from the Wyvern's back to barrel into September and Saturday, wrapping them both up in their paper arms.

"Oh, forgive us, of course we don't know you yet," said the boy, whose long, tall body was covered in blocks of text, little birthmarks of fourteen lines each. He was made of sonnets, from head to toe. His hair was a flutter of motley ribbon marks. An intricate origami looked September in the eye, folded and smoothed and peaked into a friendly, narrow face.

"But we feel as though we do!" cried the girl, whose body was the warm, expensive gold of old letters, an elegant calligraphy covering every inch of her round, excited cheeks, her acrobat's costume, her long, red, sealing-wax hair, the postmarks like freckles on her shoulders. September could make out a number of addresses and signatures, words like *Dearest, Darling, Yours Forever, Heart of My Heart*: love letters, woven together to make a girl. "I'm Valentine," she said, holding out her angular hand.

"I'm Pentameter," said the sonnet boy. "We're them." Both Valentine and Pentameter pointed their thumbs over their shoulders at a vivid sign, nailed to the pole that hoisted up the trapeze platforms. In deep scarlet it read: AEROPOSTE: WINGED WORDS AND FLIGHTS OF FANCY! Small golden wings flapped at the edges of the letters, the tail of the Y, the bar of the T.

Valentine pressed September's hand to her heart, which read: *My dearest Robert, henceforward I am yours for everything.* "We feel as though we know you because Saturday talks about you whenever he's not breathing, eating, or sleeping. And sometimes he'll make an exception for all three!"

Pentameter grinned. Silky, blackly inked words formed his top lip: *For thy sweet love remember'd such wealth brings.* The cursive line of his bottom, smiling lip curved to finish the couplet: *That then I scorn to change my state with kings.* "The contortionists call him Saturday-When-September-Comes-Back!" he said with a laugh that was pleasant and prodding all at once.

The Marid stared at his feet as though he could burn a hole in the ground and be swallowed up by it. Poor Saturday. There is nothing like a friend to blurt out what we would most like to keep hidden.

September laughed a little. She tried to make it sound light and happy, as though it were all over now and how funny it was, when you think about it, that simply not having another person by you could hurt so. But it did not come out quite right; there was a heaviness in her laughing like ice at the bottom of a glass. She *still* missed Saturday, yet he was standing right beside her! Missing him had become a part of her, like a hard, dark bone, and she needed so much more than a few words to let it go. In all this while, she had spent more time missing Saturday than seeing him.

Valentine pressed on. "Though he certainly never mentioned you being a Criminal. How dashing!" September started to argue; she even pulled off her cap. All her dark hair came tumbling out and it did feel nice to take off some part of those black silks.

"Oh don't worry," said Pentameter with his rough, kind voice. "We're a circus. We're used to rogues and charlatans and hooligans and rascals! They're our favorite sorts of people!"

In the midst of the ring, as though it were an act, part of the circus about to start, four Lunaphants busied their long trunks with setting up a banquet table. Now that September stood on the ground and could see them much more clearly than while hanging upside-down to the back of a Taxicrab, she was struck quiet by the creatures. As tall and strong and broad as a usual elephant, if a girl from Omaha could ever think of an elephant as usual, they gleamed silvery and white and twilit blue. Their bodies were costly stationary, letterheads from offices and writing paper meant for folk you wanted to impress most. Their trunks, which they used more gracefully than September could use her own hands, were twisted ropes of scratch paper, cluttered with crossed-out equations, bits of verse, telephone numbers, and the scribbles people make when testing a pen to see if it works. The glass inkwells of their eyes dripped, now and again, navy-colored tears onto the circus ring. They floated in the air without effort, nimble as sparrows—and so September could see, when she looked up, the bottoms of their feet, which each bore a miniature model of the Moon, every crater and mountain exact and exquisite.

When the Lunaphants finished with the furniture, they trumpeted all together. A shower of envelopes popped into the air between them, each sealed with a different thick wax blot. They drifted to the table and landed perfectly, one at each place set for September, Saturday, A-Through-L, Valentine, and Pentameter. Saturday and the acrobats fell to immediately, popping the seals on their post. Like lifting the silver dome on a dish in a fine restaurant, dishes appeared steaming and fragrant. September looked at her own plate. Her envelope looked up at her with an orange seal with a little wrench stamped in the circle of wax. She slid her finger under it and with a satisfyingly thick cracking noise her dish filled with a rich pie—whose crust was a riot of writing, crossed-out, rewritten, X'd out once more, written a third time, as if by a poet who could not quite get his verse to obey him, no matter how he tried, could not find the perfect phrase. The only line left un-scratched was: *Turn, Beatrice, O turn your holy eyes upon your faithful one . . .* September's stomach announced that it had no intention of turning down a meal just because someone had done their homework on it. She stuck her fork into the center of the *O*. Black, purple, and blue ink gurgled out, thick with pen-nibs, typewriter keys, and blocks of move-able type from some ancient printing press.

"I am sure to break my teeth!" she exclaimed. Saturday had already dug into his own pie. A-Through-L shrugged and bit off the whole crust of his, slurping up the filling with relish.

"Just try it," he coaxed, licking a bit of ink-sauce off of his blue lip.

September did not take much comfort—she had seen the Marid chew seastones to dust. But all the same, she lifted a forkful of key and type into her mouth, an exclamation point and a Gothic letter *H*.

They burst against her teeth like soft grapes and summer cherries, savory and sweet, slippery and rich, the crust buttery and smooth, like a shepherd's pie baked full of lamb and chocolate and nutmeggy apples. Without quite meaning to, September let out a little cry of delicious-ness. She was so hungry! Aroostook had had her lunch, but September had eaten no more than a hard butterscotch since this morning—could it really be only this morning she had set out across the fields to mend the old fence? She felt Ballast Downbound's orange fizz in her pocket and reached for it, for nothing could taste better with any sort of food than orange fizz, as far as she was concerned. But Saturday popped the top off of a squat little poster-tube and produced a pretty newsprint goblet of fine brown ink. This time, September did not hesitate, but drank deeply. The taste of walnuts and cream and cinnamon and—could it be? Yes! Moonkins! The lovely glowing fruits the Hreinn grew in the Glass Forest, distilled down into a thick brew. A little ribbon of something like the brandy her parents kept for special occasions wriggled through the other flavors. This must be what the Blue Wind meant when she waxed about the cocktails on the Moon! But it did not make September feel dizzy, no matter the ribbon of brandy, only full and strong and awake.

"Have you really joined the circus, Saturday?" she asked between wolfish, huge bites.

The Marid flushed with pride. Had she ever noticed how pretty he got when he did that? Like foam cresting on the deep sea.

"When I first came to the Moon I had no idea what to do with myself," he said ruefully. "Ell had his Library and it kept him so busy. Some days I would sit very quietly in the empty half of the Lopside and read the lonely books on those shelves so they wouldn't feel neglected. But, oh, September! I am a child of the sea! I cannot stay in one place for long without stretching and swelling and dancing and surging and crashing and rolling. I walked over all of Almanack, never taking the same path twice. It was very lonely." Saturday lowered his eyes; he could not quite say it while September looked so intently at him. "How often I wished you were there so that I could point things out to you and hear what you thought of them. Who would you have bet on at the capricorn races? Would you have liked the rice cakes the giant rabbits whack out with their silver mallets? Would you laugh at the moon-mummers in the amphitheater near my little house?"

"You have a little house?" Suddenly Saturday seemed so much older than she, though she knew he was not, not really. To have one's own little house and walk alone every night through such a great city! But Saturday went on in a rush, hardly hearing her.

"And I would come and watch the Stationary Circus. Not the performances—I came to watch them practice. They do such beautiful shows, but what I liked was to see them working out their routines, making mistakes sometimes, trying different costumes, different combinations of players and animals, different steps and leaps and flips and grips. Practice seemed like a very alive thing to me. I thought often of how much I would like to practice something like that, to shape it bit by bit, every day, to be so good at *moving* and *seeming* that I could change just a tiny turn of my toe and have it become something new, from a comedic tumble to a tragic fall, from a leap of faith to a twist ending, from a nosedive to lifted spirits. Because you would take that with you, you know?" Saturday looked up to see if she understood him. "You couldn't help it, if you'd practiced enough. Your body would remember, like how a piano player drums her fingers on her leg in the pattern of her favorite song without even noticing. You'd take it with you into everyday doing and walking and singing and reading in the Library and dreaming and sleeping. Every time you moved or seemed it would mean something, the way it means something in the circus, when you're performing and everyone below you is gasping and clapping and covering their eyes but still peeking through their fingers. Even the littlest turn of your toe." He took a deep breath. September had never seen him so excited.

Pentameter tweaked Saturday's topknot gently. "He thought we wouldn't want him because he's flesh and bone."

"But we're open minded," chirped Valentine, giving his knee a sisterly punch. September could not help reading her soft brown cheek, though she could not tell if this might be rude or not. *Sweet and incomparable Josephine, what an extraordinary influence you have over my heart . . .* "After all, he comes from the sea and the best ink comes from cuttlefish, so there's a family connection."

September marveled at how easy they were together. Saturday didn't blush at all when they jostled him.

"I did have to practice awfully hard."

"Rubbish!" said Valentine, chewing on a fat fountain pen that snapped off when she bit down, like a ripe carrot. "He did a Quad Folio Fold with a Double Dogear on his first day!"

Pentameter slid a second envelope toward A-Through-L, whose rumbling stomach, being so much bigger than any of theirs, announced a need for a second course. On his strong brown hand September read: *Then felt I like some watcher of the skies, when a new planet swims into his ken . . .* the rest vanished around the curve of his thumb. "You are wickedly heavy, though, brother. We had to bench press the Gunpowder Ghouls—in full gear!—every night just to work up to catching your big blue dumbbells in mid-air!"

"I learned to make myself lighter," Saturday laughed. "Seawater can be as light as spray and heavy as whales. And September, I did, I did find I was good at it. I practiced just the way I'd wanted to. Until then, the only thing . . ." he cleared his throat. It sounded like a wave breaking on sand. ". . . the only thing I'd practiced so much was what I'd say to you, when I saw you again." The Marid hurried on. "Though in the end I am better at Dogearing than remembering speeches, no matter how many times I've said them to myself! And, well, the way you can look at a surging ocean and feel everything from deep sorrow to bubbling delight to a giggling urge to jump right in and splash about—when people look at me, they feel those things, and I practiced and practiced until I could change my smile by half a quirk and change one feeling to the other. When I am on the trapeze, in the air, people look at me and they see me, they really see me, and they cheer like I've done something specially for them." The Marid looked up at the sparkling apparatus above them. "Up there, I am as far from a cage as it is possible to be."

September's eyes filled with tears. She remembered the first time she saw him, cramped and bent and broken in the Marquess's cruel lobster cage, penned in and forgotten. She shook her head; her tears flew aside.

"I am happy for you," she said as brightly as she could. And she was, it was not a lie. But even he, even poor beautiful Saturday knew what he could be and do in the world. Ell had his Library, the Sibyl had had her door, Ballast had her ships—and September, still, was only herself, in the audience watching Saturday moving and seeming. "Back home everyone is always asking 'What do you want to be when you grow up?' As if everyone is a Pooka and you can just *change,* from a girl or a boy into something else, a griffin or an armchair or a shark! But you have, you've changed into . . . into a flight of fancy, like the sign says. A circus man." And it was the first time she had thought of the word *man* in connection to Saturday.

Saturday looked at her strangely. His dark eyes shone. "No, no, I haven't. I'm still Saturday. A slightly more airborne Saturday is all! And I am going with you, of course I am going with you! That's what understudies are for! September, I have waited and waited for you! If you say we must go and see about a Yeti, well, that is what I want most in the world."

Valentine and Pentameter looked at each other. They grinned identical grins. Together, they leaned into Saturday and kissed him on each cheek, squeezed his arms, and dashed away as quickly as they'd come running over the ring to meet them. They scurried up the little footholds on the trapeze poles, nimble as cats. On one of Valentine's bare feet the dedication *My Dearest Pickle*—flashed. One the other: *My Own Boy*—Pentameter's heels announced joyfully: *I love thee to the depth and breadth and height my soul can reach.*

When they reached their positions, the two of them nodded to each other, and then down to Saturday and September. They swung out on their bars and as they did, their bodies opened up—but not into paper airplanes this time. Triangles of paper opened and closed along their limbs so that when Valentine and Pentameter met, grasping wrists or ankles or under the shoulders, when they somersaulted together or dropped so fast even Saturday gasped, new words formed from the fragments of letters and sonnets printed upon their bodies. As Acroposte danced above them, September read the message they acrobaticked into being:

*Be missed you
like a fish in a bowl
misses the open sea.*

As Ell flew toward the mouth of Almanack, Saturday holding onto her waist and Ell humming beneath them, September opened her mouth to talk. Several times she stopped herself. She had gotten so used to not saying what was important that she could not quite get the habit going again. The words would not come out. Perhaps she did not even know the words she wanted. *I missed you, too,* seemed such a little name to put on the bigness of the feeling inside her.

Saturday squeezed her hand. Blushing furiously, her heart battering at her bones, September leaned over and kissed him. It was a quick kiss, as though speeding through to the other side of it would make other kisses easier. When she pulled away, the Marid's eyes shone.

Ell laughed a big, rumbling, beastly laugh. He started to turn a loop-de-loop, so joyful was he. Remembering his passengers, he haroomed instead. "Next stop: Orrery, City of Lenses! Traveling by Wyverary cannot be beat!"

September suddenly realized something. "But Ell, Orrery begins with O! How can you know so much about it?"

The Wyverary soared high, his neck stretching into a long red ribbon, full of words and pies and relief and flying.

"I'm growing up!" he cried.

CHAPTER XII

NEXT SATURDAY

*In Which September and Her Friends Contract a Serious Case of
Restlessness, Get Bashed About by an Invisible Fist,
and Meet Someone Again for the First Time*

Night washed over the Moon. The scarlet sea glimmered blackly on
one side of the peculiar troupe; high mountains creased and folded
into sharp shadows on the other. A Wyverary walked happily alongside
a weatherbeaten Model A Ford driven by a girl all in black—as much as
you could call it driving when the Ford seemed happy to trundle along
on its own. A blue-skinned boy rode in the passenger seat, marveling at
the sounds of the engine, the feel of the cracked dash, the cracks in the
mirrors.

September said nothing in particular to Aroostook on the subject
of her new horn. Nor her throttle lever, which was no longer rusty and

bent but a twisted, shining ebony branch ending in a small hand carved out of gold, its palm facing upward in a friendly fashion. Tiny china mushrooms clung to the gnarls of the branch. She did not understand what the car was about. How could September possibly figure out her trouble? And was it trouble at all? She simply would not discuss it until the Model A stopped this gussying up and settled into whatever she was going to be. A-Through-L and Saturday, having never seen a car, assumed they all had sunflower-wheels and big striped phonograph horns and golden hands on their levers and were simply delighted with the noise of his engine. *No use in yelling at something till it makes sense. It doesn't work with me, after all.*

Besides, September felt shivery and strange, quite as though her skin meant to jump off and run away howling into the mountains. She fairly trembled; she wanted to *run,* not drive, or dive into the sea, or just see how far into the air she could jump. At the moment she felt certain she would fly off like a firework. She wanted to drive faster—the sooner they got over the ridge of the Moon the better, that was definitely right, why was Aroostook so damnably *slow?*

Ell looked in the window at her, grinning. His eyes danced. A little ripple ran along his spine.

"It's the Sea of Restlessness," he said. "Fills you up with *go go go,* like you're a bowl full of reaching and wanting but you don't know what you're reaching and wanting *for.*"

"When we first came to the Moon, we nearly turned around and ran off again," Saturday said. "It just *lights* you, like a candle."

"But Almanack seems so peaceful! Shouldn't everyone there be itching to leave? Shouldn't Almanack feel like this? Just . . . boiling up with *off we go?*"

Saturday laughed a little. "I think it does, really. I think maybe that's what a Restless Whelk looks like."

A-Through-L just whipped his tail up toward the stars. "Inside the shell, we're safe!"

September felt as though her heart were a kettle boiling on a stove, that screaming whistle just nearly bubbling out. She looked up toward the tip of Ell's tail, snapping like a lick of fire at the night sky. And there—*there,* suddenly—was Fairyland. September gaped. She brought her hand to her mouth. It hung in the sky like an emerald, huge and green and streaked with blue, rose, gold. But it was nothing like she ever imagined a planet could look like when she daydreamed during Mrs. Henderson's astronomy club talks. Tufts of creamy, popsicle-colored clouds drifted around the globe and out into the black like a wheel of birds. And Fairyland had rings! Like Saturn, rings like great glittering wedding bands looped round at a rakish angle, breaking through the clouds. But the rings were not just rocks and ice, they were train tracks. Jeweled and empty, with no engine in sight, but tracks all the same, with switches and trestles glowing softly. September could not even say it was beautiful. It was ever so much bigger and grander than beautiful. She had a feeling stuck in her and she could not name it. It bobbed up and down in her heart like a crystal bottle with a message inside—but she could not get out the stopper.

Many years later, folk whose names you and I studied in school went up to the roof of our world and looked down. Perhaps they could name the feeling for her. It's something like suddenly stepping out of your own skin and seeing yourself from the outside, seeing the body you live in the way it looks to the stars and the sun and the sky and everyone who knows you, without mirrors or photographs or reflections in shop windows. You look at that silly old place you've been walking around in and forgetting to brush your teeth or braid your hair neatly and it is nothing like you thought, but somehow, someway, better than you ever hoped it could be. If you want to know a secret—and

I do love to tell you secrets when no one else can hear—you cannot grow up at all until you've done it, not if you are a little girl nor a whole species.

"Stop!" September cried. And Ell did. And Aroostook did. She pointed, and Saturday and the Wyverary looked up with her. Even the Model A seemed to strain upward, ever so slightly. They looked together for a little while, and the light on their faces was as green and warm as wishing. Saturday and September put out their hands at the same time and knocked knuckles before lacing their fingers together. A-Through-L wrapped his tail in a knot around their hands and they giggled.

But they could not stand still long. The restless sea air prickled at them and tugged at their hair and their whiskers and their fenders. September broke away before her skin burst into flame, for that was truly how it felt, as though suddenly she were made of kindling the way Valentine and Pentameter were made of paper. She grabbed the Stethoscope's box from the rear of the Model A, leapt out of the car, and pulled the gleaming sapphire tubes out of the ivory.

"She said we could hear anything! Anything!" September's hands jittered like they had when Aunt Margaret filled her doll's tea set with coffee and coaxed her into drinking it. "Why couldn't we hear the paw? There's no reason! Everything makes a sound, one way or another! It could be scrabbling underground or tapping its hairy old fingers against a tree!"

September put the jeweled cup of the Stethoscope against the earth of the Moon. The soil was chalky and pale, greenish white. September remembered the Fairy newsreel ages and ages ago telling her that the Moon was made of pearl—and so it really seemed to be. The weeds and scrub-flowers grew hard and luminous and slick. They bent and snapped under her as she lay down on the surface of the Moon. But the sapphire ear-knobs were far too big for her own ears. September offered them to A-Through-L.

"Erm," said the Wyverary. "Ah." He listened very intently, tapping his claws restlessly. "I . . . I can hear noise." His great red face quivered, winced. He sucked in his cheeks and cried out: "Just the most noise you ever heard! All at once. Oh, September, it hurts!" he wailed suddenly. "It's so loud, everyone talking and sleeping and eating! Everything growing and stomping and digging! Moon-moles! And an old Wyrm eating Kappa shells! It's so thick, it's so loud! I don't like this at all!" He squeezed his eyes painfully shut, trying to listen. "I don't know how to listen for a *paw*. There's paws everywhere! Stomping and scratching and padding and pummeling! But, oh, wait, oh . . . there's a great big thumping in there. Like thunder. Boom, boom, boom. Under everything! It's down there—oh! Not one thumping but two thumpings! Hear them go! Oh, they will crush me! Boom, boom, boom!"

"It must be Ciderskin," breathed Saturday. "And his dog. Thumping on the Moon to break it."

Finally, Ell could bear it no more. He clawed the Stethoscope out of his ears and lay down, panting against the pearly scrub.

"I'm sorry, September," he gulped. "It was a good idea. I tried to find a clenching or a scratching or a tapping in the middle of it, a sound a Yeti's paw might make, but you just hear everything all at once, one thing on top of the other and it's like a radio tuned to every channel. Maybe there's a trick to Stethoscoping, but if there is I don't know it. S'what comes of consorting with things that start with S."

"I think we ought to turn inland," September said nervously. "You're liable to let your fire out after all that—I feel as though *I* could breathe fire right now!"

And so they did, veering off the long opaline beach road. Ell felt certain he knew the way and September nestled into her old trust of the Wyvern. They curved around away from the shore toward a dark thatch of forest and murky shadows. Lights flashed within it, crackling, flickering, rolling into little balls and out again.

"Oh, I do know all about Lightning!" said Ell, eager to be back on familiar ground. "When my mother was a tiny little lizard, no bigger than a castle, she lived with the giants of Thunderball Monastery. They grew lightning in their herbarium, just the healthiest, juiciest, brightest bolts you ever saw. Lightning buds off a great gleaming rod, you know. You have to pick it right after the first frost; that's when the forks are sweetest. The giants peddled their lightning all over Fairyland, sold to Winds and Witches and Writers alike. That was how my mother met her fated Scientiste—Scientists of any stripe are just mad for Lightning. Hang it in a basket, stuff it in a bottle, tie it in a bow! But that there is wild Lightning. Not the nice neat rows the giants hoed or the bushels my sainted mother carried to market in her claws. Unkempt and untamed and ungrounded!" The Wyverary ran a little harder, the Sea of Restlessness still tugging at them with its briny air, whispering at their heels: *Come back, have a swim, wrestle a whale, have you considered naval warfare as a profession?* Aroostook jumped forward and gave a little rev all of her own.

Distances on the Moon can deceive. September thought they'd be deep in the lightning jungle in hardly a moment, but it danced off beyond them still. They rumbled down a long open plain, quite unprotected. Snowy sands blew away from their wheels and their feet. The green disc of Fairyland set quickly and all went dark save stars like thousands of dice thrown across the velvet of the sky, turning up numbers lucky and not so.

It happened quickly, so quickly, unfathomably fast. But then, how else could it have happened?

A fearsome, hideous bawl broke the night open. September and

Saturday twisted around in their seats, but they could not find who it belonged to. It came from every direction and up from the Moon and down from the air as well. Another bellow exploded over the plain. Ell groaned, his ears aching already. Something vast and heavy thumped toward them—they could hear it, they could *feel* it—but they were alone on the wide moon-prairie.

A fist heaved into Aroostook and sent them spinning, headlights turning like a mad lighthouse, colliding with Ell and cartwheeling off away from him again. The Wyverary yelped piercingly; purple fire shot out into the night. September saw the dark, wild tongues of it come in and out of view as they spun and screamed. *Oh, Ell, don't!* she thought as her teeth jarred into her cheek and she bled. But she could hear his terrified *haroom*s and she knew it was no good. That awful, awful sound could scare fire from a bar of soap. Finally the spinout slowed and ground into a stop. Saturday clung to her arm miserably; September wiped her bloody lip. Her arm and shoulder crunched painfully into Aroostook's door. She yelped herself, but a girl's body is not equipped to belch fire at anything that insults it, though we might sometimes wish this were not the case. She rubbed at the windshield with her good arm; their frightened breath had fogged it up.

A figure stood before them, directly in their path, his skin dark and glossy and dancing with coiling patterns in the headlamps' glare.

It was Saturday.

But it was not Saturday. Yes, he stood quite tall and slender, like the Marid September knew. He stood looking down at the automobile and the people in it with the same curious expression Saturday used when something interested him. But the man—for he was certainly a man and not a boy—wore his dark hair long, gathered up into a top-knot. And he had the most beautiful blue skin, the color of a sea deeper than the sky. Even in the night she could see the blue of him shining.

The muscles in his back swept in broader and stronger lines. He wore no shirt above his long, black silk trousers, either, and September could see his graceful, familiar tattoos there. His face was older, so much older than fourteen or fifteen. Older than twenty. Perhaps older than thirty.

September knew him. She'd know him anywhere—but she also knew it was not him and besides, Saturday was *here,* right here next to her! Right here, digging his nails into her arm and refusing to look at the version of himself standing outside the Model A.

"Don't look, September," he pleaded, lifting his eyes to hers. They searched September, begging. She had never seen him beg, not even to be set free on that first wretched day in Pandemonium. "Don't listen to him, either. Look at *me*. Look at me and remember the velocipedes, remember when you turned into a tree, remember how we wrestled and I didn't let you win even a little. . . ."

But September could not look away from the Marid in her headlamps. Seeing the other Saturday standing there on the white plain was like looking at a photograph of your house when you are well and truly inside it. She felt a little ill, stretched taut between the two of them. Finally, September called out his name—a little shyly, a little too quiet, perhaps, for her voice to get outside the car. But the man snapped his head toward her, surprise moving like a tide on his face. Beside her, Saturday cringed and shut his eyes tighter. September called his name again, this time so unsure that it came out a whisper. The man who might have been Saturday raised his blue hand up hesitantly—and September remembered suddenly what it meant to be a Marid. They were the djinni of the ocean. They lived out of time. A Marid could meet himself many times in his life, older and younger, wiser and more foolish. He might even meet his parents before he was ever born, as Saturday had. This *was* Saturday, it was. But he was an older Saturday, one

September had never met, a grown man and strong, no longer timid or bashful. She felt very strange, seeing this person her friend would one day become. There are emotions that we have no words for, since their circumstances do not come up often enough for committees to form and decide on the proper terms. This was one of them, this time-tangled future-present unsettling recognition.

Slowly, without warning, snow began to fall.

September leapt out of the car at the same instant the other Saturday leapt toward it. Her black silks rippled, warming her skin against the icy air. They met in the snow. September looked up into the eyes of someone very grown-up. More grown-up, she thought, than she could ever be.

He said her name. He said it so gently it was as though he was holding it in his hand, trying not to crush it. Slowly, he reached out a hand and touched her hair. He smiled at her, a smile so full of knowing and warmth and merriness that what he said next hit September as though he had reached out and shoved her.

"You have to get out of my way," he said. His voice boomed deep and hard. "I'm sorry," he repeated, "but you're in my way and you have to get out of it."

September was frozen. She could not move. The awful bawl sounded again and a gust of wind blew as though someone had dashed by without stopping long enough to be seen.

The older Saturday had had enough. His arms shot out, and, knocking September aside, curled behind Aroostook's seat. He snatched the ivory casket from the backseat without a word.

"Get in and sit down," the taller Saturday said calmly. "Or this will hurt more."

September did, numbly. She pulled her legs into the car just as that walloping fist came banging into the other side of Aroostook and they twisted out into the black again. September fell forward against the hard green sunflower and did not hear the other, older, colder, stranger Marid's voice chasing her down into dreams.

"I love you," Saturday whispered after September and Ell and his own small, miserable self, and vanished.

CHAPTER XIII

ONLY THE DEAD DON'T ARGUE

*In Which September Is Troubled by the Mechanics of Time
and Fate, the Course of a Curse, the Unlikelihood of Visiting Pluto,
and a Very Argumentative Donkey*

September woke washed in light.

At first she thought she was back home and doused in a bubbling bath—light fizzed and frothed all around her, a shade of white that had great ambitions to grow up to be purple. Great tall viney stalks rose up all around, thick as trees and thicker. Balls of light clung to their sides like brussels sprouts, crackling and sizzling and popping. The white-violet brilliance turned everything brighter than day. Aroostook, battered but still sputtering, showed deep, shadowed claw marks in her doors. September had to squint; her skin looked like the slope of a lightbulb. Saturday's face leaned down over her, his teeth blinding against his lightning-shadowed skin.

"Please be all right," he whispered, and it did not take September's heart long to catch up with her memory. He did not only mean that they'd had their heads knocked about by, presumably, a Yeti with a fist like a train car.

"It was you," she said, rubbing her glowing, aching arm. "That was you, just now, just then."

Beside her, Ell groaned. He shook his head from side to side like a bull, his black horns catching wisps of light and tossing them into the air like fireflies. The whole forest hummed and snapped. September winced before she even turned her head—how many times had he breathed his fire to protect them?

The Wyverary stood up. He stood a hand taller than Mr. Powell's pregnant roan, his face perplexed and unhappy. He patted his own head with one wing.

"Is it bad?" he whispered. "Am I little?"

"No, no!" said September. "You're a great big beast, just like always!" She crawled to her feet and went to him. She put her arms around his long neck with ease, and the easiness of it unsettled them both.

"Little begins with L, but I don't want to be it," the Wyverary said as quietly as he had ever said anything.

"It's not so bad to be little, you know!" September smiled when she said it though she felt no more like smiling than like writing a composition with her mashed arm.

"Oh, it's all right for you!" cried Ell. "You're meant to be little! I like your littleness! It means I can hoist you up and make you feel big and show you all the things I can see from where I stand. But . . . but if I get much littler, who will be big, among the three of us? Wasn't it my job to be big and stomp and carry you and look menacing if looking menacing was called for?" A-Through-L's orange, feline eyes filled with turquoise tears. He whispered: "Who will hoist me up, if I am little?"

September shook her head helplessly. She did not know what to say to comfort him except to hold him tight, which is a language primates use to say: *Everything will be all right somehow.* Reptiles, however, prefer for everything to simply be all right, at once, and then they will feel comforted. Above them, a cluster of lightning-sprouts flashed a hot blanket of light like a summer storm and then quieted again. September listened for the thunder by instinct; none came. It felt very strange, this silent and thunderless storm.

"You have to try not to," she begged the Wyverary. "We've ever so much farther to go."

"Oh, September, if you tell me how I shall, I promise!" How awful it was to see fear swimming in those kind eyes!

But she could not tell him.

"He has it," she whispered instead. "Ciderskin has the Stethoscope. We hardly made it out of Almanack before he took it—and I couldn't do anything! We couldn't! We were *helpless*. And now he can hear us!" September felt sick with failure. A simple box and she couldn't keep it in her hands for a day.

"Maybe not," Ell said miserably. "It's a frightful mess when you listen to the Moon—maybe Ciderskin won't be able to sort it out, either."

"Did he come because I took the Stethoscope out of the box? Did he *smell* it? It was so fast! I should have left it where it was! I just needed to *do* something, I was crawling with it! I was so sure we'd hear the paw. . . ."

September sank into a long quiet. Finally, she took out the troubling thing that would not leave her be and opened it up like a dark picnic between them.

"But it *was* you," she said through her teeth. Saturday looked away from her. "And you were helping the Yeti!"

"Please remember that I am a Marid. . . ."

"I know you are! And that was yourself from some day a long time from now, yourself older and another Saturday and I understand that but how could you be helping Ciderskin, even a hundred years from now?"

"I don't *know*!" yelled Saturday. September jumped inside her skin. Her belly went cold. Saturday had never yelled. He had never spoken crossly to her. His voice had never hardened up along the edges like other people's voices did; the light had never gone out of it the way it went out of anyone's when the upset got too wet and heavy and snuffed it out. His first words to her at the circus drifted back: *I'm glad I found you first.*

"Oh, September, I've seen him, of course I've seen him. All of them, not just that one. There and everywhere, and sometimes he talks to me and sometimes he doesn't and I don't know why he does what he does because I'm not *him* yet. Maybe he's not even me yet! The me and the him cross over but we're not the same and maybe he knows something I don't or maybe I know something he doesn't or maybe he's just gone cold and wicked because of some dreadful thing that will have happened but hasn't *yet* happened and maybe that thing will *definitely* have happened and maybe it will tentatively have happened or maybe he got put in a cage again and he just couldn't bear it and now he's got to do whatever he can to stay out of it or maybe he just doesn't care about anything because he lost the girl he loved—I don't *know*. I can think of a million million waves he could have ridden to get to where he is but I won't find out till I'm drowning in them. No one understands this but a Marid—this is what it *means* to be a Marid. You see *him* and you think *me* and I knew if you saw him first you would be afraid because it *is* frightening! I'm frightened! I have to turn into him!

He's already been all the Saturdays it takes to be that Saturday, but whatever happened is still coming for me, I still have to stand up for the hurts and the grief that made him and I can't not do it, but knowing I will is like looking at a hot stove and knowing you're going to touch it, knowing you're going to burn, and feeling the blisters and the peeling before you even reach out your hand. I have to feel it now, all the time, and I don't even know what the stove is. You have to understand, September, you have to. I told you when we met, I told you and you liked me anyway." His voice broke a little.

September tried to be stern. She didn't like it. She didn't know what to do with it. It seemed to say something deeply wrong that she could not quite put her hand to. It sat on the floor of her heart like a toy with a thousand working pieces that could not possibly be put together. But her sternness, which was after all only a very young thing, crumbled when Saturday's voice cracked like a glass. She touched his shoulder, very gingerly, as if her hand might go through him.

"I can't talk about this right now," she whispered. "I would rather fight the Yeti. A Yeti is big and angry and you can't deny it's a Yeti. All that fur. All that snow. A Yeti is a Yeti and that's very straightforward, which is admirable in its own way!"

"I do so love arguments," came a raspy, silky, cottony voice behind them. All four of them jumped.

The voice belonged to a creature watching them, chewing an unripe lightning-sprout in her mouth like cud. She had the body of a white donkey, muscled and powerful, with electric hooves. But a magnificent peacock's tail spread out from her rump, dark green-violet wings folded along her back, and where a long horse's face ought to be, a human face beamed at them. She had dark hazelnut-colored skin and silver-black hair curling out from beneath a domed red cap festooned with copper stars and prongs. A crescent moon stuck out of the top on a slender spike. The creature was not young: wrinkles creased her skin like map-lines, little starbursts near her dark eyes, deep trenches on her brow. September realized she had not seen many old folk in Fairyland.

"You can call me Candlestick, if I can be in your argument," she said, trotting closer. "I once argued with my fate until it clapped its hands over its ears and bellowed for peace—and that means I am very good at bickering. My fate behaved itself after that. It would tie itself up in a bow and walk to the sun barefoot if I looked at it crosswise, and that's the sort of attitude you want in your fate if you ask me, which you should, because this is my jungle and you should defer to the sorts of people who run whole jungles."

September's head felt heavy and fuzzy. She had put so many things out of it to consider later. They crowded in at the edges, buzzing, insistent. But she would not let them in.

"Miss Candlestick, if you please, we do not mean to barge into your very nice jungle. We are on our way to Orrery. If there is a toll or something we might be able to pay it, but we must get through and on." September twisted her hands.

Candlestick reared up, turned round, and trotted off, her peacock tail fanning darkly in the stormy light. For a moment September thought she had left them. But her thin, pointed face appeared again around the side of a lightning-yew.

"Come on then," she said.

They followed the pale donkey through the winding paths of the Lightning Jungle. A-Through-L nudged Aroostook's bumper with his snout, rolling her along behind September and Saturday, who felt it rude to drive while their host walked. Long shapes that might have been vines and might have been some brand of thundery snake coiled through the canopy overhead.

"How did you make your fate talk to you?" Saturday asked Candlestick. His voice sounded low and bruised. "I suspect a Marid's fate is a very obstinate thing, and not at all social."

Candlestick shook her gray hair. "In my younger days, I was the most cantankerous Buraq you should ever like to meet. If the sun came out in the summertime, when it had every right, I raged at it because I wanted snow. If the stars shone bright, I let forth with a diatribe on the virtues of darkness. My mother and father thought me wretched; my cousins said I was the most unhappy creature to walk the Moon and could, the next time I wanted to harangue them on the subject of their faults and their choices, go and soak my head. They did not understand me! Though it is true that no one understands other people. Other people are the puzzle that will not be solved, the argument that cannot be won, the safe that cannot be cracked. They just could imagine the truth: I was happiest when I was arguing! When you argue with verve in your saddlebags, you are *extremely* alive. That is why you yell and holler and shake your fist—could there be anything sweeter than convincing someone to see the world your way? What else is talking for, or jokes, or stories, or battles? The Loudest Magic, and how I loved it. They saw a jennet red in the face—they could not see me red in the heart, so full of knowing that I had to make them know it, too. Until I changed my mind, of course. There's no fun in arguing if you never get shown up. Who plays a game if there's no chance they'll lose? I do so *crave* to be proven wrong. It is as sweet as proving yourself right, when done properly. The trouble is, most people only argue with their friends and their family, which a real sportsman knows is no way to practice. If no one you know can prove you wrong, you're in peril and that's the truth. Well, I do go on—the devil of a thesis is digression! When my herd could no longer get a word in edgewise—and that's the best way to get a word in, where no one can see it coming—I flew off to find the Sajada, where all the things worth knowing are kept. There, someone would best me, I was sure. After all, growing up is nothing but an argument with your parents on the topic of whether or not you are grown. You scream *am so am so am so* from the moment you're born, and they fire back *are not are not are not* from the moment they've got you, and on it goes until you can say it loudest. I won my argument by lighting out for parts unknown—it's a good rejoinder, but a last resort."

Is that what I've done? September thought. *Lit out?*

Candlestick pawed the brilliant earth and went on. "You know what a fate looks like, don't you? It's just a little toy version of yourself, made out of alabaster and emerald and a little bit of lapis lazuli and ambition and coincidence and regret and everyone else's expectations and laziness and hope and where you're born and who to and everything you're afraid of plus everything that's afraid of you. They're all kept in the Sajada. And I went all the way to Pluto to find out where they keep the Sajada!"

"There's a Pluto here? We have a Pluto in my world!" September exclaimed.

"Oh, every place has a Pluto! It's where a universe keeps the polar bears and last year's pickled entropy and the spare gravity. You need a Pluto or you're hardly a universe at all. Plutos teach lessons. A lesson is like a time-traveling argument. Because, you see, you can't argue until you've had the lesson or else you're just squabbling with your own ignorance. But a lesson is really just the result of arguments other people had ages ago! You have to sit still and pay attention and pantomime *their* arguments over again until you're so sick of their prattle that you pipe up to have your own. You can't learn anything without arguing."

"What does Fairyland's Pluto teach?"

"That's for it to teach and me not to step on its toes. I could tell you, but you won't learn it, because you haven't been to Pluto and you haven't fought the ice-ostriches and you haven't even ridden the

Undercamel until he collapses in a heap of his own dreamsweat so it'll be just words to you. They'll only mean themselves."

"But who knows if I'll ever get to Pluto?" September countered. "I'd bet the state of Nebraska it'll never happen in my world, and I don't get much choosing in where I go in Fairyland!"

Candlestick stopped in her tracks, her hooves squishing into a crackling electric mud.

"That's a fair point, girl. But it doesn't sit right. The Undercamel would spit in my eye and I'd never stop weeping. I shall give you half of it—the other half you'll have to race down proper. Very well! Here is the great lesson of Pluto: *What others call you, you become.*" The Buraq's eyes danced with mirth. "Very helpful indeed! I hope you feel edified."

They continued on through the trees. September thought on this as hard as she could, but without an ice-ostrich, she supposed, it was rather hopeless.

"You do love to distract me!" said Candlestick. "I was saying that I went to Pluto to find the Sajada, which is a secret place known only to that very Undercamel, an extremely ill-tempered individual with great heaps of black fur and frozen humps and eyes like a slot machine and big hooves made all of terrible iron nails that bleed him even though a fellow can hardly get away from his own feet. Also he spits. And not like you spit or I do. He spits sorrow. One glob and you'll never get off your knees again. You'll weep until there's no water left in you, just another mummy blowing around the plains of Pluto like a tumbleweed."

"That's dreadful!" cried Saturday.

"That's sort of the point of an Undercamel," agreed the Buraq. Her peacock tail shimmered in the stormlight. "Well, I'm sworn not to tell you the trick of doing it but you have to ride him till he breaks. Only then will he spit out his secret. I'm hardly equipped for dressage, having no arms and far too many legs, but I drove him seven times around

Pluto, pole to pole, chasing his miserable tufted tail and dodging his bubbling green spit until he fell down half-dead. And I bent down to his slavering undermouth and he told me this: The Sajada is a planet, too, all covered with a mosaic of every possible color and a few that got kicked out of the family for being too wild and unruly. The mosaic makes the most radiant pictures, so many you can never see them all. The Sajada rises up from the tiles, a thousand thousand domes stuck over with stars like pincushions. And under every little pebble of the mosaic is somebody's fate. No place more holy in the heavens. And do you know what I did then?"

"No," breathed A-Through-L, who had quite forgotten his own trouble in the Buraq's tale.

"I laughed. I laughed like the whole world was a joke and I was the punchline. And the Undercamel did not appreciate my sense of humor, I can tell you. I laughed because I knew just where it was. I knew a planet with a mosaic exactly like that."

"Where?" asked the Wyverary eagerly.

"Well, not to put too fine a point on it," Candlestick said, "but here."

They stumbled out into a clearing in the Lightning Jungle. The sharp whip of ozone snapped at their noses. Lightning sprouts buzzed and tingled all in a ring round a thousand thousand domes like a pincushion—and quite the size of a pincushion, too. The Sajada spread out before them, the domes gorgeous and ornate and no bigger than toadstools. Crescent moons pronged up from their tips just like the one on Candlestick's diadem. Little courtyards and fountains and walkways dotted the meadow between the domes. The fountains made a tiny trickling sound like the lightest rain. The domes flashed in cascading patterns, flickering pale colors, bright and dark, bright and dark.

Candlestick looked over it with pride. "I grew up on the Moon. If I don't know my own mother I don't know anything." She kicked at a tuft of charcoal sod with her pale hoof, digging deep into it, pushing down and in and scrabbling against the soil. It popped and steamed like boiling cake. The Buraq finally flipped up the divot—and underneath it gleamed a mosaic pattern of gems. "Oh, it's thin here. You'd have to dig down ages most everywhere else. Scientists used to come up here all the time trying to suss out the secrets of the Moon, but I kept them away. The Fairies never cared. Fairies don't have fates, you know. I've heard it told that they stripped them off, eons and eons ago, like winter jackets. No one tells a Fairy what to do! Held a bonfire in the place that became Pandemonium, and if you looked too close at the pyre, you could catch one of them, one of the fey fates. What a dangerous day that was! A glow worm became Queen of Fairyland, though she died within the week, poor, short-lived creatures. One of the hillside towns caught the reflection of the flames in the windows of their houses and their baths and their chocolate shops and their water mills and their museums and the buildings revolted, hauling off to the long plains to live together and love each other and dance at the full moon with their foundations hitched up like skirts and have heaps of little baby amphitheaters and post offices. But everyone else, everybody else's fates are here, under the skin of the Moon."

September stared at the mosaic. *Is mine in there? What does everybody mean, in Fairyland?* Candlestick noted her gaze.

"In the old days it used to take the patience of a planet to find your own. Most everyone gave right up. But not me. I'm stubborn as the last word. When I found my fate, under the smoky stone eyeball of a caladrius posing rampant near the equator, we sat down for a long jaw, the longest I've ever had. I sweat so much I soaked right through to my bones. Finally, when that little Candlestick had had enough, well, we agreed to disagree, and I returned triumphant. No, I would *not* die young quarreling with the heart of Fairyland! What a load of bunk! Dying is a very poor way to end a conversation. No sportsmanship at all. Instead, I went on a Grand Rhetorical Tour, had a foal or two, wrangled with the Woodwoses's anxieties, mediated the theologicals between the Manticore and the Ant-Lion, and galloped for a decade in the Centaur Rodeo—before coming home and here. To mind the storms and to mind the Sajada. Lightning is the only thing quick enough to trip me up. Such clean, brilliant logic a lightning-tree has! Reveals folly in a flash. It was just crumbling, no one to look after it but the Weathercock Elks, and if their arrows are in a tizzy there's no getting them on task. So I rinsed the place with static electricity and soaped it up with hailstone lather and hung it up to dry with the sheet lightning. Now it shines. The Sajada is how the Moon remembers all those thousands and millions of fates. It is a sacred place. It keeps a record. Every dome you see is a catalogue, every sparkling crescent a Dewy Destiny System, organizing our fortunes so that one, out of all, can be called up and hollered at."

"What an extraordinary life!" September breathed, and Saturday stared at the luminous ground.

"And more yet to wrestle," neighed Candlestick.

"I . . . I think I should like that," said September. "To dash about and do a hundred things, to do anything one might call Grand."

"Then you ought to pick a bone with your fate. Nothing like it for the constitution." The Buraq brandished her donkey's chest: broad and strong and thick. Had she a fist, September felt sure she would have thumped it. "I could take you. I took a fine gentleman once—longest beard you ever saw."

"I fear I haven't time for a journey—"

"A pilgrimage. That's the word, dear."

"A pilgrimage. But you see I'm already journeying! We're heading to the other side of the Moon to find the Yeti Ciderskin."

Candlestick's wrinkled face wrinkled further. "Oh, isn't he just the sourest old ape? My poor lightning-larches lose their tempers when he shakes the place and it takes weeks to quiet them. They go darting off to dally with delinquent thunderheads, cruising the canyons for masts and crowns and turrets and golf clubs."

Saturday said, "We mean to get him to stop all that."

Candlestick laughed. It was a nice laugh, a grandmotherly laugh, a laugh that said: *Isn't it sweet when the little ones try to reach the tallest shelf?*

"You'll be sure to come back and tell me how that went, won't you? As best you can with your heads rearranged and your torsos on backwards."

Ell puffed out his scarlet chest—but his heart did not seem to be in it. It was so strange for him to have no one to tower over! "We've managed Feats before, I'll have you know! They begin with F and they are our speciality!"

The Buraq considered for a moment. "I should very much like to argue with a Yeti! A first in the histories, and that's what I call a thing worth doing."

September ducked as a lightning-sprout streaked through the air. "If you'd like to come. . . ."

"Oh, no, no, child, that's not at all right! Don't just let me muscle in because I feel like it! Tell me to stick to my own business! I could be anyone! I could be an agent of destruction, and a slowpoke besides. Resist! Resistance is the beginning of the truth."

September fretted. "I would like to, ma'am, because I know you like it frightfully, but you're much older than I am and you've done many more things, so I expect if you think you'd like to come along then who am I to argue?"

"*Who* are *you* to argue?" The Buraq flexed her tail in astonishment. "Who are you to *argue*? Why, you are yourself! You are. . . ." She drifted off expectantly, not having been introduced.

"September."

"You are September!" Candlestick roared. "And whoever that is, it is somebody! Who are you? You are the person with something to say! Only the dead don't argue. And even then there are exceptions. Didn't anyone tell you? Respect your elders is just a secret weapon, and like most secret weapons, it's a cheap trick. It shuts everyone else up for free, without having to break a sweat. And she who shuts up first loses."

"But," said September with a grin, "I don't want to argue. The more we have with us the better, for even standing on our shoulders we couldn't look a Yeti in the eye. Just because you tell me I should argue with you doesn't mean I should, if I get what I want without it! If you wanted to quarrel, you shouldn't have offered the best outcome right out of the gate! The object is to be the one who's right, and I'm right when I say what I want, because who could know that better than me?"

Candlestick opened her green wings—lightning-sprouts flew from all over the jungle, tiny and burning and bright, to huddle up near her skin. She folded her wings down over her charges. The jungle darkened and seemed to sigh around them.

"Well done," the Buraq said with a wink. "We'll make a brawler of you yet. But that is what we call a Fallacy. No one knows themselves very well. Who has the time these days? Have you been formally introduced to yourself? Made the effort to get to know your faults and your strengths, sit yourself down to tea and listen to all your troubles, answered the call when yourself falters? Then how can you say you know yourself in the least? You must be so careful with Fallacies. They're contagious, you know. Pustulant. I call an end to this argument at once on the grounds that I am no longer entertained and would rather harangue the sheet lightning as it comes out of its nap. You have lost! Don't feel bad. You're bound to, in the beginning. And in the end. And the middle, too. I've no doubt you're capable of Feats, and that getting on your way is most important! But it's when you're dead set on your way that you most need a pilgrimage. Going straight in a line to any-place is the saddest path. Come now, wouldn't you like to have a word with your destiny? Skip to the end and have a peek at how it all works out? Maybe your fate has written an academic paper on How to Defeat a Yeti, you never know. And I've streamlined the process—very mod-ern now! I keep records, coordinates, cross-references! I can find you quick as a rod draws a bolt in a rainstorm."

September glanced at Saturday. If she went, if it was as quick as Candlestick said, then they might be even. She might be able to under-stand him a little, if she saw her own life the way he saw his. She could make it better between them. Make it straightforward. And after all, hadn't she been trying to grow up? Wouldn't it be a relief to know what she had done in the end, what she had turned out to be good at, who she would be when she grew up, a griffin or an armchair or a shark? Wouldn't it be easier to know how she'd solved the trouble of the Yeti before she tried to do the solving? Or know it just wasn't solv-able, not her fault, no shame in it, nothing to be done? She had only just gotten to the Moon. She had time. She had to have time, Septem-ber reasoned, or else Almanack would have hefted its shell and run back down the road to Fairyland. It would never let its folk come to harm, even if a thousand Yetis rained down their fists on its prongs.

But then September saw her Wyverary watching her uncertainly, ever so much smaller than he had been when he met, ever so much more uncertain. Saturday lifted his eyes to hers and she saw the same plea there: *Don't leave us. We've only just found each other again.*

"Don't you worry about them," Candlestick crooned comfortingly.

"A girl's fate is her only possession, her unflappable friend, her truest mate. When everyone else has gone, her fate remains. Closer than a shadow, kinder than a death. Some things are to be done in private, such as weeping, praying, embezzlement, and the writing of novels. I'll set them up with a nice spread and they can watch the storms come in from their shifts."

"I suppose it's far too late for afternoon tea," sighed A-Through-L. September did not feel particularly hungry for once, but a Wyvern's belly has many rooms, and it is impossible to fill them all at once.

"It's rude to discuss religion," the Buraq sniffed. "But I don't hold with Teatimers. I'm of the Midnight Snack school. You have tea because it's three o'clock and that's what's done and yes, yes, it's pleasant to have a nice cup and a sandwich with no crusts on, but pleasant is not enough for me! When you tuck into a Midnight Snack, it's because you're hungry in the dark. You want that bit of roast you couldn't finish at supper and you want it now. Midnight Snackery is primal, like a wolf in the wood, hunkering down over her kill."

Candlestick quivered her tail and stomped the ground. A sparkling cloud of round white-violet sparks as big as apples came sizzling through the wood with a willow-wood basket hefted on their backs. They set it down and nuzzled the Buraq excitedly while Saturday opened the basket. Inside lay drumsticks wrapped in wax paper, a flagon of brilliant, sparkling, glowing something, and a large clutch of lightning-grapes. When he opened one of the wax papers, she saw that the drumstick came from no chicken. A storm cloud flashed and rumbled around a stark white bone.

"Teatime can be nice," A-Through-L said, nosing at the grapes, resigned. September was suddenly reminded of his shadow, deep down in Fairyland-Below, who had been friends with the Duke of Teatime and the Vicereine of Coffee, and let their children ride on his back and pull his ears. She shivered.

"Ell," she asked quietly, as though if she said it soft enough it would be somehow as if they were alone together, as they had been once, in a field of little red flowers and trees that were rather like persimmon trees but not persimmons at all. "What made you cry, in the Lopsided Library, when we opened the box?"

The Wyverary clawed the thin charcoal soil of the Jungle with his scaly foot. His orange whiskers flicked once, twice, like a horse's tail swatting a fly. A-Through-L wrapped his long crimson tail all the way around his body, as tightly as he could, as if to hold himself together.

"You mustn't laugh at me. I am a large beast, and very fierce, and I've been alone plenty in my life. I can face alone and punch it in the nose."

September nodded solemnly, though she wanted to smile very much at her dear lizard and his own fierce nose.

A-Through-L's fiery eyes pierced the dark. "I thought of that day in the glowerwheat field. When you wished for us all to be whole and well and we woke up with the sun shining on us."

"But that isn't sad at all!"

"Oh, September," the beast sighed. "We woke up and we were whole and well and the sun was so warm and you disappeared right in front of us like you'd never been there at all and it was *years,* it was three years of the world going on like you'd never been in it! And maybe you were dead or maybe you just didn't feel like coming back or maybe it was even longer in your world and you'd gotten big and mated and forgot me and I *missed* you. And when we did find you at the other end of three years, dancing with the shadows in that green valley, well, you up and vanished again like vanishing was the thing you did best in the world! I didn't get an hour of not missing you before you were gone again! Saturday took it hard, too, of course he did, but before we ever saw him you rode on my back and called me yours. Do you remember saying that? I remember it. I felt . . . as though I'd grown . . . I felt as though I'd grown forepaws. Like I wasn't a Wyvern anymore but something just a little different because my forepaws were shaped like a little girl and with them I could grab up the whole of Fairyland and shake it till everything good fell out. But as soon as I had them they got cut off and I missed you which is a funny word and starts with M but you can't blame it because it's the *right* word. I *missed* you; you were *missing* from me. Like forepaws. Like flying."

September put her hand on her chest. Her heart squeezed, clenching up, trying to hide within her and burst out of her at once. But she would not cry. She would not. Ell was very fierce, after all.

"Well then," she said thickly, straightening her shoulders. *See what you see and face up to it.* "Let's go." The Wyverary and the Marid seemed to deflate like a red balloon and a blue one. They nodded a little, as if to say they had always known it should be this way, after all. It was, after all, September alone, in the end. It always had been and always would be.

"All of us," September said gently, and held out her hands. "I know what you said, Miss Candlestick, but however you count it, our fates are stuck together and stitched up good." She paused for a moment, looking down at her flowing black silks and her own small hands. "Closer than shadows, she finished."

The Buraq, her wings and her tail flickering with the fitful lights of concealed lightning, cantered off. Ell ran to keep up with her, abandoning the midnight picnic without a thought, his heart bouncing boisterous in his chest, not left behind, not alone, but leaping through the stormgrowth, squashing the tangled floor of the Lightning Jungle underfoot. With every clawfall, he thought he would bellow fire, so great was his exhilaration—and with every clawfall he hiccuped, a purple bubble popping against the rows of his long teeth. The Wyver-ary could feel it rising up inside him, the rope of fire getting bigger and thicker and hotter and more inevitable, like a loaf of bread baking within his belly, but a loaf as heavy as an anchor. It was going to hap-pen, he could feel it, and no matter how he tried to make it not happen, he could hardly breathe for the heat in his throat. A-Through-L surged ahead of his friends, of the Buraq. Some things are to be done in pri-vate, the donkey had said. He would not let them see or be scorched. Lightning cracked and spangled and knifed around the Wyverary as purple flame finally bloomed out of his snout, curling and writhing into the forest canopy.

But the trees did not burn. The Lightning Jungle seemed to drink up the flame like fresh water. After all, it was nothing but fire and light and surging itself. Baobabs full of firebolts flared even brighter, wash-ing the air in clean flashes, crisp forks.

September and Saturday, having legs nothing like a donkey's or a Wyvern's, bounced along behind in Aroostook, who roared under branches and over blackened trunks, squall-vines whipping at the wind-shield. The whole of the Lightning Jungle sounded in September's ears like static from the walnut wood radio in her living room at home. The throng of them hurtled toward the edge of the tree line, the last squat black trunks showing starkly like lowercase letters. Finally, with a last forked snaggle of light snaking out ahead of them, Aroostook burst clear, into a field of pale silver scrub, a meadow of tiny raindrops frozen in the act of splashing upward, growing from the ground like grass. Round, black lakes opened up in the ground, lightless and deep as blood, leading up into the mountains like a sentence without an ending. . . .

CHAPTER XIV

No

*In Which September Meets a Pair of Lunaticks, a Peculiar
Computational System, Several Fallacies, and Her Own Fate,
Whereupon Our Heroine Performs a Drastic Deed*

September followed the line of pure black ponds as far as she could
with her wide eyes—they curved away into the mountains and
disappeared long before she could spy an end to them. Each one perfectly round, each one depthless and darker than sleeping. The strange,
growing crystal rain that covered the ground, frozen in up-slashes,
made stark weeds and reeds and seedpods, as pale as the ponds were
not, and crunched delicately under their feet, under Aroostook's
wheels, under Candlestick's hooves. They stood between two large
ponds with but a narrow wisp of pale grassy earth between them.

"We call it the Ellipsis," the Buraq said. Her steely curls glittered with lightning-dew.

"Oh, Ell," Saturday sighed. The Wyverary still stood taller than the Marid, but not by so terribly much now. He hung his head mournfully.

"It's all right," said September, stroking his long neck. "It's not so bad. I always wanted to take you home to meet my mother. Now you could fit in our house! Don't worry, oh, please, don't be afraid! After all, little begins with L . . ."

A crashing, echoing, ear-skewering boom shot through the night. September's hands flew up to her ears. Her eyes squeezed shut and her whole body stiffened—Ciderskin had come back for them, that terrible fist would sweep through the meadow and the ponds and this time she did not have Aroostook's door to protect her, she would be crushed. Saturday leapt toward her with his new trapeze-man's swift strength, covering her with his arms.

The boom rang out again, clapping sharp against the cold.

No paw followed, any more than thunder followed the lightning in the Lightning Jungle. September opened her eyes. A third rolling, smashing blast sounded, and what followed it was neither blows nor storms but laughter, tinny and thin. Through the ponds of the Ellipsis, a cannonball flew, beneath the water, the color of Jupiter, all cream and fire. The shot began in a pool some ways farther off from them and barreled through the waters, streaming bubbles behind it, disappearing when the little lake ended and reappearing once more in the next. Finally, in the dark circle nearest them, it found its target. The ball exploded against the grass basket of a great striped hot-air balloon suspended down beneath the rippling surface. The perspective made September feel a little sick; the balloon hung down deep into the water as though the water was the sky and they stood on some strange circus platform higher than the heavens, looking down on the creatures of the air. The balloon's basket rocked back but did not break. A hissing blast mark blossomed on its woven grass, joining many other smoking star-shapes already there.

"Call that a love letter, do you, Marigold? Smells like a burnt bug-bear's least favorite beehive." The tinny, thin laughter tittered out again. It came all the way up through the pool, softening and quieting and thinning out along the way. September peered down into the pond. The balloon's stripes gleamed white and teal. Jets of bubbles burped out of its neck now and then, keeping it aloft, or submerged, however one ought to measure a thing that flew underwater. But she could not see anyone in the basket. Someone hid there, surely! A small door in the charred grass opened; the mouth of a cannon popped forward, silver so pure it looked like glass, blown into the shape of a man's head, mouth wide to fire true, every curl of his hair a strand of silver butterflies. The body of the cannon, his arms, bound back and down into a hospital straitjacket. A second cannonball roared out of the man's silverglass mouth, the color of Neptune, hot turquoise and boiling white.

But this one did not speed through all the ponds and up far off into the range of mountains beyond—another balloon bobbed into the dark of the second pool, turning on like a lightbulb where it had not been before. The second balloon was more nimble; the Neptunian shot careened off the basket's bumpers, skipping up through the ponds like a stone, but never disturbing the surface. A second voice giggled, muffled, as if they had their ears against the bottom of a glass tumbler pressed up to a locked door.

"I know you miss me, Tamarind, but you miss me by so much I wonder if you love me at all!"

September peered down into the other pond. She could see the owner of this voice, under her gold and wine striped balloon. It be-longed to a thin, pearl-colored insect shaped like a wintry twig, deli-cate and coiling, but hard and brilliant. She peered over the side of her basket eagerly. Her antennae, chartreuse and much longer than her body, snapped like horsewhips. She crawled around the edge of her basket, her body softening and arching and inching along like a cater-pillar. When she stopped to speak again, she hardened back into her branch-like posture.

"It does sting so to miss a person!" the insect cried, her tiny sap-phire eyes blazing. "The only solution is to be doubly careful with one's trajectories!" An identical door opened in the basket, and an identical cannon showed itself—but the head was a woman's.

Candlestick cleared her throat. No cannonball burst from the twig-insect's balloon.

"Good evening, Marigold," the Buraq said. She turned to the first balloon, the first pond. "Tamarind. How lovely to see you getting along so well."

Saturday frowned. "They're shooting at each other!"

The tinny, thin, invisible voice floated up to them out of the depths. "Hold still, my darling! I'm going to kiss you right in the face!"

September, and Ell beside her, peered closer till their eyes felt like peeled grapes—and finally saw that the first duelist was a grasshopper, his wings iridescent, his great bulging eyes black as the water, sparks gleaming dully within. He was so nearly the color of the grass balloon-basket that he seemed no more than grass himself.

"Don't mind them," Candlestick said. "They're Lunaticks."

"Oh, that's unkind!" yelled the grasshopper.

"*Princess* Lunatick to you, you old mule!" cried the wintry twig.

September sighed a little.

Marigold drew herself up to her full frosty height. "Don't you sigh at me, young lady! I suppose you think Princessing is nothing more than dresses and blushing and dancing and the occasional side-job as a distressed damsel! Young people today, why, they've no more sense than a gumdrop!"

September winced—for that was precisely what she had been thinking. The Duke of Teatime had wanted to make her a Princess, and she'd felt then just as she felt now—that if one had to be in the kind of stories that had Princesses, it was much better not to be the Princess, for they were given very little to do other than weddings and distresses, neither of which offered much in the way of excitement or exercise.

"Where I come from, being a Princess is a job, young primate!" huffed Marigold. "A position in the civil service! We are Executive Branch, child! Why, I never wore a dress except on a dare! I wore a suit, like any government employee. And a fine suit, too, with a hat to match! I had more ties than a railroad! A Princess must be serious and calculating, she must learn Fiscal Magic and Severe Magic and Fan Magic, both Loud and Shy Magic as well as Parliamentary Procedure, Heraldry, and Constitutional Conjuring. I had a desk at the castle like all the other Princesses, and we ate packed lunches every day, I'll have you know. Of course I had ten fingers then, it's much easier to run a kingdom when you have fingers. I was an excellent Princess, one of the best. I loved my work! I personally negotiated the peace of Parthalia, despite the ogre-of-record eating the first, second, and ninth drafts. The Fairy Queen Tanaquill herself gave me my first double-breasted jacket. I don't suppose she is queen anymore. But how proud I stood that day! She saw Princesses for what we are: the engine that fuels Politicks. No Devious Dragon or Knavish Knight would dare tower me up as long as I wore my suit of armor, my sharkskin shield! Ah, but then, but then!"

Tamarind's wings buzzed. "Then we came to the Moon. We'd

only just married, we were young and bald and had all our limbs! We wore our hearts on our sleeves!"

"That's what you wear to your wedding if you're a Lamia, which we are," chirped Marigold. "To show that you mean it, to show you know that love means wearing your insides on your outside. And under the first waxing moon after the ceremony, you swap."

Tamarind chittered. "You swallow your love's heart, and they swallow yours. Then forever after, your heart is living inside your mate, and theirs lives inside you."

"You're not in love if you keep your own heart bricked up behind your bones. You're only playing." Marigold gazed across the thin strip of raingrass between her black pond and her husband's, and her gaze shone deep and warm.

"But you're not a Lamia!" scoffed A-Through-L, who counted Lamiai safely within his alphabetical kingdom. "A Lamia is a beautiful person with long shining hair who has a snake's tail and sharper teeth than you want to know about. They drink blood!"

Marigold snapped her antennae. "Don't be superior. Everyone drinks blood. Blood is a word that means alive. You can do without almost anything: arms, legs, teeth, hope. But you can't do without blood. Lose even a little and you grow slow and stupid and not yourself at all. We are all of us beautiful and complicated vessels for carrying blood the way a bottle carries wine. I suppose you think there's no blood in your roast beef? Life eats life. Blood makes you move, makes you blush, makes the pulse pound in your brow when you see your love walking across a street toward you, makes your very thoughts fly through your brain. Blood is everything and everything is blood. That's the law of the Lamiai."

There must be blood, September thought, and rubbed her finger where she had pricked it, so long ago, and bled to open the doors of Fairyland.

"Don't act like you've never eaten anyone's heart," Tamarind said.

"I haven't!" cried September. Saturday opened his mouth, but thought better of it. He rubbed at the backs of his blue hands.

"Then I'm sorry for you," the grasshopper sighed. "It's a dreadful world with only your own heart to drive you."

"But we couldn't wait, you see," Marigold whirred in her balloon. "We couldn't wait for the waxing Moon. So we took the road all the way up—when you're on the Moon, we reasoned, it's all the Moons together, waxing, waning, new, old. We met here, with a little flask of fizzing whipwine, to devour each other's hearts and begin our lives together. And just as we'd held our rite and Tam started back toward the Jungle, just as I'd called him husband and he called me wife, that Yeti, that terrible Yeti, came bawling and brawling out of the wood, clutching his bleeding wrist and caterwauling like the stars had gone out."

"His foot came down and I was under it," wept Tamarind, shaking his head.

"His next step took me, too," whispered Marigold. "And the Yeti's blood filled up his prints and caught us in their black cups. And here we stay, separated by a step. We cannot get from one pond to the other. We cannot even see each other properly. The balloons crashed down into the water during a Thaumaturgists' duel some time later. The cannons are all that's left of the duelists—they can break through, but we cannot. And now my heart's living over there in that old grasshopper and what am I supposed to do?"

Tamarind went on. "We had no plans to live forever! But blood is everything; everything is blood. The Yeti's blood got old, too. It's not exactly blood now, though I suppose that's obvious. It pickles us, preserves us, pumps through us and keeps us running like a couple of old clock towers. We live and live, but it doesn't keep us young. We started shrinking and shifting and warping, the way anything does when it ages enough, turns to stone or dust or stories. Only we became—well, first I was an iguana, wasn't I? You were a water dragon. Oh, wasn't that nice! Halcyon days! Then I was a salamander and she was a rattlesnake, then she was a turtle and I was a boa, then for a long bit we were both frogs and it was like we were young together again, then I can't remember, sometimes she was the male of the species and sometimes I was, sometimes I was female and sometimes she was, sometimes I had legs and sometimes I didn't, sometimes she had a mouth and sometimes she had mandibles, and then on our anniversary we suddenly got wings and I was a butterfly, she was a dragonfly, I was a bat, she was a moth, I was a ladybug, she was a beetle, and so on and so forth and at the moment she's an inchworm and I'm a grasshopper."

"It never bothered me any, you being a grasshopper," sighed Marigold. "Marriage is a wrestling match where you hold on tight while your mate changes into a hundred different things. The trick is that you're changing into a hundred other things, but you can't let go. You can only try to match up and never turn into a wolf while he's a rabbit, or a mouse while he's still busy being an owl, a brawny black bull while he's a little blue crab scuttling for shelter. It's harder than it sounds."

The Buraq nodded sympathy. "It's Yeti's blood, you see. Time speeds down there like it's racing against the world. For them, it's been thousands of years. More. Thousands of thousands. They've gone a bit mad, started firing broadsides and counting obsessively—which is how they're useful to me."

"Are we going fishing?" cried the inchworm with delight.

"If you're not to tired after your cannonades."

"Never!" buzzed Tamarind.

Candlestick beckoned September forward. The Buraq instructed her to put her hand down into the ponds, one after the other. When September did as she was told, her fingers disappeared as though they had been severed. The cold black pond drew closed over her wrist like a curtain. Tamarind and Marigold's antennae quivered and snapped in their private pools. Then without warning, the balloons shot out twin clouds of blue-white bubbles, collapsed down into scraps of cloth, and disappeared wholly.

"The mosaic covers the whole of the Moon," Candlestick explained, her peacock tail waving in the starlight. "Even with the records in the Sajada, it would take months to find the little pebble that hides your fate. But once I met the Lunaticks, I discovered they'd counted everything on the Moon, every tile of the mosaic and every root and every fish. The pools have seeped down and down and down until they run all over the insides of the Moon like veins, and they've had so long to look for some little place where their waters might meet. When I want a fate, I send my lightning-sprouts through the Sajada to find the record and light it up—for the Sajada has veins, too, and roots as well. But if I want it faster, I send the old kids fishing—they get a taste of you, a smell of you, and race down through the Moon to find the lit-up tile that tastes and smells like you and bring it back fast as thinking."

Sure enough, Tamarind's balloon bounced back up underwater like a lightbulb coming on. Marigold's appeared a moment later.

"I win!" the grasshopper cried. "That's three in a row! You're losing your touch, dear!"

"It was in your hemisphere, that hardly counts," huffed the inchworm, and crossed two of her wintry, spindly arms. Her cannon slid out from the grassy basket and fired as sharp as a retort. Her Jovian ball blasted through the inky water, arcing beautifully, like a comet—and landed squarely, precisely, in Tamarind's own basket. It smoked and rolled, gleaming. And it had knocked something free: something small and glinting, rising up through the pond toward them.

"Oh," sighed the grasshopper, "oh, it's still warm where you loaded it into the cannon. It still smells of your perfume." Tamarind laid down upon the cannonball and closed his wings around his green body.

September knelt and caught the small, glinting thing as it bobbed up out of the black—though it was not so small after all, almost as long as her own arm. Saturday got down into the grass to help her haul it out and get it upright on the shore.

It was a Leopard.

It was *her* Leopard. Imogen, the Leopard of Little Breezes, the cat who had borne her to Fairyland that first day. September would know those whiskers and those spots anywhere. Yes, she was smaller than she had been and entirely still and silent, but all the same it was her. September cried out and threw her arms around that dear, wooly neck.

But it was not the Leopard of Little Breezes. It was not a living Leopard at all. September's arms found no wool on that neck, but cool brass, pocked with onyxes, a statue of her Leopard, with a flat, stony gaze.

"I thought you said it would be a little toy version of myself," said September, a little embarrassed. "I am not a Leopard or a Little Breeze."

"I . . . I don't know why it isn't!" Candlestick's face creased in confusion. "Perhaps it's on account of you being human. I've never dredged up a human fate before. That will teach me to make assumptions! Assumptions are the enemy of logic!"

September looked the Leopard over. It did not seem to be in the least alive and she had no notion of how it might talk to her, let alone argue.

"Hullo, Leopard," she said shyly.

At the sound of her voice and the tiny gust of her breath on the brassy muzzle, the Leopard's eyes softened and turned toward September.

"Hullo, Tem," the beast growled, but it was not an unpleasant growl, nor loud, but cozy as a purr.

September startled as though she had been struck. Her mother and father called her Tem, years and years ago, when she was tiny. They never did anymore, she was too big for small names, her father always said.

Saturday squeezed her hand comfortingly. A-Though-L pressed his red forehead into her shoulder just exactly like a cat. And then both of them took a few steps away and turned their backs. It was her fate. They would not leave her, but they would give her privacy. Candlestick followed their example, though she thought not a one of them ought to have come along in the first place. Only Aroostook watched September and her fate, her headlamps illuminating the glittering Leopard's spots.

Neither girl nor cat said anything else for a long while. September stared. Everything she could ever be or know was inside this brass creature. What could she possibly say to it?

"Try the Appeal to Probability," Candlestick called over her shoulder without looking. "It's a good opening gambit with fates. It's a fallacy, of course, but what isn't? Such and such will probably happen, wouldn't you agree, Leopard? That sort of thing."

But September could not stop staring. She thought of the older Saturday, standing in front of her car, blocking her way. She thought of the Blue Wind laughing at her. She thought of the Fairies, speeding through time so that they never, ever had to wait to find out what happened next, never, ever had to long for anything before they had it in hand.

Candlestick cleared her throat. "I do like the Fallacy of Many Questions as well, mind you. Loaded questions, leading questions, lying questions . . ."

The Leopard stared back at her. September thought of the Sibyl, how surely she had known what her life would look like all along and all through. She thought of Saturday in the circus, how gorgeously he'd flown. She thought of Ell in his Library, shelving romances. And she thought, she could not help thinking, of the awful night when she wrestled Saturday on the Gears of the World, and burnt his back with iron, and how when it was done they had looked up and seen someone. September had seen a little girl with blue skin and a mole on her left cheek—but of all the things she had tried not to think of since she first knew about Fairyland, she had tried hardest not to think about that. She didn't like it. She didn't know what to do with it. It sat on the floor of her heart like a toy with a thousand working pieces that could not possibly be put together. Their daughter, Saturday had said, as out of time and out of order as any true Marid.

Slowly, September said: "A Yeti is frightening. Frightening and strong and so much bigger than me. But not half as frightening as thinking your whole life has already happened and you don't have any choice in it."

The brass Leopard curled and uncurled her tail. "I didn't think we frightened so easily," she purred. "Aren't we ill-tempered and irascible? Isn't that us?"

"Is there a way to defeat Ciderskin?" September whispered, and once she had asked one question the rest tumbled out after. "What will I be when I am grown-up? Will my father ever really be well? Is the war really going to end? Will the Marquess wake up? Am I going to have that daughter no matter what, no matter how, no matter which way I go? Will I like the version of myself I will be if I have her? Is everything done, done and decided and all there is for me is to wait for it to happen to me? The Green Wind said I chose myself. Please say he wasn't lying. I do know winds lie, I do know it, but please let that have been true, of all the things he said."

"Dodgy attribution," the Buraq coughed. "Quoting from a biased and frankly fanciful source."

The brass Leopard said nothing. She lifted her paw and pressed it into her spotted breast. A little door came open, a patch of brass fur and jewels with a darkness inside it, and empty space.

Within that empty space lay a book.

The book was a very deep and very vivid red, with curling gold shapes stamped in the corners. It had a lock upon it and many, many pages clapped up within. It glowed in her fate's chest like a heart.

September reached inside and took out the red book. It was heavy. A girl's face graced the cover, finely embossed, but it was turned away, gazing at some unseen thing. Perhaps it was her own face, perhaps not. A miniature version of herself, after all. Was it an answer? Was it everything already written?

"You can't argue with something that's written down," she said, stroking the red locks of hair on the cover. "If the heart of my fate is a book, there's nothing for it. Once it's written, it's done. All those ancient books always say 'so it is written' and that means it's finished and tidied and you can't say a thing against it."

Oh, but September, it isn't so. I ought to know, better than anyone. I have been objective and even-tempered until now, but I cannot let that stand, I simply cannot. Listen, my girl. Just this once I will whisper from far off, like a sigh, like a wind, like a little breeze. So it is written— but so, too, it is crossed out. You can write over it again. You can make notes in the margins. You can cut out the whole page. You can, and you must, edit and rewrite and reshape and pull out the wrong parts like bones and find just the thing and you can forever, forever, write more and more and more, thicker and longer and clearer. Living is a paragraph, constantly rewritten. It is Grown-Up Magic. Children are heartless; their parents hold them still, squirming and shouting, until a heart can get going in their little lawless wilderness. Teenagers crash their hearts into every hard and thrilling thing to see what will give and what will hold. And Grown-Ups, when they are very good, when they are very lucky, and very brave, and their wishes are sharp as scissors, when they are in the fullness of their strength, use their hearts to start their story over again.

Has she heard me? Have I tilted my hand? I cannot tell. Look close—she is not moving. Well, my powers are not infinite.

September held the red book of the Leopard's heart tightly. Her fingertips turned white. She looked past it, not to the grass but to her black silks, flowing around her body, clinging and warming her and announcing its own purposes to everyone she met. *I chose myself,* she thought furiously. *I did choose.* Some distant night-bird called. She did not know if she could do it. Candlestick called this place holy. What would that make her? This was no way to win an argument, certainly. The lesson of Pluto sounded in her heart, heavier even than a brass Leopard. Perhaps she was, in the end, a Criminal. A breaker of laws. A vandal.

September lay the red book on the raingrass. Blades shivered and broke beneath. *You cannot argue with fate,* whatever Candlestick says, she thought. *You can only defy it.*

"You can only say *no,*" she said aloud. "*No* is how you know something's alive."

Out of the pocket of her silks she drew her last possession, the one thing the Wind would not take when he demanded Everything She Had. Her iron hammer.

With a great deep breath and a choked cry, September lifted the hammer high and brought it singing down onto the red, red body of her fate.

The book shattered.

A roaring, rumbling, blossoming sound shook the world—a moonquake, splitting the ground and shaking like nothing would stop it.

What others call you, you become.

THE BLACK COSMIC DOG

In the city on the inside of the Moon, the Black Cosmic Dog has found something.

It is a very large something.

In fact, the Black Cosmic Dog has occupied himself with nothing but digging it up for some time now. It is a big job. When the Dog furiously claws at the soft lunar soil, bits of glittering stardust show under his fur like burrs. He uses both his front and back legs. When he sleeps, he sleeps curled up against the steep curve of his prize.

A scarlet boil, hot and painful, has grown on the waxing slope of the Moon, in the place where a city used to bustle and thrive. The red of it glows against the night and the Black Cosmic Dog. He pants all the while he digs around it, exposing it to the air and the wind. The Moon is so white and the boil is so red it looks as though the whole world is bleeding. The Black Cosmic Dog grins his cosmic grin and goes about his work. He is happiest when he is digging.

The red boil grows day by day as he scrabbles at it, moving great heaps of Moon-dirt like drifts of snow.

In the end, even the Dog cannot say how big it will be before it bursts.

CHAPTER XV

THE TYGUERROTYPE

*In Which September and Her Friends Enter the City of Orrery, Meet a
Gentleman Tiger, and Perform a Spectacular Optical Trick*

The Moon owns many mountains. Some are so tiny you and I
would step over them without a thought—yet on their infinitesi-
mal slopes, wee invisible sheep chew lumps of microscopic snow. Some
line the rim of the Moon like a spectacular fence, and there you will
find frog-footed rams stripping painted bark from twisted tapestry
trees. The highest and most fearsome of these mountains is the Splendid Dress, which opens up from its snowy bright peak like a skirt, flowing in stripes and swirls and patterns and tiers all the way down to the
plains. I will share a secret with you: once, a girl really did wear this
mountain like a dress. She was a very serious young strega and stregas
are not to be meddled with, for they can hex as easy as they can tie

their shoes. She wore glasses and her hair hung very straight. She had a highly developed sense of humor, which in some lights looked a bit like a sense of justice. She would not like it much if I told you how she got so big, so I will hold my peace and keep my hat.

At the foot of the Splendid Dress many brass rings and tracks circle the stony frills and ruffles of the Underskirt, the crags and cliffs that announce: *A mountain is about to put on its heights, so hitch up your pride and get climbing.* Here and there on the tracks, bright glassy bulbs as big as battleships open up like lotus-flowers whose petals have only just begun to yawn and open up to the day. Inside the many-colored flowers you can find anything a town might like to have for its very own. The tracks click and move every so often, but it's done smoothly, and only a few people fall down, the way you and I will when riding a tram in a new city where we do not know the stops and starts. This is the place the Ellipsis leads to, the very last, small black pools and ponds no bigger than rabbit-holes.

"Are you sure this is the easiest way to the inner edge?" asked September. Everyone had walked softly after the Ellipsis and the moonquake, each in their thoughts. Great cracks in the Moon showed now, where the quake had cut them. But even so, September felt strangely light and eased since leaving the night and the Lightning Jungle behind. Once you have done a thing like that, she supposed, the only thing for it was to pick up your feet and get moving. She chose, and she chose now to be pleased with herself. Candlestick had not come with them after all, turning up her peacock tail and refusing to speak further with any of the lot of them. Vandals and sophists, she called them, and that was all she would say.

A-Through-L furrowed his orange brow. "Easiest, no, no, September, it surely isn't. It is the shortest, though, and the two are rarely the same. When you've scared off all the patrons you can get so much reading done, and I read over all the maps of the Moon I could find. We could go the long way and walk up the whole lunar curve with hardly a bump in our way, a few very nice rivers with party manners, meadows full of teatime roses that bloom at exactly three fifteen every afternoon, full of iced cakes and sandwiches and cups and tablecloths. And it would take us a year and by that time Ciderskin will have cracked the crescent in half and used the horns to pick his teeth. But this is Orrery, and the way to it is done."

September fell quiet. Dawn broke over the Splendid Dress, a black and white sort of dawn, stark and sudden and crisp. The craggy colors showed only as shades of darkness on the slopes. Saturday held out his hand across Aroostook's cabin to take hers—a desperate sort of taking, as though if their hands touched, the Marid could believe that everything was all right. September let him, but she did not lace her fingers in his or press her thumb against his knuckles. She did not want to be cold. But she did not know another way to be just now. She had missed him so much. She could feel the hurt coming off him like heat. Who knew what he had done, who he had been, without her? A circus performer, and a boy who smiled the way she'd seen him smile on that platform. September had never made him smile like that. But she had seen more than that smile. She had seen *him,* grown-up and stern and unyielding and how could she bear knowing he could be like that? That he could be the man who stood beside the Yeti and did his work? No, no, that wasn't it, and she knew it. Everyone can be stern. She had done it herself, though she felt very tired afterward. But she could not look her worry in the eye just yet. She folded it up and put it somewhere else, to be peered at later.

"It's awfully quiet," Saturday said, hiding his hurt like a wound. The brass rings stood cool and silent in the early light. Nearest to them, a pale yellow cup with swoops of quartz in it rose up against the peaks. A space between its petals showed the tips of gables and garrets inside.

"It's a wind-up city, September," Saturday said shyly. "An orrery is like a map of the sky, only it moves like the sky and spins like the sky and you wind it every day to keep it on the same schedule as the sky. Each of those stone cups is a neighborhood. They click around, and when they line up, the neighborhoods talk to one another, hold markets and barn dances, say hello to old friends, and then circle apart again. There's planets up in the sky for every cup, and every cup fashions itself as a miniature of its planet. This one is called Azimuth." He flushed with pleasure, to be the one who knew something. "It's in the constellation called Wolf's Egg. Do you remember?"

September smiled. In remembering, the unpeerable thing in her softened and she held out her hand. "Yes. The night we slept by Calpurnia Farthing's fire. *Ain't what's strong, but what's patient.*" Calpurnia was a Fairy, no different than the Fairies that had cut off a Yeti's Paw years ago. She hadn't seemed like the kind who could do such a thing, with her changeling daughter and her quiet way of talking. Perhaps she couldn't—she still lived and chewed tire-jerky and rode the plains, after all, when her folk did not.

A long pair of slatted tracks led up into the brass rings from the earth around the mountain. Uncertainly, slowly, painstakingly, September fitted Aroostook's wheels to it like a roller-coaster car. Ell flew above them as the automobile rolled upward and slid gracefully around the rails. After a moment, a great rumbling broke the birdless morning— for an awful, sickening moment, September thought it was another moonquake, Ciderskin shaking them off like a dog with fleas once more. But it was Orrery, clicking forward on its track. The yellow cup moved closer, and they saw a lovely carved gate in its side decorated with apples and sunbeams.

But inside the yellow glass petals, Azimuth stood empty and quiet. The pleasant, narrow little streets held not so much as rubbish; rows and rows of silver houses all had open doors and windows and no one inside. Ell had told it true—Orrery was a city of lenses, and Azimuth boasted so many that the morning sun seemed to explode in all directions. The fountain in the central square was a great, mad, jumbled mass of a telescope, bristling with eyepieces and earpieces and mirrors and bulging glass globes. Every roof hoisted up crystal discs and tubes and plates pointed upward and upward, toward the spire of the Splendid Dress, toward the stars, and further still.

"Would you stay, if a Yeti gave you an eviction notice?" asked Saturday. "How nice it would have been if we all could have seen the Moon and all her millions, dancing so that the whole thing bounces and singing up the earth below! But then I suppose that's a lot of noise, and I did so miss your talking."

"There's a light on up there!" cried Ell, circling down toward them, his great red wings banking. "On the hill! A whole house lit up like a cake!"

With a sigh of relief, September's little band turned toward the steep, tottering hill that reared up on the north side of the bulb. Aroostook took the hill in stride. His carburetor knob slowly melted into a moondial, carved with figures all in tiny opals, and the gnomon shining like a blade. September did not see it change. She saw only the road ahead, thin and straight with no hope of turning off or away.

The light gleamed ruddy and very home-like out of a peculiar house. September knew instantly what it was made of—not bricks, not wood, but silver plates, photographic plates. The delicate black lines and shadings and angles of a picture of the outside of a house showed stark and detailed on the surfaces of the plates. Every few moments the lines flickered and a new sort of house appeared: now a sweet cottage with roses in the window, then a forbidding stone fortress, still again a fisherman's shack. Near the door-plate, before a tall window, an etching of a very handsome gentleman tiger stretched on the silvered glass. He bent down to pull a few beans and strawberries out of a negative garden. He wore a rumpled tweed suit with patches on the elbows and papers sticking out of the pockets as well as a dark paisley cravat. His stripes and whiskers rippled on the silver surface of the house.

"Visitors!" he cried when he saw them, putting one furry black and silver paw to his forehead. "Welcome, welcome! How nice to see a full-color face! Or four! What can I do for you this fine morning, and if you don't mind my asking, why haven't you skipped off like the rest of them? Good for your health, you know. Such peril in being three-dimensional!"

"Excuse me, Sir Tiger," began September. The houses around them were all the same, silver plates with black images flickering over them like shadows on water.

"Oh, no sirs between the object and the gaze!" he said, his teeth showing beneath that striped muzzle. "I'm the object for the record. You're the gaze. But calling someone an object is rather rude, so you can use my name, which is Turing and not Tiger, for I am not a tiger at all but a Tyguerrotype. Accuracy is next to godliness."

"How is it you haven't skipped off?" asked Ell. "Where has everyone gone? They want very much to talk to a Glasshob about the use of that great heap of a scope back there. But there seems to be nobody left in Azimuth but yourself."

Turing the Tyguerrotype scratched behind one round ear. "What a funny thing to say! Everyone *I* know is still here. Azimuth is as busy and bustling as ever! I can hardly walk down the streets most days!"

September and Saturday looked around at the deserted cobblestones, stretching away into more and more empty blocks.

"Subjects are cowards, is what I think," the Tyguerrotype went on.

"It's what comes of having to pose and look one's best all the time. Me, I am what I am. Fixed and finished. A little shaking doesn't worry me."

A soft, velvet-shoed boom blossomed out of the mountain. Rain began to fall in thin, gauzy ribbons.

"Might we come in, please?" asked Saturday politely. "If you and yours have stayed behind, we must find someone to let us use the telescope—and tell us how! We mean to stop the shaking, you see. And for that . . . well, we need to see. Far and deep."

"I wouldn't recommend it," answered the Tyguerrotype, moving like a filmstrip over the plates of the house into the door-plate. "If you came in you'd be photographed and that's a dodgy business."

"I've had my picture taken." September shrugged. "It's not so bad, only you never come out looking quite like yourself."

Turing ate a silver strawberry in one bite, and looked a bit guilty eating in front of them. "You don't come out looking like yourself," he said with his mouth full, "because by the time you come out, you're *not* yourself. You've gone through a whole country, in through the lens, out through the chemical bath. Everything that's ever photographed does. But it happens so fast you don't remember it. It only shows in the photograph—the lines of your face, the set of your eyes, just a little different than you see in the mirror. Life outraces memory. It's on account of how memory dawdles and smells the perfume of a long-lost love or sings the same song over and over again instead of getting right to the important bits, whereas life just steams right through, one thing to another, episode to episode. That's why photography got invented in the first place. To help memory catch up. I was a tiger, though probably not a *Sir* Tiger, once upon a time. A professorial tiger with a big, predatory brain! But some fellow took a picture of me at the presentation of an academic medal and sent me into the Country of Photography."

"I thought you said you come out the other side on the quick," interrupted Ell, searching for a hole in the logic of the tale.

"Oh, most all of you does. You'd never notice the difference. But some of you stays and lives in the Country of Photography forever and ever. That's why you never look quite like your picture—when you're done being pictured you're a new person. Part of you is living in the Country of Photography and not in *you* anymore. It's lovely here—all kinds of people and houses and trains and horses and apple orchards and smiling people and frowning people and old people and young people all together, everything that's ever been filmed or photographed. If you sat for a great lot of pictures, there'll be heaps of you running around, if not, maybe only an out-of-focus background shot. And Azimuth, *photographed* Azimuth, is a metropolis. Packed full—the biggest city in all of Fairyland, except that no one counts us in the census. The Glasshobs had a lens for everything, and lenses are for capturing, and they took more pictures like blinking before they bolted off at the first sign of worry. As I said, subjects are cowards."

"But your house isn't a camera; it's only plates," said September, her hair beginning to drip.

"The inside of this house is a darkroom, and that's the same as saying a tunnel from one Country to another. I come to look at the scenery in the mornings. Though it's been ever so lonely lately. I don't know what the fuss is about. We've got eleven Ciderskins in Country. They're harmless! Still, if you came in I couldn't vouch for your safety. A photograph doesn't die; it only fades a little—we don't fear much. But you are very fragile."

"Do you mean to say you're not . . . well, not quite alive?" asked September, who thought better of the question as soon as she had said it.

"That's very interesting, you know!" The Tyguerrotype scratched under his cravat with one claw. "I suppose it depends on what you mean by alive. Do I *seem* alive?"

"Oh, yes!"

"If I were *not* alive, do you suppose I would sound or seem or behave very differently than I am doing?"

"I don't think so. . . ."

"If you shut your eyes and only listened to my voice and didn't *know* that I was a Tyguerrotype and not a Tiger, if you couldn't see that I am an image on a silvered plate and not a fat, roly, orange and black gentleman with an advanced degree, would you assume that before you stood a real and living Great Feline? With a noble constitution and an eye for composition?"

"Yes, I expect so. . . ."

"Then I am as alive as makes no difference. I do all the things an alive thing does," said Turing. "Do you know another test for living?"

September could not help looking at Aroostook. She changed by herself, into sunflowers and golden hands and phonograph bells. Only living things could change without someone changing them. She drove himself when he saw fit and she had said no to the Blue Winds (though that might have been a jammed lever) and she had to eat or else she would stop, just like her. She Had Rights, if the King was to be believed. But September could believe a photograph of a tiger was alive more readily than that her car was.

"It's a handsome machine," said Turing, following her gaze.

"Do you think—" September cleared her throat. She had said nothing to her friends about Aroostook and his changes. "Do you think it might be alive as well? You seem to know something about the business, is why I ask."

The Tyguerrotype roared laughter.

"Do I know about living? Do I know about Alive? I know about *seeming,* little primate. I know about how a thing *looks.* It looks like a handsome machine. But then, so do you. And I wouldn't, I really wouldn't come into the house. I'm sorry you're wet and hungry but if you stood where I stand and ate my strawberries you'd come down with a fantastic case of mercury poisoning at the very least. If you came into the house you'd end up in my Country, backwards and upside down and black and white."

"You said when a picture's taken a body goes all the way through the Country of Photography," said September slowly, trying to figure out where her mind was tugging her. "As fast as a shutterclick. But that country has to be as big as anything that's ever stood in front of a camera. How long have folk been taking pictures in Fairyland? They've been at it for quite a while in my world. Have you seen a Fairy city in there? With a great giant paw on display in the middle of it?"

The Tyguerrotype stroked his striped cheeks. "It's possible. I can't be sure. There are ever so many cities in Country. But I think I saw a place like that when I was first developed."

"Don't you see?" cried September to her friends. "We can do better than the Glasshobs' lenses! It all has to be in there—the Paw, Patience, even the Fairies! If we are lucky, we can see what happened to it. When you live as fast as the Fairies did when they could Yeti away anything they didn't like you'd just have to take pictures! Their lives outraced memory, kicked it, and jumped on its head."

"But we couldn't really," protested Ell. "You go through in a blink. The tiger said so. There'd be no time to look around."

The Tyguerrotype shoved his paws in his pockets. "I suppose you know about Physicks, little one. They don't work the same way in Country. Seeing is magic. A lion I once knew called Werner, photographed in a zoo for chessmasters and scavengers, well, he told anyone who would listen—but no one would. Seeing is magic. When you look at something you change it, just by looking. It's not an apple anymore, it's an apple your friend Turing saw and thought about and finally ate. And it's worse than that—anything you look at changes you, too. A camera takes a picture—but the photographer can't escape the picture. She's there, even if you can't see her. She's the one holding the box."

"It's like what Candlestick said about Pluto. People see my clothes and they say I'm a Criminal," September said, chewing over the Physicks of it. "And I know I've acted like one—but only when I had to!" *Or when I desperately wanted to,* she thought, a flash of guilt bursting in her stomach over what she'd done.

The Tyguerrotype nodded. "They see you and they change you and you change because you've been seen and you change them because they've changed you. I hope that sounds very confusing because it's much worse in Country. There's nothing but seeing and being seen in the Country of Photography."

"That's all very well. But you haven't said there's no point in it because we'd flit through in an instant. So there must be a way not to," said Saturday shrewdly, tugging on his topknot.

Turing the Tyguerrotype furrowed his furry brow. "I should have to catch you as the flash goes off," he said, "to stop you silvering right through. But I *am* very vivid. A strong image, clear and dynamic!"

Saturday looked longingly at the silver-plate house. "It sounds like home in there. Everyone all together, all of themselves round the supper table, baby pictures and holiday portraits and wedding albums."

"And perhaps I will be safe in there—you can't photograph a curse, after all," added Ell softly. "But I do not like it. I do not want to be flat and colorless as well as small. I like my own country. I like being red in it, and warm, and round."

"But photographic processes are caustic!" whispered Saturday.

"We shall certainly be scorched, and what if we should come out a mile into space or back in the Jungle? Let's not be reckless!"

Turing had already pulled an old studio camera out onto his silver plate. He positioned the tripod and peered through the lens, pulling a curtain over his striped ears.

"I am reckless," said September to her friend. "You have to be, in my line of work." She paused. "Our line of work."

"Scoot together now," called the Tyguerrotype. "Around our hand some machine. I've got to get you all in frame at once!"

Turing spread his great, wide arms as wide as he could. His fierce mouth opened, showing silver teeth and a silver tongue lined in black. In one paw he squashed the squeezebulb.

"Everybody say 'Observer Effect'!" he roared.

At the last moment, Ell could bear it no longer. His flame burst out in fear and doubt and great lizardy distress. The violet jet arced over the silver-plate houses, sizzling and hissing through the raindrops.

The flash exploded like a star.

CHAPTER XVI

THE COUNTRY OF PHOTOGRAPHY

In Which September Is Observed and Observes Herself

September saw nothing but blackness.

Her feet stood in something warm and wet—at first she thought it was a puddle where they all dripped together out of the storm. But as the wetness rose up, past her knees, past her waist and her tummy and her chest, panic rushed up, faster than the wetness, clutching her throat so tight she could not cry out. Liquid flowed over her face in the dark, seeping into her eyes and her mouth. September thrashed and beat at the stuff, but she could see nothing, feel nothing, move nowhere.

And as suddenly as it had engulfed her, it left, draining away into nothing. September opened her eyes, wiping at them, coughing. And everything was full of light.

The Tyguerrotype's house had no rear wall; it opened up onto another Azimuth, wide and silver and black and white, shade upon shade of charcoal and ash and pearl and oyster and gunpowder and smoke. Not just another Azimuth—many Azimuths, lying one on top of the other like the pages of a book. Everywhere September looked, she saw images wriggling together and apart. A Glasshob—she could not be anything else, her heavy lantern hanging down on a seaweed-wrapped stalk before her eyes, her goat-legs furry and gray—took one step toward them. But a dozen copies of her leapt out in every direction, bolting off in every direction. Houses vibrated, their images layered three and four and eight deep. Yet you could not really call it *deep*. Depth seemed to have fallen asleep and forgotten to set its alarm. The Tyguerrotype, the thirteen bouncing Glasshobs, the quivering houses—and September and Saturday, A-Through-L and Candlestick—had a little thickness, but no more than a thick sheet of paper. They were all black and white, the Marid swirling with dark and light like tarnished silver, September a floating pale face in the sea of her inky silks. September looked down at Ell. It took her a moment to realize what she'd done—looked down. Down, at a Wyvern. He was the size of a wolfhound now, just a hair below September's own height. White tears welled up in his silver eyes—but did not fall. She put out her arms and pulled Ell into them, and in her heart she thrilled a little, for she had always wanted to be able to hold him all entire this way, snuggle him even though she knew very well he was not a dog. But the poor Wyverary turned his face away in terror and shame and the thrill died away in an instant.

"Don't cry," she said with a voice her mother used when September was disconsolate. "You have to teach me to be the bigger one, out of the two of us. I daresay I won't be very good at it, at first." Ell straightened a little at that, but not much.

Not all was black and white in the Country of Photography. September did see in the distance a sepia spriggan lecturing to a throng of brown-and-cream gnomes. And there, sitting against the wall of a shivering cafe, sat a single fat man all in the brightest blue, a brocade coat that fell to his toes, his bushy black beard swallowing up a round brown face with wide brown eyes. But he was the only colorful soul in that corner of the Country of Photography.

"They've been showing up here and there," said the Tyguerrotype. "Someone somewhere knows the secret of color photography. I should very much like to meet them, whoever they may be."

September took a step forward—and stopped short. When she moved, images scattered before her like autumn leaves. Layers of Azimuth peeled off—this one showing Glasshobs standing before the great telescope, straight-backed and dour-faced. That one showing a tired-looking witch waving in front of the same telescope, yet another showing a little boy with a bobcat's face asleep in the telescope's plush chair. Wherever September turned her feet, more of the city skittered out in front of her, separating into still frames and blowing out across the very streets they captured. It was like walking through autumn leaves—the leaves scattered before your feet, blowing into the forest where more leaves waited.

"Am I hurting them?" she whispered.

"Oh, no, my little soft-focus dear," said the Tyguerrotype kindly. "That's how it is here. The world is an album of pictures, with everyone flipping ahead to see what comes next. When you move, you move the world. Now, it was a Fairy city, wasn't it? I know I saw one in here somewhere."

Turing put up his tiger's paw and tucked his claw into a bit of air. It peeled back like the corner of a stamp—and at the same time he strode forward forcefully. As he flicked his claws and pounded the cobblestones, the city around them flipped and shuffled like pages. Turing walked right through the ruffling images of Azimuth—and then places that were not Azimuth—a wide lunar meadow, a silvery Pandemonium in the afternoon with pookas sipping ices near the Briary, sepia hamadryads picnicking in the Worsted Wood, Groangyre Physickists throwing their heads up into the air at a graduation ceremony. September and her friends hurried after the Tyguerrotype, for behind him the photographs drifted back up, layering on top of one another, shivering back into their shapes and becoming solid once more. Turing descended, or ascended, or dove through, the Country of Photography like a dolphin in water.

September halted, realizing that she had forgotten Aroostook, puttering away patiently behind her. Several images of identical horses grazed around her fenders, their hooves in mid-gallop, not touching the ground. September took a deep breath and decided to try something. She patted her hip. She gave a little whistle, like she would to her little dog when supper was ready. At first, nothing happened. The Model A idled without concern. She whistled again, more sharply.

And Aroostook bounced a little. She rolled forward, tagging along behind her, sticking close to her side. September gave her car a long, concerned look—then dashed after her friends. Aroostook's horn *squwonked* joyfully. Photographs burst and riffled before them, blowing aside so fast they blurred together.

Suddenly Saturday cried out; September saw it, too, and without thinking they clutched each others' hands, their hearts racing together away from the thing they saw.

"What?" yelped Ell. His voice had gotten higher in his shorter, thinner throat. The sound of it pierced September's fear.

"Did you see that?" she hissed as they ran after the Tyguerrotype, through family portraits of Dodos in the safe mountain cubbies of Walghvogel and unfamiliar canyons draped with silk sails and garlands of drums and stranger still farmhouses and silos and men in stovepipe hats and stern-faced mothers with children on their knees that would have been unremarkable in the world September knew.

"Did we see what?" called Candlestick.

"There it is again!" Saturday gasped.

And then they all saw it—a huge blur passed before them as a photograph spun away. A mass of streaky gray with black bulges within it, a glimpse of teeth, a flash of horns.

"Oh, don't worry, it's only a Yeti," Turing yelled back over his monochrome shoulder.

"How can we possibly not worry?" panted September, who, even though she had no more depth than a playing card, seemed still to possess lungs that could burn and ache. A tiny whelk shell next to a great dark sea floated past and away.

"I did say we have eleven of them in here! No details, though. They're too bloody fast for that game. They hulk on through like stormclouds, but they've got no mouths to complain about the quality of breakfast or eyes to narrow at those they take an unkindness toward. They're out of focus and that means out of everything."

September turned her head to look at the blur, receding through the crinkling photographs behind them. She felt an instinct sit up inside her and set its jaw.

"I want to follow it!" she hollered after Turing. The Tyguerrotype stopped. Photos settled and drifted around him like seedpods. "Don't you think—don't you think a Yeti, even a blurry one, might want to be near the paw we're after? Like a magnet, they might be attracted, even if they were so out of focus they couldn't think sharp."

September tore off from her pack, dragging Saturday by the hand, bashing back through heavy frames and cellophane films of Ifrits firing meteors through thin silk zeppelins, straining toward the great white blur staining the Country of Photography like spilled ink. Finally, a sound like a shutter cracked, not in her ear but in her mind, in her bones. And September, Saturday, the Wyverary, and Turing the Tyguer-rotype all tumbled forward, pitching into a silver-white photograph.

Eleven white blurs ringed a city of blooming, vine-tangled, thorny, lush spires. A gentle curve of land held towers of twisted white wood and black blossoms, boulevards of long gray lawn, pools like mirrors sunk into the streets. In the midst of it all lay a broad pavilion ringed with toadstools, and there, out of a tiered pedestal, rose a vast, withered, ancient, crooked paw, the great dark hand of an abominable snowman.

They had found Patience.

Fairies poured out of every house and turret and garret and hall. They, too, were too fast for a camera to catch—shimmering blurs whipping around the paw like veils in a strange dance, misty, spar-kling. Only one had enough focus to show on the film: a young girl, something like the Fairies September had known, like Belinda and Calpurnia and Charlie, wings unfolded and full of prisms, smiling and strong, stretching up on tip-toe to bite the leathery skin of the paw. Her hair was bound up with rowan-berries and six knives hung from her willow-belt.

"Is this all?" asked September urgently. "The only picture of Patience?"

The Tyguerrotype scrabbled at the air again. And suddenly, aw-fully, the eleven blurs howled. It was the selfsame bawl they had heard on the plain before Ciderskin came to batter them. It was muffled; if a sound could blur, this one did. But it sounded all the same. Several Pa-tiences stripped away like birch bark. The Fairies' blurs only thickened into a creamy stain that blotted out half the city. The light of them was so bright September shaded her eyes.

And then the blurs were gone. The paw was gone. Turing pulled up a Patience as crisp and clear as ever—and empty. The image settled around them, lines and shapes opening out to let them walk through. September dashed to the pavilion, but nothing remained of the paw or the Fairy girl about to bite it. A thin wind whistled through the gently growing and roughly abandoned place. Across the lawn-roads and toadstools and brambly, rooty palaces, nothing remained but rubbish, useless belongings left where they lay, as if a whole city's pockets had been turned out onto the ground.

"That's it?" September cried. "Where did it go?"

"We are all at the whimsy of those who observe us," said the Tyguerrotype kindly. "We can never know what will move someone in your world to photograph something. Why was it worthy, and not this other thing? Folk choose what to observe, and what they observe, at last, becomes all there is."

The eleven blurs bawled again, all together. Saturday shuddered. September shook her head. She opened and closed her hands.

"I don't know what to do now," she said helplessly. "I was so sure I was right, that the answer was here." September put her hand on her cheek. Her skin felt hot—and somehow sour, if skin can feel sour. She pulled her hand away. Black paint smeared her palm, inky and bubbling. But it was not paint—it was her palm, dropping away into a burn of nothing. She looked at Saturday—his chest was a lightless bruise of nothingness. Ell's tail splotched with dark holes.

Turing's stripes wriggled in distress. "I did say. I did say it was dangerous for you. I couldn't vouch for your safety. I was very clear! You aren't meant to stay so long in Country—you aren't meant to stay more than a second, half of a second, half of a half of a half of a second! I think . . . I think you're overdeveloping."

She felt something tug at her sleeve, but her mind was too busy trying to right itself, to find a new grip on the whole of it.

"What happened to the Fairies," she whispered, "happened here. We just saw it happen—one moment here, the next gone. Abecedaria said that the Fairies came to the Moon by the thousands—it must have happened to them *here*. In Patience." The tug came again. "And if it happened here, then no one *could* know where the paw is, because there's no one left *to* know."

September yanked her sleeve away in irritation.

And looked down into her own eyes.

CHAPTER XVII

LAST SEPTEMBER

*In Which Two Septembers and Two Wyverns
Reveal Two Paths Forward*

September stared up at herself.

September stared down at herself.

Only it was not herself, quite. The small, flat, silver-faced September tugging at her sleeve was exactly five years old, wearing a puffy dress with lace on the skirt that she remembered very clearly had belonged to an older cousin and had a tear under the sash. It was meant to be a sunny Easter yellow. The sash had been light green. She remembered it because the edges of the tear scratched her skin when she had to sit still for a portrait with her mother and father at Christmastime. Now, the dress, all black and white like the photo that still sat on their mantle at home, had a black and white girl in it and the girl in it was looking up at her expectantly.

"Hello!" said little September.

The bigger September did not know what to say.

"Don't we look just alike?" her younger self said. "I saw you running—you run very fast! If you don't slow down you'll fall!"

Ell looked at the child with delight. "Wherever did you come from?" he asked. "I see you have both shoes. Well done, you!"

Little September pointed back over her shoulder—through several gauzy layers of photos, September saw her parents as if through glass, her father's arm around her mother, her mothers hand outstretched to rest upon her daughter's hair just as it did in the portrait at home in its brass frame on the mantle. She wanted to go to them, to run to them and tell them everything that had happened, to show them her silks and—and to have them see her, really *see* her, as she was when she was in Fairyland. Not a child in school. A Professional Revolutionary with a hammer on her hip and plans in her pocket.

"Come play with me!" the child cried. "Come away with me to my room and we'll play robbers. I'm a very good robber."

At this, September smiled faintly. But she did not feel at all well. Speaking with oneself causes awful headaches.

"I can't," she said softly. "Though I am sure you are a good robber."

The small September made a grimacing face. "Grown-ups are the worst people I know," she said confidentially. "And you have something on your face." September's hands were almost gone now, lightless lumps at the ends of her wrists. She began to feel very thin and hot all over.

The child looked at Saturday with big black eyes. "Hullo," she said shyly. The Marid smiled at her, ear to ear and not an inch less.

"This is what it's like," he said excitedly. "Looking at yourself, your younger self. I've done it. All Marids do. It makes you dizzy at first, that's normal, don't worry. But what you're feeling now is what the other Saturday felt when he looked at me, or what I feel when I come upon a tiny me running around the shoreline laughing at the werewhales." September frowned. Saturday spread his hands. "Just look at her. Look at her," he begged.

A great shape flickered up behind the child September. A-Through-L stared, dumbfounded. He began to rock from side to side and September knew his flame would come before it did—forking out in hot white bursts, not truly fire but flashbulbs popping away.

Little September had a Wyvern, too.

Her scales shone dark and silver in graceful patterns; her chest the color of pearl, her wings black as fireplace pokers. All along her back, great plates bristled like a stegosaurus—and that is how one knows a female Wyvern from a male. Her great silver eyes danced and her claws scratched like paper tearing. Small September giggled and put up her arms; the Wyvern nuzzled her with her broad gray nose.

"Hullo, Tem!" The other Wyvern haroomed, and nuzzled the child with her enormous long muzzle.

A-Through-L looked up at both Septembers. He was the size of a strong, lithe fox—but even the strongest and lithest of foxes is not very big. Terrible dark holes opened up in his little wings, glowing at the edges like holes in film.

"I found her in a picture that said *Fantastic Lizards from Around Fairyland Gather for Annual Picnic!*" recited the younger September carefully. "Her name is Errata. Isn't that a funny name?"

"It begins with E," whispered A-Through-L. His voice was so awfully small and high now—nothing at all like the big deep voice September so loved. She couldn't help it—September gathered A-Through-L up in her arms and snuggled him close, as she'd done with her small and amiable dog at home when a thunderstorm came and it was feared. But her blackened, sizzling hands went right through his splotched, scorched ribs, and she had to balance him on her forearms.

"You can't stay," the Tyguerrotype said. "You'll burn away to nothing." He opened his paw, which still held the squeezebulb of his camera.

"No wait!" squeaked Ell. "I don't believe I've ever had my picture taken, so there won't be any of me in here, but there's her and I so rarely meet other Wyverns. . . ."

"There's quite a few in Country," Errata said. Her voice thrummed deep and heavy. "People do like to snap photos of themselves standing in front of us, though I'm sure I have no idea why."

"But there *will* be one of me here, when the picture's done taking itself?" Ell said breathlessly.

Errata's scales blushed a darker shade of charcoal. "I'd be happy to show him the Negative Gardens," she said. "You have a very nice flame, though you're quite small—but I don't judge. It's not my way."

"I have a curse," Ell sighed.

"Mating season can often feel that way," agreed Errata, her silver tail coiling and uncoiling.

"Mating season?"

"Of course! Didn't you know?"

"I was raised by a Library," Ell squeaked, by way of apology.

The lady-Wyvern shrugged her massive shoulders. "Fire is always within us, but when the time comes for eggs and dancing, it isn't content to roast our hearts. It must out."

"*We* must out," begged Saturday. His face had gone indistinct, his nose and eyes and cheeks swallowed up in a cloud of inky darkness.

"Not yet!" cried Ell. His tail shriveled into darkness. "How long does it last?"

Errata flicked her thick tail back and forth. "As long as it takes to find a mate. That's what the Annual Picnic is for, of course. Lizards are solitary sorts, by and large. Always sulking in lairs or brooding on hoards. Wyverns are quite the most social of the genus. Oh, we make our beds of bones but have you ever known one not to have radishes for company or a comfortable vertebra for lonesome travelers? No, and you never will. I met a very fine gentleman at the Picnic—bright gold with a blaze of green! He read me poetry, couplets like strong hind legs. And I knocked a tree down with my tail to impress him. But he fell asleep in the briars by the time the photograph was taken, and he isn't here at all. But the rest of us have a nice time in Country, when those spoilsports feel they can leave their hoards to their own devices for the afternoon."

September's parents were getting closer. She could almost see them clearly now, moving through the layers of film like mist.

"Mom!" she cried. "Dad!" And waved her arms, which had started to sizzle away into silver fumes. Her father walked so straight. Her mother held his hand.

But little Tem was already skipping away through the photographic fields, laughing heartlessly as she burst through the blurred and motionless Yetis, beckoning the pale Wyvern behind her. September watched as her younger self leapt up into her parents' arms, laughing as though she had never heard the words *war* or *shift* or *hospital*. Errata looked back and forth between the two Septembers. Her whiskers flicked and quivered—but she went with her girl, as any beast would. She waved her tail at Ell as she skipped after her Tem—and September saw her own mother, out of focus and black and white though she was, reach up to pat a Wyvern's neck fondly. She saw her father lift her child self up onto his shoulders as he used to. Tem screamed with giggling and kissed Errata's offered nose. Like a needle in her chest, September saw their ease, their smiles, and all of her leaned toward them, as if by wanting it she could be Tem again.

I have missed Saturday and I have missed Ell and I have missed Fairyland— but how can I miss myself? September clenched her fist against tears that longed to well up and spill out. Instead, drops of searing, mercurial fluid dripped down her face, burning her skin away as they fell.

Ell stretched his neck forward, straining after Errata in his own way, calling for her to stay even as his eyes darkened to nothingness. The little Wyverary shook his head from side to side wretchedly. He had already started to hiccup.

"Oh no, no, Ell, you must try not to! Hold your breath or try to swallow it . . ."

But A-Through-L's fire burst forth in a long, glowing stream of longing and she could feel him wither up in her arms.

The Tyguerrotype closed his paw around his squeezebulb. "We can't wait any longer. You came for Patience and you got what there was to get."

"Wait!" cried September. Her cheek yawned inky wetness, flushing down over her chin even as she spoke. "Don't! Couldn't we somehow come out here, here, in Patience, the place in this photograph, and not in Azimuth? Couldn't we punch through this very film here and now, and come out on the other side of the Moon? If you don't take the picture, if you don't finish taking it, we could go some other way?"

"I don't see how," said the Tyguerrotype.

"I do," whispered Ell miserably. "After all, photographs are only light and light is only fire."

"Ell, you can't." September clutched at him. He fit into the palm of her hand. All of him. His red snout, his whipping orange whiskers, his long scarlet tail, his broad chest the color of old peaches. Like a new-born kitten, his tail snaking over her thumb. How much smaller could he bear to get?

As A-Through-L shut his eyes, blackness swallowed up his snout.

"No," September said, and her voice was deathly hard. She put her hand over his mouth and stopped him.

Instead, she pulled her hammer from her pocket once more. It was iron. Nothing in Fairyland could bear iron.

She turned to Saturday. His face diffused into darkness. She felt herself fading, fading, hardly able to stand.

September raised the hammer, teeth first, and brought it shredding down into the image of Patience. Slowly, sickeningly, the photographed city melted around them. The Tyguerrotype fell backward through crisping and peeling layers of Country, batting them out and scowling. A picture of a fire brigade bristling with ladders shuffled through the prints.

"Where are you going?" came a voice behind them.

September turned. Flickering and popping in silver and black stood the Marquess as she had seen her long ago, in a newsreel, her velvet and silk and flowered and jeweled hat tilting to one side.

"You wicked little thief," she said slowly, her mouth forming the words as though she were swallowing cream.

The picture of Patience swallowed them up before September could answer.

CHAPTER XVIII

The Heart of the Moon Is a Month

In Which Much Is Revealed

The edges of the world sizzled silver, then black, and then vanished. September's eyes burned; suddenly everything had color again and depth, too. The Moon seemed so much brighter and harsher. Afternoon spilled out over the bowl-curve of the inside edge of the Moon, turning the pale soil to gold dust. She felt her face, her throat, her chest, her hands—all whole, all full of color. In her lap, A-Through-L sat shivering, tiny, helpless. September held him close. She did not know what to say—so she ripped a scrap of fabric from her blouse and another from the long leg of her trousers, knotting them into a necklace with a black silk basket for him to ride in. A-Through-L climbed in, his eyes round and frightened, hardly knowing his own body, coiling his tail up through the cord and gripping the rim of the pouch in his claws.

"See? I will hoist you up, when you are little," she whispered. Ell put out his red paw. September lay her finger inside it, and his claws closed round.

Aroostook struck the edge of a rise in the land and sprayed earth before them like a splash of seawater. Saturday gripped the dash as they crashed through the moongrass and down into a long valley. His blue fingers clutched the rough loops of a vivid tangerine-colored scrim-shaw that had taken over the whole of the dashboard, the sort of carving old whalers once did on the long baleen teeth of their catches. They nearly crashed before they saw the creature who had been waiting for them, looking up from a lunar sandbar with piercing, intelligent eyes.

A broad, polished, black and white checkered crab.

"Spoke!" cried September.

"That's me," the Taxicrab chuckled amiably.

"But you're so far from Almanack! What are you doing out here?" September asked.

"Didn't I tell you? Almanack takes care of all your needs before you know you have them."

"But I'm not one of Almanack's folk," September protested.

The Taxicrab nodded at Saturday and little Ell in his silk pendant.

"They are. And you're theirs. Family is a transitive property. Almanack wants you all safe in the shell. Even when Almanack's given up and headed on down the road with the rest, to weather it out by some strangely named sea in Fairyland and who knows if it'll be a kind one. Even when the shell is gone. 'Course, *I* knew you'd be needing an escort ages back. I'm right on time, as usual and I don't mind saying! Follow me!"

Spoke skittered off in his madcap fashion, his ten legs scrabbling against the barren dunes of the Moon's inner edge. Aroostook bounded down the rocky valleys after the Taxicrab. Sprays of fine pearly soil shot up around her wheels and September believed that if she could, the automobile would be whooping with joy. They wound through ashen crags and riverbeds hardened into hematite and wide, curving salt flats and finally, finally, out onto a scarred plain they had seen only in pictures.

Down below them lay a city.

Down below them lay something awful and red rising up out of the surface of the Moon. Its hump swelled into the sky like some terrible fish cresting in a sea of light. September touched the little basket around her neck where A-Through-L rode, stroking his tiny head with her thumb.

The city was Patience—it could hardly be anything else. The towers and clocks and halls and theaters had no leaves or blossoms, but the branches of them twisted into the same shapes, bare and brown and black. Dried grass flowed into streets where fresh, thick grass had done in the photographs. The awful red blister rose out of the place where a certain pedestal had once been, shattering the ground around it and buckling cobblestones and squares of ancient lawn in its rising. All around it rubbish lay in heaps and scatters, flotsam and jetsam and ruin.

Someone was moving down there. Patience was not wholly abandoned.

"Thank you, Spoke," Saturday said. "Please give Valentine and Pentameter—and Almanack—my care."

September put out her hand and Spoke shook it with one checkered claw—service rendered and done. He scuttled off back over the edge of the world, toward the road and the shell already tottering down through the stars like a long, bright train.

. . .

At first September saw nothing living except rushes of wind and the rustling it made as it passed over dead weeds cluttering the rim of the red dome. Shadows bloomed up on that scarlet surface like handprints— and faded just as quickly. But as Aroostook roared down into the valley, pouncing through the lunar flats, September clinging desperately to the green sunflower of the steering wheel, she could feel her heart twist strangely. It felt as though the whole of the Sea of Restlessness poured through her in a great huge swallow, prickling along her limbs and in her blood and to the ends of her hair. Saturday felt it, too—the tattoos along his back wriggled and swam, braiding and unbraiding themselves.

"September," he hollered over the crash and bang of the automobile. "When I climb up high, onto the highest platform, and the lights are on and the seats are full and I have the trapeze bar in my hand but it hasn't started yet, when my toes are hanging over the edge and I can see all the way down and there's no practice net and for a moment I forget everything I practiced and my stomach wants free of the rest of me—this is what it feels like!"

September smiled. She remembered his flying through the air above the Stationary Circus and the ringmaster below blowing peonies, before he knew she was watching, before they'd touched again. Could it have only been this morning? She wished they could have stayed there and eaten typewriter pies and fallen asleep in the contortionists' tent.

She brought Aroostook to a halt in the great pavilion of Patience. She hardly had a choice—all that junk crowded every inch of street and courtyard. Aroostook's wheels ground over sledgehammers, rakes, chisels, straight-edge razors, sickles and scythes, spades and hammers, jewelers' glasses, telescopes, wheels, abaci, longshoremen's hooks and seamstresses' tape, wrenches, knives, swords, fishing rods, and wrenches, shears and knitting needles and frying pans and brooms and axes and typewriters and film projectors and dead lightbulbs and clocks. Yet though the bulbs at the very least ought to have shattered, they held under the weight of car and girl and Marid and tiny, thimble-light Wyverary. The knitting needles ought to have snapped, the clocks burst, but they did not. Still, September had to press on the brake with both her feet and all the strength in her legs to stop them. The Model A hummed and thrilled as though she did not want to stop. Did she feel it, too? The terrible tumult, the terrible *quickness* soaking them all like electric sweat? The red dome soared up, patterns of dark bloody shades and shimmering fiery veins moving over it like fish under the water. A handprint blackened one side of the great orb, vanished, then appeared again a little ways away. Finally, without warning, the hand that made the print popped into view, and then the body attached to it, the cause tripping over itself to catch up with effect.

It was a Yeti.

He stood taller even than Ell once had, a dizzying tower of tangled, matted white-blue fur and muscle. Black horns curved around his shaggy, heavy head, almost wrapping up his whole skull. Deep ruby eyes glowed within the dark folds of his face and his wide, long nose sniffed deeply at the air of the Moon. His left arm hung to the boulder of his knee, ending in a monstrous hand, black and six-fingered, nails dark and shiny as onyx, his palm a vast blank page.

The Yeti was missing his right paw. His arm ended in a stump overgrown with mossy, snarled fur knotted up around his wrist like an old bandage.

September stared. It was him. It had always been him. It had always been Ciderskin, his own paw, stolen and used to batter the Moon through time.

Ciderskin moved around the dome, touching it, sniffing at it, prodding it with his long, many-knuckled fingers, pressing his horns up against it, listening intently. He kicked a typewriter out of the way, sending up a clatter of shovels and brooms. Every so often he would growl at the strange marbled blister, a crooning, rasping, chewing sound that rubbed hideously along September's bones. But the dome seemed to like it; it rippled and flushed when he rumbled. A black shape darted around the Yeti and the dome, between his massive white legs and over the garbage heaps of long-dead Patience.

September could not speak. Her throat held itself as closed as a fist. A single, almost childish thought repeated over and over in her mind: *He's so big. He's just so big.* She had never been afraid of Ell's size, but then, he had always crouched down to her, lay on his belly in long grass, let her ride upon his back, bent his head when she spoke. Ciderskin had no reason to make himself reachable to a small human. He stood at his full height, even standing on his tiptoes to reach some invisible, vital part of the dome he had not yet examined.

But she could make her feet work. September opened Aroostook's bent door and stepped out onto the far side of the Moon. She took one step and then another, pretending that she was still walking up toward the broken fence her father had never gotten round to mending, the hot June sun still singing on her skin, Skadi still choosing her husband from the dancing-girl lineup of the great gods' legs, one butterscotch toffee still to be eaten. That she had never heard the words *war,* or *shift,* or *hospital.*

Saturday took her hand. She had not heard him come round to her. His fingers shook a little in hers. She was glad of him then, so terribly glad. That she did not have to stand alone in that lonely lunar city, as she had stood with the Marquess, as she had stood with her shadow.

The black shape saw them first. It stopped, quivering with the effort of stopping, peering at them from behind the blood-colored curve of the dome—was it bigger than it had been? September could not tell. The black shape sniffed the air. It was a huge dog, wet of nose and long of ear, his curly fur lit strangely, tangled up with tiny white stars like burrs. The dog bounded out from behind the moon-blister, spraying dusty pale pearly soil from his hind legs. He was tall enough to look September in the eye and he did it then, both Saturday and September, one to the other and back again. He stared with depthless black eyes. His tail swept back and forth through the air.

"You can't have it," September whispered, for it is easier to speak to a dog with conviction than a Yeti.

"What's that?" came a bassoon of a voice, a long blare of sound full of frosty echoes and windswept notes. Ciderskin turned toward them, his wrinkled face crowded with white wool, his horns glinting in the misty ruby light.

"The Moon," said September, and tried to put into her voice all the bravery she did not feel. She had no paw, no weapons, no notion of what to do except to stand and say what must be said. "It's not yours, or at least not only yours. I'm very sorry for what happened to you but you must know the Fairies are gone now. I know you must feel awfully sore about it." September glanced at Ciderskin's severed paw. Could it really have been this same Yeti, all those years ago? "But you'll shake the place apart and it'll rain Moon and fire and stone in Fairyland and I can't let you."

"Begging your pardon," groused the Yeti, "but I believe you haven't the first idea of what's happened to me or the weather in Fairyland or the least fact about the least thing in the known universe. Just my opinion, of course."

The black dog opened his mouth. His pink tongue flopped out, panting through a wide grin. September could see straight down his dark throat.

September cocked her head to one side. "Are you a Capacitor?" she asked the dog.

He yelped a little, the way a person would give the kind of short, sharp laugh that isn't really a laugh but punctuation. "That's not my name but it's not a bad one. Not bad at all," he barked.

Ciderskin crouched down and put his great blue-black paw on a swirling patch of the red and rising dome where it met the cracked, chalky lunar earth, slabs of stone and peat bursting and buckling wretchedly. As September and Saturday watched, paralyzed by fear and a large and attentive dog, the Yeti moved his fingers in strange circles, each fingertip tracing its own path. A wind picked up; the light of afternoon went out like a book snapping shut, gold to black in less than a gasp. Stars bustled quick and hurried over the arch of the sky. Gold returned and was gone again, whipping by like those little books where a little figure dances if you flip through the pages fast enough. September felt the terrible restlessness in her heart pick up speed and put on muscle. The Yeti glanced at them. His face rearranged itself into a craggy, weather-beaten smile. It looked out of place, like a volcano smiling.

"It works better when it's attached," he said with a bit of sheepishness hidden in his growl. He held up his good hand. "Better still if I had both, but I haven't in a long while. You can beat time about the head with a hacked-off hunk of flesh, but my body is my own. No one can use it better than me. Time is no one's friend—time has no social niceties and holds the door for nobody nowhere. But I hold the door for time, with my one good paw." The stars slowed up above, and dark settled down over the open dust bowl of the Moon. "I was very young when I lost it. And I did lose it—I was careless. I know that now. I was meeting a mountain. I meant to kiss her in secret. I meant to wed her under the midnight dark. The prettiest mountain you ever saw, sparkling with snow in all the right places, rich with granite and tourmaline and silver, sturdy and sensible and weathered by the experience of eons. When she saw me, my mountain's pine trees bristled and the wind in her heights whistled my name. When I saw her, I felt rivers break through the rock of my heart and carve me into a new shape."

"Do all Yetis wed mountains?" asked Saturday softly.

Ciderskin smiled a private smile. "Only the lucky ones," he said. "She agreed to meet me, to pick up her skirts and come to me away from her brothers and sisters who watched over each other with unclosing eyes. I came early. I was eager. I was young. I was lost in my dream of living quick and slow and quick and slow on her slopes, being near her every day, hearing the small mountain particulars of daily living: which foxes had kits and which had fallen off of cliff-faces, which avalanches wanted to come round for tea, what still meadows had business with alpine hypnodaisies, a thousand dropping pinecones. Some look at a mountain and see only the peak. I looked with a lover's eyes and saw every tremble of every pebble. And so lost was I in contemplating the future happiness of my life with and on my mountain that I did not see the trap—the crude, stupid, idiot trap that would not have caught a bee-addled bear—until it crunched into my wrist. My mountain heard my screams of rage and pain and ran, the tremors of her going quaking me apart. I was angry at myself. A body is never so vicious as when it has only itself to blame for its trouble. And so much grief came bubbling up from my single thoughtless snap of a clock-hand." Ciderskin pushed one of his fingers, as long and thick as a sapling, into the flesh of the blister with infinite slowness and patience. He dug inside like a lemur scratching for insects. A distant thundering, quivering sound bubbled up around them, from everywhere and nowhere. "Yetis are better than that. We have to be. We are the Moon's children."

"If you're the Moon's child," September cried, "how can you hurt it so? What *is* that thing coming out of the ground? I should never crack my mother's bones and shake her limbs the way you've done!"

As if to support her argument, the land gave a sickening lurch.

Ciderskin scrabbled at the innards of the red dome. September nearly fell into the body of the black dog; she and Saturday clutched for each other as the moonquake tore through Patience.

Ciderskin laid his head to one side. "Do you know what the Moon is, little girl?"

"A Moon is a Moon. It orbits around an Earth."

"Well, yes, that's true. Just as it's true that a girl is a girl and orbits around a life. But the Moon is many things. Nothing is only itself. The Moon is the Moon, forever and always. But she is also alive. And like anything alive, she ages and grows and has rebellious years and takes up with passing planets and has her moods and her stubborn ways. It is only that her ways are so big they become our ways. She changes her face over the course of a month, well, who doesn't? Who is the same creature on the first as on the thirty-first? Anything might happen, in such a space. But when the Moon changes, she keeps the time for the world below. She pulls the tides up like a blanket when she is cold and pushes them down again when she is too warm and thus rolls out the hours of the day and night. I will tell you the truth: The heart of the Moon is a month. She is an Engine, and as she turns she spins out month after month, like the pages of a book flying free. And down below, folk pack them up into a calendar and understand the rhythm of the world. Full Moon to full Moon and twelve of those make a year. I hope you understand: The Moon *makes* time. All Moons make time. And a Yeti, born on the Moon, fed of the rocks of the Moon and the water of her snows, is like a clock full of blood and bone that walks and talks and sings rhyming songs at eternity. When the Fairies took my hand—and it *is* a hand, you know. A hand and not a paw. A hand that uses tools and manipulates objects and touches the face of a beloved and counts off the years until joy."

"A paw is not so useless as all that," growled the black dog. It could speak—a rolling, rough, raveled voice.

"The Fairies called it a paw because they wanted to believe I was an animal—and not the sort of animal that discusses junkyard philosophy and enjoys Turkish coffee and knows Bone Magic and holds down a mortgage, no, the kind you can cut up for meat and only feel bad about it on Fridays. It's easier to use somebody if you can think of them as mute and dumb and made for your pleasure." Ciderskin's mouth twisted; he rubbed his furry stump. "That is how Fairies think of everyone, you know. They used the world as a tool for their delight. We hated them so much and they could never see it. Our hate was a great red beast scraping the walls and they could not see it."

September could not bear this further. "I have met Fairies and none of them were like that. They have helped me; they have been kind! How shall I believe a monster stabbing at the Moon over my own friends!"

Ciderskin shook his woolly head. "If you have known Fairies, you have known only those who heard of a Yeti's Paw on the Moon and did not come. Who heard of a way to lash time to a sleigh and whip it till it bled, and did not wish to drive it. Rare creatures. There is no such thing as a people who are all wicked or even all good. Everyone chooses. But even they, even they looked at people and saw only tools. No one is a cup for another to drink from. And yet the Fairies sucked deep of us all."

And September did remember that Calpurnia had a changeling girl, a child who could not have been her own child. And that Charlie Crunchcrab ruled Fairyland with a hand heavier than she could ever have thought.

"I will answer your question before you ask," continued the Yeti, pulling his fingers out of the blister and bending to clear more slabs of white stone from its growing body. And September could see it swelling now, pulsing a little, even, as though it were taking a long, deep breath. "And the answer is: You are wrong. The Fairies are not gone. But they are no longer what they were. I watched it and did not help them, though I could have. I cheered. I cheered and I wept and I was glad. Perhaps I should not have been. Perhaps laughing at agony is a Fairy's game and I should not have moved my pieces on their board."

"What happened?" asked Saturday and September together.

"No one will tell us!" September went on alone, her fear outboxed by her curiosity. "The Fairies seem to think it is a secret, or else they do not know."

The Yeti shrugged at the mounds of rubbish around them. "They are not gone," he said again. "You are surrounded by Fairies. Pressed in on all sides and crushed by them. You have held them in your arms, I have no doubt, and carried them on your back. You have thought them precious, sought them, found them, lost them." Ciderskin pulled from the depths of his impossibly thick fur the long blue length of the Sapphire Stethoscope. He put the knobs in his ears and the cup against the red blister. "I suppose you've noticed the Moon has no Queen, nor any King, nor a Marquess nor a Prime Minister nor even so much as a hedgehog perched on a barstool with a paper hat. The Moon is anarchistic—she has her own mind and will not be told what to do by folk less long lived than she, which is no one. Some say the Moon hated the Fairies as much as anyone. That she did not take kindly to being ridden about by a bunch of overgrown dragonflies fueled by the elixir of thinking you're in charge. I'll tell you for nothing, that's the worst sort of drunk you can get. When people tell it now, they say that the Moon wanted to shake off the gadflies on her haunches and so she whipped up a Thaumaturge. Just pushed her up out of the ground, made of the Moon's own pearl and the cold breath of that eternal month ticking by inside the lunar depths. It's true that she took after the Moon: long silver hair and stars dancing on her black skin. Her eyes were panther's eyes, they whisper even though they never met her. In their slitted pupils, if you looked closely, you could see the soft boom of magic detonating within. She called herself the Pearl, no different than the stuff of the Moon. I suppose she had a school of magic, but who could guess what it was? Everyone tried to claim her later—Dry Magic, Severe Magic, No Magic, even the Quiet Physickists. But she, like the Moon, had no kind of heart for rules. The Fairies welcomed her and squabbled over whether the Seelie or the Unseelie ought to get to drive her mad by dancing or turn her head into a cockatiel's. And all the while my poor hand had time draped over it like a cat's cradle. When the Pearl first appeared she was young, but the Fairies kept her dancing and squawking in their parlors until she was a woman grown, who'd spent more of her days as a toy than a girl. And finally, the booming magic the Pearl kept tied down in her burst out. In the midst of Patience, she smiled. That was all. She stood next to my severed hand and leant into it like it was a throne made just for her. And she smiled. The Pearl went dark, like a lamp going out. All to silky black. Stars blazed briefly in her skin, like wishes falling. The Pearl smiled and the Fairies disappeared."

The black dog picked up a long silver scythe from the wreckage of the city. Grinning wolfishly around it, he shook it in his jaw like a bone.

"Oh!" cried September, understanding in an awful instant.

"They used us as tools," whispered the Yeti, though his whisper was the shout of a human child. "So the Pearl made them tools for the use of all. There is poetry to thaumaturgy, or else what fun would it be? You've met half the fey nation. The Sapphire Stethoscope was the Mayor of Patience, Barnabus Broom, if I remember the color of his jacket correctly. The Bone Shears were his wife Monkshood. I believe old Tanaquill turned into a wrench. Her sons clattered to the ground as wooden spoons. There were more Fairies than flowers in the fields, and they all became what they always were—" Ciderskin's voice darkened with old, creaking rage. "*Junk*. Useful junk, but junk all the same. I am quite sure you've used a Fairy to do a job. They can never break or wear out, the Pearl made sure of it. Of course, not every instrument has a hideous history, but there are so many, so many."

"*My* wrench?" said September with a sick heaviness in her stomach. "The Witches' Spoon . . ."

"But are they awake?" squeaked Ell suddenly from the basket round September's neck. "Are they awake inside their wrenches and their spoons?"

September put her hand to her mouth. "The Pitchfork said no," she gasped. "In the giants' country, in Parthalia. In Parthalia, a Pitchfork said no. That's why King Charlie decreed that Tools Have Rights. Of course they do—Tools are his cousins and friends and aunts and uncles! But then, but then, something must be happening, that they're waking up, that the Fairies are stirring. And Mr. Yeti, if you pressed me on the subject, I might say it's you, wrecking the Moon for no good reason but your own hurt! If the Moon made the Pearl, then breaking the Moon would break the spell. Maybe. It feels like logic, even if it sounds like nonsense."

The Yeti laughed. He laughed so long and so hard that September had to clap her hands over her ears. She tried to turn her chest inward to protect little Ell. But even then, his laughter did not stop. It kept rolling and pealing and battering the towers and the night air and finally the rolling and the battering was not just his laughing but the whole of the Moon, quavering in torment, whining and wheezing erupting from the surface like icebergs grinding away from each other.

Chasms opened up into long black. A Fairy church all of dried bitter-sweet vines and frost tumbled into a yawning canyon without a sound save a little sad, resigned rustling. The blister suddenly ballooned higher and wider than ever before. The shaking went on and on, only surging harder. September crouched to the ground, holding her balance as best she could. Finally, mercifully, the moonquake ebbed away.

"You are not as I thought you would be," snapped September, her nerves a-jangle. "You talk like a good and kind beast, but you break things just by laughing!"

"Why do you think *I* am causing this, lowlander?" roared the Yeti.

"You've stabbed the Moon with the Bone Shears!" September yelled right back. "You slapped Aroostook across a plain like she was nothing! You laugh and the world shatters! You're so big, bigger than anything but a mountain, and your eyes are red and angry and your hand is cruel and I am afraid of you—I shall not be ashamed to be afraid when I am about to be crushed along with my friends. If I should draw a picture of a villain, I daresay it would look a great deal like you!"

The Yeti looked meaningfully at her. "You are dressed as a villain also. Does that make you one?"

September looked down at her black silks. "That's not the same thing!"

"You are a baby," sighed Ciderskin. "And you only see what's small enough for you to crawl toward. The Moon hurts, but I am not hurting her."

CHAPTER XIX
TIME IS THE ONLY MAGIC

*In Which One Becomes Two, Two Become One, a Half Truth Becomes
a Whole, Everything Is Transitive, and Everyone Was Mistaken*

The red dome in the great pavilion of Patience began to move.

It twisted, slowly, straining. It swelled, and shrunk, and swelled again. It made strange, soft noises as it stretched toward the empty sky. Under the skin of it, shadows blossomed.

"It's nearly time," growled the black dog. And as soon as he did, they were no longer five but six. A tall man with blue skin and black tattoos clouded into being—clouded, because he came in a thundercloud as gray and dark as summer storms, and when the cloud had cleared he stood there, wet and bright and strong. And holding a pair of shears made all of bone, long and white and sharp. He looked at September for a long moment, and not less long at Saturday, his younger self, whose eyes were filling with gray and cloudy tears.

"Why?" the younger Saturday whispered. But the older did not answer.

September watched the tall Marid as though from somewhere very far away. She knew she ought to holler at him—he would listen to her, probably. Her own Saturday did, usually. But once again she felt a terrible paralyzing stillness flow over her. This Saturday was the future. Didn't that mean it had all already happened? Didn't that mean there was nothing to be done? How could she argue with all the Saturdays ahead? She had smashed her fate with a hammer—didn't that mean something?

The elder Saturday moved swift and sure. Ciderskin moved his fingers in the pearly soil, and once again the stars wheeled as though on a racetrack, dashing after some poor, hopeless rabbit. The sun rose and set in flashes like photographs, faster and faster. Time spasmed and dragged them with it. And in the flashbulb dawns, September saw Saturday open the shears and slice into the Moon itself. He cut in long lines away from the horrible red boil, using all his weight to lever the handles up and down. The black dog capered behind him, biting the edges of his cuts and peeling them back.

The red blister began to rise.

A final, profound, spine-severing quake shivered up under them. It seemed to begin in the back of their minds—and bloom forward, crumbling and convulsing. September fell to the ground, catching herself at the last moment so as not to crush Ell beneath her. Saturday caught her up, put her on her feet. But then he dashed off, trying to catch his future self, vanishing into his own stormclouds and out again after him.

Out of the wounds made by the Bone Shears, the black blood of the Moon seeped up like deep oil. It shimmered, hot gold and crimson and violet patterns over the dark of it. And still the red dome rose up out of the wreckage of the Moon.

September screamed, clutching Ell's basket. She tried to crawl to Aroostook—but she no longer recognized the Model A at all. She seemed to have turned wholly to stained glass and striped, wild pelts, no longer a car but a creature, her sunflower wheel glinting within, her ebony and mushroom lever, her scrimshaw dash. Only the Aroostook Potato Company burlap sack still flapped over her spare wheel—no longer a wheel but a long feline tail coiled around itself. The Model A's horn sounded, and it was no longer a *squwonk* or an *ah-ooga* but a voice, a thin and thready voice like a trumpeter blowing with his mouth only half fixed to his instrument. A voice saying that other word an alive thing must learn, that other word as necessary to living as taking in fuel and making of it movement, music, leaves, roots, dimetrodon spikes, dancing, libraries, children:

Yes! Yes! Yes!

The curving, swirling, swollen red dome burst free of the Moon. It tore away with a sound like a thousand bones shattering—and floated up into the dark, the dark flashing into day and out again as the sped-up world stuttered forward. The red dome drifted free like a great balloon.

But it was not a dome, nor an orb, nor a blister, nor a boil.

It was a crescent.

A tiny version of the great pale Moon, dark red and new, wafting up and up and up. A long, pulsing rope of stone, shimmering quartz and opal, connected it to the bubbling sea of Moon-blood below. The scarlet crescent seemed to twist and tug but could not get free of the rope, the thick braid connecting the little Moon to its mother.

September had seen dogs get born, and sheep and cows as well. She could not mistake what was happening for any other thing.

The Moon was having a baby.

The Black Cosmic Dog gave a great leap, arching in the air like a perfectly fired arrow. He caught the marbled rope as he passed it and caught it with one savage snap of his powerful jaw. The little Moon rocked onto its side, the points of its ruby horns tillting upward, making the shape of a smile, or a cradle. But the cord did not break. The dog fell back with a yelp.

"I am not a villain," said Ciderskin when the quaking had stilled. He watched the red Moon kick and gambol at the night, learning to turn and phase as fast as a just-born deer. Already it had grown bigger. Perhaps two people together could fit on its surface now and make a house there. "I am a midwife," he finished. "I told you, the Moon is alive. No different than your mother. It takes a long time for a Moon to come to term. Longer than many quick lives down below. And who will help a planet in her birthing bed but a nurse who can hold time in the palm of his hand? All I have done has been for this little one, to bring her out of her mother safely. The Moon quaked—but I did not shake her. She was in her labor."

"But Abecedaria said—"

"I should have paused in my duties to explain to a wig that I needed the Sapphire Stethoscope to listen to the heart of the new Moon? It was good that they left! She needed her privacy. The Moon couldn't worry that her contractions would hurt her folk, terrify them, even shake them off into the black! I couldn't do my work with the Moon crowded full. I'd be no better than a Fairy, kicking time forward so that the little one can get big fast enough so that the first comet by doesn't kill her. So I let them look at me and say what they pleased. Call me a monster, call me a menace. Call me a villain. It doesn't pain me. I've been to Pluto. I learned my lesson."

"What others call you, you become," said September worriedly. "So you are a monster. A villain."

The Yeti stared at her. "That's just the first part. *What others call you, you become. It's a terrible magic that everyone can do—so do it. Call yourself what you wish to become.* I'll have to have a word with the Undercamel, he's clearly gotten lazy."

September's breath caught. Her heart flooded with words, with callings: *Knight, Bishop, irascible, ill-tempered, wicked little thief, Criminal, Revolutionary, child, autumnal acquisition, small fey, jaded little tart*—and more, worse, whispered names behind brick school buildings, in the backs of classrooms, in the halls. Each one of them like a spell cast on her. What would she call herself? September reached inside for a new word, for her own word. She found nothing. She just didn't know.

But A-Through-L had listened, too. He peered out of his little silk basket at the infant Moon, pulling at her cord pitifully. He, too, looked into his many-chambered lizard-heart for something to become. He saw the Black Cosmic Dog worrying his muzzle, his teeth broken where the cord that bound the Moon to her child had rebuffed him. And he looked down into the Moon, the great cracks that the Shears opened in her. The red crescent had stopped growing. It twisted and writhed in whatever pain a Moon feels, bruises forming where the long tether vanished within it.

Ell said nothing. If he said anything at all September would stop him. The Wyverary flapped his tiny wings and darted away from September. Even if he ended up no bigger than a dragonfly, well, at least the little Moon would live and grow up and people would make a home on it and build cities and libraries and circuses and make it feel Necessary. He would not let a whole Moon go wondering why no Papa came to help it, as he had once done when he was small and did not understand that his father was the Library all around him.

Ell took a deep breath. He let the violet flame build within him, caretaking it, stoking it, holding it till he was close to the cord and ready. Till he chose to let it free and use it as he wished. The ropy, glistening stone that connected the two Moons hung much bigger and thicker than he. But he would try. The Wyverary opened his small scarlet mouth and bellowed out a long, glorious, rich stream of fire, steady and controlled and hotter than any he'd made before. It seared into the cord, broiling and scorching it. Ell did not know how long he could keep it up. He steeled himself and roared louder. The flame bubbled and flared and sang—and the cord snapped. The red Moon floated free, rolling up into the shape of a smile, sidling through the sky.

Ell gasped, empty and exhausted.

And very, very big.

The Wyverary swelled up like the red moon itself, the size flowing back into his body, his neck, his wings, his claws, his dear, sweet eyes, his great nostrils, his snapping, waving, splendid orange whiskers. He was already harooming with joy when he felt his basket burst, and the haroom grew with him until they were both their old size once more. A-Through-L roared with glee—and no fire came. He felt the curse snap in him like a bone.

"Fire begins with F and Child begins with C and I begin with A!" he called from his height, but they could not hear him. "I seized my fire and it didn't seize me and I am myself again and that starts with B and that is Big! And look! Mating season ends when the hatchlings break their shells and just look at that pretty red kid with her horns on straight!"

The Wyverary landed next to September, towering over her as he loved to do. "Family is a transitive property," he laughed, and his laugh rolled rich and full from his enormous throat.

September stared up at her friend's laugh and his height and his joy. She reached up and he put his warm, huge cheek into her little hand, just as Errata and Tem had done. September's heart eased, just the tiniest bit. Just enough to let the rest happen.

For Saturday had returned.

Both of them.

The older Saturday put down the Bone Shears, blackened with Moon-blood. He looked very stern indeed. Very much like a Grown-up. Terrifying and huge and full of an impossible and unimaginable future. September raised her hand in the smallest possible hello. The younger Saturday clouded up before the other version of his life. He stared up at himself, his eyes hard and unreadable.

"Tell me," he said. "You can tell me. If she'll ever look at me again without seeing you."

Saturday sighed, a sigh both weary and amused. "I am sorry. I am. I know I was frightening. But I was here when I was you, and I was frightened, so I had to be here when you were you. And because the Moon is our mother, too. The Mother of all the seas in Fairyland, our great-grandmother. We should always be happy when cousins arrive. We should always help. But I can't help you, because I didn't help me when I was you."

"Does that mean nothing can change?" asked September. "If what you said is true then it's all a circle and I'm stuck in it. And I'll have a daughter with Saturday because I already had one that I haven't had yet and the verbs are very difficult but they seem to add up to the future is a fist and it won't let me go even if I put a hammer through it."

"September," the younger Saturday said. He lifted her chin so that he could see her eyes, see her hear him. "Listen to me. Listen. You can't ignore me because you're afraid of who I'll be or who you'll be or who we'll be together or of something silly like predestination, which is only another way of saying you have certain appointments that must be kept. But appointments are nothing! You're always late because you had such a lovely lunch or got lost down some sunny alley. And I have never thought it so awful to live knowing your future and your past, having them so familiar you set a place for them at dinner and give them gifts on holidays. It's your present you've always got to be introduced to, over and over. I like being a Marid and that is what it means. You make me feel as though it is wicked, but it isn't. Yes, he is here because he was always here—but the farther out you go, the less calm anything is. An ocean, September, you have to think of an ocean. The depth of it, and the waves. Storms spin up in the open sea, wrecks and pirates and doldrums and they come out of nowhere and go back to nowhere when they've done. There's Saturdays out there like schools of fish, thousands and thousands, flashing and swarming, each leaping and turning and diving alone—but all together they look like one shape and that shape is me. A school of wishes and decisions and comings and goings and circuses and cages and shadows and kisses and we get where we're going but none of us can see the whole shape at once. But you can't be afraid of that, you can't, because you're just like me."

September blinked. "I am not!"

"No, September, don't you see?" Saturday smiled and it was like a blue flower opening. "You move through Fairyland backwards, forwards, and upside down. You come and go, vanish and appear. You miss years that go by for us, and we miss years that go by for you. We never know when we will find you again, or if we will! You meet us out of order, and sometimes we're the same age and sometimes I'll be older and sometimes you will because that's the kind of story we're in. It's all jumbled up on the outside, but it all makes sense in your head. It all flows the right way in your heart." Saturday grasped her hands. "And you *saw* her, you saw our daughter standing on the Gears of the World. You saw yourself, in the Country of Photography, wanting to play robbers. Just like a Marid sees. You are like me, you are like me, we are the same, and you have to understand."

September saw the red book shattering in her mind, over and over, like a thousand photographs. She thought of her father disappearing and coming back older, more hurt, and how once he was back it seemed like he'd only been gone a minute—except there was the older version of him on the couch with the plaid blanket, the more hurt version. How when she came home from Fairyland, never more than an hour had passed in Nebraska. How Saturday was not a fish but a boy, a boy who could fly through the air like a long blue arrow, a boy who practiced so carefully that when he finally did a thing, it was perfect.

Ciderskin spoke up suddenly, as though he had all along been discussing fate with them. *I forgot a Yeti,* September thought. *I was listening so hard I forgot a Yeti.*

"Time is the only magic," he said. "And Marids swim through time like the sea. Think: If you hurt yourself, and I bandage it, and after weeks and weeks it gets well and there's no scar, that's not magic at all. But if you hurt yourself and I touch you and it heals in a moment, you'd call me magic before your skin closed. It's not magic to cook a feast, roasting and baking and frying for hours and hours, but if you blink and it's steaming in front of you, it's a spell. If you work for what you want and save for it and plan it out just as precisely as you possibly can, it's not even surprising if you get it on the other side of a month or a year. But if you snap your fingers and it happens as soon as you want it, every wizard will want to know you socially. If you live straight through a hundred years and watch yourself unfold at one second per second, one hour per hour, that's just being alive. If you go faster, you're a time traveler. If you jump over your unfolding and see how it all comes out, that's fate. But it's all healing and cooking and planning and living, just the same. The only difference is time."

September turned this over in her head. "But the trouble is, I do want to be surprised. I want to choose. I broke the heart of my fate so that I could choose. I never chose; I only saw a little girl who looked like me standing on a gear at the end of the world and laughing, and that's not choosing, not really. Wouldn't you rather I chose you? Wouldn't you rather I picked our future out of all the others anyone could have?"

"I chose you," he said simply. "All the fish of me turned toward you at once."

September felt panic burn through her like gasoline. Why couldn't he understand her? "But I didn't! I have hardly had a chance to breathe since I got here and it's always like that in Fairyland. Everything is always happening and all at once. And I am growing up, Saturday! I am growing up and I have read books, so many books, and I know that growing up means you can't keep going to Fairyland the way you did when you were a child! Something happens to you and suddenly you have to keep a straight face and a straight line and I am afraid! I want something grand and I don't want to know what it is before it happens!"

"There are grown-ups in Fairyland," Saturday said. "Who told you you couldn't come back when you're grown? Was it the same person who told you grown-ups don't cry or blush or clap their hands when they're happy? Don't try to say otherwise, I've seen you fighting like a boxer to change your face so that it never shows anything. Whoever told you that's what growing up means is a *villain*, as true as a mustache. I am growing up, too, and look at me! I cry and I blush and I live in Fairyland always!"

And he was blushing, bright frost on his cheeks. *She who blushes first loses*, September thought. She put her hand on his cheek, the place where the Blue Wind had slapped her once. *But what does she lose? What contest is on that I never even knew about before the Blue Wind said I'd lost?*

September tried to pull on her sternness. It was becoming a habit. She could show her sternness and think about this another time, when it was quiet and no new red Moon turned somersaults in the sky. But when she reached for her sternness, all September found in her heart was the bar of a trapeze, swinging wild, inviting her to catch it.

The older Saturday fixed his dark eyes on her. They had kind little wrinkles at their edges, where smiles had gotten stuck and never left.

"It's a terrible magic that everyone can do," he said. "So do it. Breathe. Choose. Something, anything, whatever you want. Or don't choose. Or choose and if you don't like it later, it'll be all right because when you were very young, you took a hammer and smashed your fate into a hundred pieces."

September did not even look at the Saturday with kind wrinkles. She looked at her Saturday. The present she had to meet over and over. He was right. She lived out of order and upside down, a jumble of time and girl. He was right. September blushed. She blushed and she let herself blush. There was no losing in it, only feeling. *Fairyland,* she thought. *Fairyland is what I have where a ship has ballast. In high seas it keeps me upright. And maybe growing up only means getting bigger. As big as Almanack, as a whelk on the moon who can hold a world inside it.* September's heart sat up inside her and spoke.

She leaned up and kissed her Marid and hoped it was the right thing. Her heart caught the bar and swung out, swung wild, over the lights and the gasps below, reaching for a pair of sure blue hands in the air and willing them to find hers.

When they separated, the older Saturday put his long blue arms around the child of himself. He beckoned to September and she went to him. He smelled of cold stones and the sea. It was a good smell. "Listen to me," the older Saturday interrupted. His voice was Saturday's voice, but deeper and roomier, with space inside to curl up in.

But he did not get to finish.

I have been many things in our time together. Sly and secret and full of tricks, cruel and heartless in my own way. But for now I shall be kind. Saturday, the Saturday who has seen how it all comes out, wanted to tell himself a thing, and September, too. You and I, as we get on in years together, will many times wish to take our past selves in our arms and stroke their hair and tell them how the world is, how it is made, what can be done about it. Saturday could not be allowed to do it, any more than we can, and that is why I caused the Moon to shudder just so. I do have some small privileges.

But I will tell you what he meant to say, because we are friends and the space before an epilogue is a sacred place, soft and full of possibilities.

Saturday wanted to say: *Listen to me. Love is a Yeti. It is bigger than you and frightening and terrible. It makes loud and vicious noises. It is hungry all the time. It has horns and teeth and the fore of its fists is more than anyone can bear. It speeds up time and slows it down. And it has its own aims and missions that those who are lucky enough to see it cannot begin to guess. You might see a Yeti once in your life or never. You might live in a village of them. But in the end, no matter how fast you think you can go, the Yeti is always faster than you, and you can only choose how you say hello to it, and whether you shake its hand.*

Ever So Much More Trouble

*In Which Many Things Forgotten Are Recalled Rather
Suddenly and With Alarming Effect*

But Saturday said none of these things, and neither September nor his young self heard them.

Another quake shuddered out from the wound in the middle of Patience. It felt shallower, but it snaked sudden and sharp across the ground. September tottered and stumbled, falling into the two Saturdays. They both caught her, and for a moment all three of them held each other, clinging together with the stars like promises overhead. But then the quake sheared back the other way, a terrible aftershock, a terrible afterbirth, and September fell backward, away from the Marids who loved her.

As she fell, September saw the yawning black chasms shudder in the surface of the Moon. The cuts made by birth and the Bone Shears spat out their last blood and shivered toward closing, faster and faster as Ciderskin and the Black Cosmic Dog moved the heavens like a spinning ball and performed the only magic, the kind that heals all. Far off in the distance two bright balloons popped up out of the long, deep wounds, firing cannons as madly as fireworks in summer. The older Saturday winked out like a lantern, back into the open sea of timelines and flickering, turning fish.

September landed hard on her side against the metal edge of a typewriter dusty with lunar weeds. The keys mashed hard, whacking some incomprehensible word onto the roller. The impact jolted her teeth. She felt something break in her thigh and had time to think *Oh no, no, I've broken my leg again* before she began to bleed. Hot wetness soaked through the black silks of her trousers in a moment and seeped out onto the keys of the typewriter. Pain sparkled up along her hip. She put her hand against the wound gingerly—and it came away bright with color. But it was not quite the right color for a human wound. Some streaks of true red blood ran down her fingers, but they drowned in the hot fluid oozing dark orange over her hand, thick, syrupy, the color of a campfire. It still bubbled a little.

Ballast Downbound's orange fizz had shattered in her pocket. The sunlight of ancient days, of giant ferns and dimetrodons and werewhales and memory, remembering everything it ever had been and longing to return to being it once more. It spread out hungrily, crimson and thick and shining, dripping into the guts of the typewriter, splashing onto the carriage.

September laughed with relief—and then winced, for the shards of glass still stuck in her thigh. She rolled off of the soaked typewriter only to splash into a river of the Moon's own blood, still oozing from a canyon not quite yet stitched shut. She was not careful enough— September tried to keep her leg out of the warm planetary fluids and leaned too far over, crunching again against the typewriter, soaking it in orange fizz, in impossibly ancient light.

The typewriter began to smoke.

September thought at first that it was on fire. The deep orange stuff bubbled and oozed over the keys, spotted like a leopard's skin with September's own blood. It sizzled and sparked, beams of sunshine ribboning out and spooling back again, the sunlight of some long-vanished day when Fairies were young, stealing their first wings, when werewhales and dimetrodons and apples of immortality and cyclopses soaked up the heat and warmth of it into their skins. Sunlight that wanted only to make things bigger, to make them what they had been long ago, bigger ferns and more dimetrodons and orchards covering all the hungry earth like armies. Ballast's fountain-drink melted into the keys, its sugar and sirop dissolving the letters. It smelled like deep goodness, growing and living and working and ripeness. But beneath it the typewriter was coming apart, shrinking and surging at once until it erupted like a well-loved mountain.

And then, the typewriter turned into a girl.

She was enormous, so much taller and stronger than any Fairy September had seen or imagined. Her wings unfolded into vast prisms of fire-colors, their glassy membranes glinting green-red in the light of the still-wheeling stars, the still-flashing dawns flicking by like cards shuffling. Overhead, the small red Moon had grown broad and wide, wide enough for lakes and seas to crash into foam on its face, wide enough for snowy peaks already catching the light of the new Moon's mother below. The Fairy's hair streamed out around her head like a crown, twisted with green vines and fronds and roses bursting like stars going nova. Vermillion jewels covered her copper-colored body from throat to toe.

The Fairy looked down at September. Her eyes were black, as

black as the beginning of the world. And they were filled with white, burning stars.

The Fairy seized September in her great hands like a doll. And she began to laugh.

September looked down, her head spinning. Saturday was climbing onto Ell's back to come after her. Ciderskin had sunk to his knees, his ruby eyes full of terrible tears. She wanted to cry out to them but could not. Her throat would not move. Aroostook glittered and shone in her new glassy skin and long stripes. September reeled in the Fairy's hand. The searing, living, growing, bright, and earthy smell of the Fairy made her dizzy. *What happened to you, Aroostook, while I was smashing and yelling and running after Yetis?* Suddenly it seemed important as September drifted in the fog of perfume and laughter and thin, thin air. *I will find out, I promise, we'll have a sit down, just like the Blue Wind said.* But she could not make her lips and lungs work together to say that, either.

And then September felt a pulling in her, a hook in the heart, and she knew the feeling, she knew it but it was too soon, she had been in Fairyland but a moment, only a moment! Over the Fairy's terrible shoulder, she could see the Blue Wind coming, as the Green Wind had come for her twice now, sailing over the edge of the world to snatch her out of it and send her home.

"I only had a day!" September whispered, her voice strangled in the Fairy's endless gaze. "Don't make me go!"

Dawns popped and spun over her face at once as the Yeti went about his childrearing, moving time to give the little red Moon a chance to grow. Her skin felt hot, tight, too small for her, as though some hideous hand pulled at her hair and her feet to stretch her as far as she could go. September screamed.

The invisible hook in September hauled at her and the Fairy

laughed her booming, wild, savage laugh, and Saturday reached for her and A-Through-L roared in panic—

September fell out of Fairyland like a drop of spilled blood.

And fell back in again.

She felt it, she *felt* Fairyland push her out, away from Saturday, away from Ell, away from Aroostook, away from everything.

But the Fairy held her fast, and kept laughing, higher and louder until it became thunder, until it became a squall, and even Ciderskin quailed. The Blue Wind, her puffin vast beneath her, her shaggy blueberry-colored coat flapping in the lunar winds, flew merrily around the Yeti's head, grinning like Christmas morning. She rested her brocade elbows on the puffin's glossy dark head and rested her chin in her hands.

"You can cause ever so much more trouble by taking folk seriously," she crowed, her blue eyes dancing. "And doing just as they ask."

September was stuck fast in Fairyland, like a nail driven home.

CHAPTER XXI
THE GIRL WHO WAS GONE

Twilight made the rounds on the prairie, turning the lights on and sounding the bell for supper. The ruined fence was mended now and all well. A few strands of greyhound fur matted into the wire of the patch. The sun set over the main road, over to Mr. Albert's farm, the Powells, September's own small house. The night came on proper, full of familiar, happy stars. The moon, her own moon, our dear moon with its old face in it, came up in the south, full and bright as life.

In the Powell barn, the big roan groaned and sweated and pushed. A tangle of horse came tumbling free. Pure white against the red matted fur of her mother. The colt kicked wildly—and almost immediately tottered upright, her ghostly white body shining in the dim light, so bright against the red of blood and roan and barn.

The full moon rose passed the high barn windows, spilling in like milk.

But September was not there to see it. The next day's sun will peer in on an empty bed, a woman with engine grease under her fingernails and yelling with panic in her voice like bright paint for her husband to wake up and call her sister, call her now, use Mr. Albert's telephone and call her sister, stop asking questions—and a little dog nosing through the pillows for a girl who was gone.

Thank you for reading this FEIWEL AND FRIENDS book.
The Friends who made

possible are:

JEAN FEIWEL, publisher

LIZ SZABLA, editor-in-chief

RICH DEAS, senior creative director

HOLLY WEST, associate editor

DAVE BARRETT, executive managing editor

LAUREN A. BURNIAC, editor

NICOLE LIEBOWITZ MOULAISON, production manager

ANNA ROBERTO, assistant editor

FOLLOW US ON FACEBOOK OR VISIT US ONLINE AT
MACKIDS.COM.

OUR BOOKS ARE FRIENDS FOR LIFE